KICKING THE AIR

KICKING THE AIR

Graham Ison

Severn House Large Print
London & New York

This first large print edition published in Great Britain 2008 by
SEVERN HOUSE LARGE PRINT BOOKS LTD of
9-15 High Street, Sutton, Surrey, SM1 1DF.
First world regular print edition published 2005 by
Severn House Publishers, London and New York.
This first large print edition published in the USA 2008 by
SEVERN HOUSE PUBLISHERS INC., of
595 Madison Avenue, New York, NY 10022.

British Library Cataloguing in Publication Data

Ison, Graham
    Kicking the air. - Large print ed.
    1. Brock, Detective Inspector (Fictitious character) -
    Fiction 2. Poole, Detective Sergeant (Fictitious character)
    - Fiction 3. Police - England - London - Fiction
    4. Detective and mystery stories 5. Large type books
    I. Title
    823.9'14[F]

    ISBN-13: 978-0-7278-7657-7

Printed and bound in Great Britain by
MPG Books Ltd, Bodmin, Cornwall.

One

Nine o'clock on Wednesday evening.

'I think we'll call it a day, Dave,' I said to my sergeant.

We'd been making our brains hurt trying to put together a report for the Crown Prosecution Service on a guy we'd arrested for murder, a task often more difficult than solving the murder itself.

That's when the call came in.

The car we normally used had a sticker from Transport Branch on the windscreen declaring the vehicle unroadworthy due to a transmission problem, whatever the hell that meant. Why not fix it instead of going about plastering little notices on the damned thing? We both muttered oaths and took a cab for the half mile or so to Waterloo Bridge from our office at Curtis Green.

Not many people – including, believe it or not, the police – know that Curtis Green is tucked away behind Richmond Terrace Mews, just off Whitehall, and long, long ago was part of New Scotland Yard. Before the Yard got overcrowded and was shifted to Victoria, that is. Unhappily, however, the new headquarters is similarly overcrowded, and is also called New Scotland Yard, a decision that confuses those tourists who rely on outdated guide books, and who trot down Whitehall in search of it.

But even fewer people – and that still includes the police – know that Curtis Green houses Serious Crime Group West and that it has the responsibility for investigating all major crimes from there to Hillingdon.

Well, nearly.

Just for the record, that responsibility excludes what is known – daringly for the now terrifyingly politically correct Metropolitan Police – as 'black-on-black' crime, which is dealt with by something called Operation Trident. The onus of investigating serious sexual crimes falls on Project Sapphire. Oh, and there's something called Operation Emerald that looks after witnesses and victims.

And there are probably one or two other 'specialist' squads that I have yet to come across.

What's left is down to poor bloody sharp-end coppers like me. And Dave Poole, my black sergeant bag-carrier. Why he hasn't been snapped up by Operation Trident is a mystery, but he reckons that if he stays in the shadows they won't be able to see him. Dave has a quirky sense of humour, which is why he sometimes refers to himself as Colour-Sergeant Poole.

Come to think of it, there are so many specialist squads at the Yard now, it's a wonder that there's anything left for the Serious Crime Group to deal with at all. I've even heard there's a squad that spends all its time – well, Monday to Friday, nine to five – dreaming up new code words for new squads. But that might just be a malicious rumour put about by those who do the real work, few of us though there are these days. Nevertheless, I think I must have gone wrong somewhere to finish up where I am. I know of one superintendent with twenty years' service who, after his two years of 'foot' duty – which he did in a car – has been ensconced in a nice, warm office ever since.

However, enough of this philosophizing. As it turned out, we needn't have rushed. When we got to Waterloo police station there was just a body bag – with a body in it – on the landing stage.

In case you're wondering where a landing stage fits into all this, Waterloo is London's only floating police station and is manned by what used to be called Thames Division. Until, that is, it was renamed the Marine Support Unit by the aforementioned 'new names and total confusion squad' at Scotland Yard.

The victim had been found floating in the river by the observant crew of a police launch. They are always observant in such matters because they get a bonus for recovering bodies from the murky waters of the Thames.

As it is beneath the dignity of the Water Rats

– as river coppers are known to us of the elite – to hang about guarding a dead body, two police officers had been summoned from Charing Cross police station to ensure, presumably, that it didn't fall into the hands of a latter-day Burke and Hare.

One of the officers, I subsequently discovered, was 'learning beats', which means that she had just emerged from that forcing establishment they call the Hendon Training School, doubtless still starry-eyed and intent on working for a safer London. Good luck. She was a girl with a blonde ponytail that reached her shoulder blades, silly bitch. She clearly had yet to discover that some yob would seize it and swing her round like a rag doll at the first punch-up in which she got involved.

Her male companion – optimistically styled a 'tutor constable' – was chatting to an unsavoury youth in what used to be called plain clothes, although there was nothing plain about his ensemble. I assumed, and later discovered, that he was a CID officer, God help us.

Dave immediately set about asking questions of this trio in the hope that they might have something useful to tell us. A vain quest.

In the meantime, I unzipped the body bag sufficient to study the victim's face. She was a young brunette – about twenty-five, I reckoned – and pretty, and there was something that looked like a bootlace tight around her neck.

'Find out anything?' I asked when Dave returned.

'The clown in fancy dress claims to be a CID officer from Charing Cross police station, guv.'

'How fascinating.' I beckoned to this vision to join us. 'And what's your part in this drama?' I asked.

'The DI sent me down to liaise, sir.' Preening himself slightly, the youth announced that he was a detective constable.

'So liaise, my son. What, for instance, d'you know about this?' I asked, waving at the body.

'Er, nothing, sir.'

'I see. Well, now that you've played a significant part in this investigation, you may as well go back to the nick and do some work.'

Somewhat relieved, I imagine, the DC scurried away.

'According to the "feet"' – Dave gestured at the two PCs – 'the river police spotted the body just opposite the Houses of Parliament.'

'She's not an MP, I suppose?' I asked hopefully.

'Doubt it,' said Dave, glancing down at the girl's face. 'She's too good-looking.'

'Pity. Which side?'

'Which side?'

'Which side of the river,' I repeated patiently. 'If the body was nearer the Lambeth side than the Westminster side, it'd be down to SCG South.'

'I don't think the commander will let us get away with that, guv,' said Dave thoughtfully. 'After all, it's on our side now.'

I didn't think we'd get away with it either.

9

But I should mention that the commander, a life-long Uniform Branch wally, had – in the twilight of his career – been turned into a paper detective by someone in the Human Resources Branch at Commissioner's Office, as we of the cognoscenti call Scotland Yard. Unfortunately for me and my colleagues, the commander had a misplaced notion that the more murders his officers investigated, the greater would be the glory reflecting upon him. And would doubtless culminate in the award of the Queen's Police Medal for Distinguished Service, or something even more prestigious. Naïve fool! The only award I'd ever received was my Woodman's Badge when I was a Boy Scout. Apart, that is, from my Police Long Service and Good Conduct Medal, which the governor handed me one day when I happened to be passing his office.

'Has someone sent for the pathologist and the rest of the circus?' I enquired, looking round.

'I have.' Dave had clearly been busy on his mobile. 'The crime-scene examiners are on their way, guv, and so's Henry.'

Henry Mortlock, an exponent of black humour that rivalled that of most detectives, was the Home Office pathologist who always managed to turn up for my dead bodies. Perhaps he enjoys my company. On the other hand, it may just be that that's how the roster works out.

And, as if on cue, Henry arrived.

'Well, Harry, we meet again.' Mortlock

rubbed his hands together and looked at the woman's face. After a moment's contemplation he undid the body bag fully. 'Hmm!' he said, and for a few moments gazed at the naked body. 'Well, there's not much I can do here. No good taking her temperature.'

'I suppose not,' I said. 'She doesn't look as though she's sickening for anything. Not any more.'

As usual Henry ignored my flippancy. I think he thought he had the monopoly on smart remarks. 'Get it to the mortuary, Harry, there's a good chap.' He stood up and hummed a few bars from Mozart's *Figaro*.

There wasn't much I could do either. The absence of clothing would make identification that much more difficult, and I had a nagging suspicion that it would be some time before we found out who she was. But, unusually for me, I had a bit of luck there.

Two of the scientific lot's white vans arrived on the road just above the police station. After a short delay, during which time I imagined that the technicians of murder were donning their white overalls, Linda Mitchell, the chief crime-scene examiner, appeared on the landing stage.

She looked down at our body. 'I understand she was pulled out of the river, Mr Brock?'

'Yes,' I said. 'That's why she's wet.'

'In that case, photographing the victim is about all we can do on site,' said Linda. She too had a tendency to ignore my smart remarks.

'And fingerprints,' I suggested.

'Of course,' said Linda, and shot me a withering glance that implied I was doubting her professional competence.

Meanwhile, Dave was busy making telephone calls to God knows who, arranging for the removal of the body to Henry Mortlock's butchery.

I went into the front office of the nick. 'I'm DCI Brock, Serious Crime Group West,' I said to the station officer, a weary sergeant who looked as though he wished he were ten years older and thus eligible for a pension. 'Where's the boat's crew that found this body, Skip?' I cocked a thumb towards the door.

'Back on patrol, sir.' The sergeant's expression suggested that I'd just made a fatuous enquiry.

'Did they, by any chance, happen to mention the ligature around the victim's neck when they brought her ashore?' I didn't try to disguise my sarcasm.

'Yes, sir, they did mention that. That's why we called Wapping.'

'What's Wapping got to do with anything?' I asked. This was obviously going to be a tortuous conversation. 'That's the headquarters of the OCU, sir.' The sergeant pronounced it 'ock-you'.

'The what?' I knew what he meant, but I hate acronyms. Along with all the other things I hate about today's Metropolitan Police.

'The operational command unit, sir,' said

12

the sergeant slowly, and in such a way that implied he was treating with an idiot.

'And?'

'They said to refer it to CX. That's Charing Cross nick, sir. Er, police station.'

'I see. So the boat's crew, well knowing that this was a suspicious death, decided not to wait for me, and went back on patrol. Got that right, have I?'

'They got a shout, sir,' said the sergeant, playing his trump. 'Bit of a punch-up on a gin palace, down near Blackfriars Bridge.' He turned to his computer screen. 'All quiet on arrival. They're on their way back as I speak, sir.'

'Obviously a priority,' I muttered, and walked out of the office just as a launch was tying up. A sergeant and a constable stepped lightly on to the landing stage.

I introduced myself and Dave. 'What's the SP?' I asked. SP is a piece of verbal shorthand that the police have culled from the racing fraternity and means 'starting price', but when a policeman uses it he means 'What's the story?'

'We were patrolling upstream, sir,' said the sergeant, 'when we spotted the floater just abeam the Houses of Parliament. Taffy' – he nodded towards his PC – 'got her inboard, but she was already dead.'

'Probably because of the ligature round her neck,' observed Dave mildly.

'Given the tide at this time of year, Skip, where could she have gone in?' I asked.

13

'Ah, that's a good question, sir.' The sergeant took off his cap and scratched at his thinning hair. 'And I can't answer it until I know *when* she went in.'

'Thanks a lot. You've been a great help. DS Poole will take brief statements from you both.'

And then everything happened at once. Henry Mortlock went, the crime-scene white-suits left, the body was removed and the boat's crew continued their patrol, no doubt to sort out a few more revellers who were polluting the environment with their drunken carousing.

Thursday morning. An unidentified murder victim, no idea what to do next and the commander poking about in the incident room. What more could one ask?

'What d'you think, Mr Brock?' enquired the commander.

'I'm waiting for the result of a search of fingerprint records, sir,' I said. 'Until we know who the victim is, we're a bit stuck.'

A bit stuck! We haven't got a bloody clue. Literally.

'Mmm! Yes, I suppose so. Er, any thoughts on the cause of death?' This despite the fact that Linda Mitchell's team had already produced blown-up photographs of the dead woman, including a close-up of the ligature around the girl's neck. All of which had been posted on a notice board by the ever-efficient Detective Sergeant Colin Wilberforce, the

14

incident-room manager.

'At a rough guess, sir,' I ventured, with just a hint of irony, 'strangled with a ligature.' I pointed at the close-up with my pen. 'That ligature. But, of course, we'll have to wait until Henry's finished.' I glanced at my watch. 'I'm just about to leave for the post-mortem.'

'Who's Henry?' The commander knew fine who I was talking about.

'Dr Mortlock, sir. The Home Office pathologist,' I said.

'I see.' The commander wrinkled his nose. He always treated highly qualified medical practitioners with some deference, and would never dream of referring to them by their first name. Perhaps he feared that one of them would one day declare him unfit for further service. Then he wouldn't know what the hell to do with himself.

Henry Mortlock was always at his best when he was conducting a post-mortem. Attired in all-over white – tunic, trousers and rubber boots – he was lovingly sorting through his collection of ghoulish instruments when I arrived.

'Ah, Harry, you've got here. Now I can begin.'

After some consideration, he selected a scalpel and opened up the body from throat to pubis to the accompaniment of his very own hummed version of some obscure symphony. Well, it was obscure to me.

15

It took an hour of incision, muttering and the occasional operatic aria before Henry declared himself reasonably satisfied. He was never more than *reasonably* satisfied. 'I'll let you have my report, Harry,' he said, 'but on the face of it, my professional opinion is that this young woman died as a result of strangulation with a ligature and was dead before she entered the water.'

What a coincidence. I'd more or less worked that out for myself.

'There's some post-mortem grazing on the woman's back,' Henry continued, 'and I'm of the view that she'd been dead less than twenty-four hours when your fishermen dredged her up. Oh, and she'd indulged in sexual intercourse – probably consensual – shortly before dying. I've obtained a sample from the victim's vagina. Might be a good idea to send it for DNA analysis.'

'That *is* a good idea, Henry,' I said, but my sarcasm escaped this eminent pathologist.

All I had to do now was find the guy who'd had it off with her. He might be the murderer, but knowing my luck, maybe not.

Dave and I grabbed a quick bite to eat and then hastened back to Curtis Green in time for Colin Wilberforce to announce that a piece of good news had flooded in. The woman's fingerprints were on record and we now had a name: Patricia Hunter.

'What's her form, Colin?' If she was on record she must have been convicted of a crime within the past seven years. Otherwise a compassionate government would have declared it to be a 'spent' conviction and rubbed it out. Bit like the victim herself.

'One previous five years ago for shoplifting in Oxford Street, sir. Fined three hundred pounds plus costs. Her antecedents show her to have been an actress at the time.' Colin looked up and grinned. We both knew what that was a euphemism for. 'And they also show that her fine was paid by a guy called Bruce Phillips. There's no address for him.'

'Have you got an address for the woman?' I asked.

'According to this' – Colin waved the print-out –'she was living at nineteen Saxony Street, Chelsea, sir. But, as I said, that was five years ago.'

'Age?'

Colin had no need to refer to the woman's record again. 'She'd've been twenty-six now, sir,' he said promptly, having already worked it out.

I glanced at the clock: half past two. 'Know where Saxony Street, Chelsea, is, Dave?'

'Not offhand, guv, but no doubt I'll find it,' said Dave with a sigh.

Saxony Street was not far from Chelsea Embankment, which, given that Patricia Hunter had been found floating in the river, was interesting. But probably irrelevant.

We introduced ourselves to a svelte brunette of indeterminate age who told us her

17

name was Clare Barker.

Once seated in her plush sitting room, we explained that we were trying to trace any friends or relatives of Patricia Hunter who had, according to our records, lived at 19 Saxony Street five years previously.

'Is she a missing person?' asked Mrs Barker.

'Not any more,' said Dave.

'Oh!' That seemed to mystify Mrs Barker momentarily. 'Well, my husband and I bought this house about two years ago,' she said. 'The previous owners had converted it into three flats, but we changed it back and refurbished it, and now we occupy the whole house.'

'So the name Patricia Hunter doesn't mean anything to you?'

'No, I'm sorry. I've no idea where you'd find her now.'

'We *have* found her,' said Dave. 'Floating in the river.'

'Oh, my goodness!' Mrs Barker looked shocked and put a hand to her mouth. 'Was it an accident?'

'We don't think so,' I said. 'She'd been strangled.' That'll give the Chelsea set something to chatter about, I thought.

'How dreadful,' was Mrs Barker's further contribution to the conversation.

'Can you tell me who you bought the house from?' I asked hopefully. The death of Patricia Hunter was already showing signs of developing into a complex investigation. But little did I know then that it was going to get

18

considerably more complex before we found the woman's killer.

'I'll ask my husband.' Mrs Barker rose from her chair. 'He's in the study and he dealt with all of that,' she added over her shoulder as she glided gracefully from the room.

A few moments later she reappeared followed by a man in a Paisley shirt and chinos. 'I'm Sandy Barker,' he said. 'How can I help you? Clare mentioned something about a murder,' he added with a frown.

I repeated what we knew and what we wanted to know.

'As Clare told you, we bought the house about two years ago.' Barker handed me a business card. 'That's the estate agent who handled the sale – they're in the King's Road – and the people we bought the house from were called Mason. I think that was their name.' He glanced at his wife and she nodded.

'Any idea where these Masons moved to?' I asked, hoping to short-circuit a visit to the estate agent.

'No, sorry,' said Barker.

'Does the name Bruce Phillips mean anything to you?'

'No, sorry,' said Barker again.

Oh well, it was worth a try.

'There's nothing we can do until the morning, Dave,' I said as we drove back to Curtis Green. 'We may as well have an early night while we've still got the chance.'

Not that Dave ever minded working late. His gorgeous wife Madeleine was a principal ballet dancer, and rarely got home before midnight.

As for my girlfriend Sarah Dawson, a scientist at the Metropolitan Forensic Science Laboratory, she's grown accustomed to the bizarre hours I work. I think she even believes me now when I tell her I've been working late at the office.

Two

The ligature had been sent to the forensic science laboratory, and I decided to go there myself. For two reasons. Firstly to see Sarah and, secondly, to see if I could hurry up the analysis of the ligature. Which *also* meant seeing Sarah, because she is the rope, yarn, string and miscellaneous ligatures expert. I do love combining business with pleasure.

Sarah is thirty-one and gorgeous. She has long black hair, long legs and an hour-glass figure. But now, perched on a stool at her bench, she was in her professional mode, emphasized by the white lab coat she was wearing, and the heavy black-framed glasses.

'I thought you'd be here sooner or later, Harry,' she said.

'So, what can you tell me, darling?'

'About what?' Sarah didn't smile, just appraised me rather severely over her glasses. I got the disturbing feeling that she didn't want to see me today. Perhaps it was just that she was rather busy.

'The ligature.'

'Ah, the ligature.' Sarah swung round on her stool, revealing a black nylon-clad knee. 'You can have all the scientific mumbo-jumbo if you want it, Harry, but it's some form of thin electrical flex, and it was tied in a running slipknot.'

'A running slipknot, eh? Were you a Girl Guide?' I asked.

'Yes, as a matter of fact, I was.'

'You never told me about that.'

'There are a lot of things you don't know about me,' said Sarah. But, despite the banter, I detected something tense about her this afternoon. And her enigmatic comment was to prove truer than I knew.

'It was obviously tied at the back of the neck then,' I mused. 'There was no knot visible from the front when I examined the body.'

'That would be right,' said Sarah. 'The CSEs said it was tied at the back.'

'What sort of electrical wire was it?'

'Fairly standard, I should think.' Sarah smiled. 'But finding out's your job, Harry. You're the detective. I've no idea where it came from. And there's one more thing which is bound to excite you.'

'Apart from what usually excites me, you mean?'

'There was the slightest trace of greasepaint on the piece of wire,' she said, making no attempt to match my badinage.

'That's interesting. The victim, Patricia Hunter, was an actress.'

'That should be easy then. There are only about fifty theatres in London.'

That sort of sarcasm was alien to Sarah's

character and I wondered what had ruffled her feathers. I found out almost immediately.

'Thanks.' I started towards the door, but Sarah stopped me.

'Harry.' She turned back to her bench and toyed with a pair of callipers.

'What is it?'

It was some seconds before she answered, but then she faced me once again. 'I've resigned from the lab,' she said as she took off her glasses.

'Resigned? But what are you going to do? You've got a brilliant career ahead of you and—'

Sarah held up a hand. 'I'm moving to Poole in Dorset, Harry,' she said simply.

'Christ, that must be a hundred miles away,' I said. I was completely taken aback by her bald statement. 'But why? I thought that we – you and I – were going to make something of this relationship.'

Tears welled up in her eyes. 'It can't be helped, Harry. My father's seriously ill and my mother can't cope. They're both in their late sixties and...' She paused for a moment. 'I don't think my father will last too long. It's one of those things that can't be helped,' she said again. 'I wish to God there was some other way.'

'But I thought your parents lived in Cornwall. Helston if I remember correctly.'

'They did, but they got fed up with Cornish winters. I persuaded them to move to Dorset. There's a flat in their new house that I'm

23

'going to occupy ... for a while anyway.'

'For a while?' I didn't like the sound of any of this. 'But what about your sister? Can't she do anything to help out?' Sarah's sister Margaret lived in Staines with her carping little husband David, an air-traffic controller at Heathrow, and their two kids.

'There's no way she can get to Poole on a regular basis, not with David's job and everything. The best that he could do would be to get a transfer to the air-traffic control centre at Swanwick, but that's still fifty miles away, and even so, Margaret's never been one for worrying about our parents too much. And she's got a job and the children to ferry back and forth to school.'

'But what about us?' I asked. I was at the beginning of a tricky murder investigation that I suspected would go on and on, and the last thing I wanted was the sudden departure of my girlfriend. Call it selfish if you like, but I'd nurtured high hopes that we would get married. Now, however, Sarah had suddenly announced that she was moving over a hundred miles away. The implication was that I might never see her again.

'Why don't we have dinner tonight?' I said. 'See if we can't sort something out.'

Sarah shook her head. 'Are you seriously suggesting that you'll have time for dinner with all you've got on your plate, Harry?' She obviously hadn't intended the remark to be funny and neither of us laughed.

Suddenly the awful truth dawned on me:

she was trying to let me down lightly. 'Have you met someone else, Sarah?' I asked, hoping to God I was wrong.

The tears began again, and she nodded as she fumbled for a tissue from the box on her bench. 'I'm sorry, Harry.' There was a pause. 'But my father really is ill and I do have to go there to look after him. I wasn't making that up.' She paused again. 'But yes, I have been seeing someone, and we're getting married.'

'Do I know this guy?' I asked lamely.

She shook her head. 'No, he's in the army.'

'Oh, not again.' Her previous fiancé, Captain Peter Hunt, had been killed a few years ago during some footling exercise on Salisbury Plain and I didn't think she'd ever recovered from it. But now ... 'How did you meet?'

'At Bovingdon Camp. That's in Dorset too.'

'I know. I was quite good at geography.' I tried to keep the sarcasm out of my voice, but failed miserably.

'Last April, I had to go down there to do some work for which the military police hadn't the resources. I stayed overnight in one of their messes and this major took me in to dinner. It just went on from there. I'm truly sorry, Harry.'

'You mean he's a military policeman?' I briefly considered making some trite remark about jumping out of the frying pan into the fire, but thought better of it.

'No, he just happened to be there. He's in the Hussars and he lives in the mess.' Sarah paused. 'I won't invite you to the wedding, Harry. It wouldn't be fair.'

'I hope you'll be very happy, Sarah,' I said and turned on my heel. I was too choked to say anything else.

'You're looking decidedly fed up with life, guv,' said Dave, when I got back to the office.

'Yeah, well, a complex murder is not exactly designed to cheer you up, Dave,' I said, deciding against telling him about my break-up with Sarah. At least, not yet. I knew that very soon he would come up with another invitation to see Madeleine performing in a ballet. Time enough then. I suppose I still nurtured a vain hope that it would all come right again, and that the bold Hussar was an infatuation that would go away as quickly as it had arrived to disrupt our bliss.

Fortunately I was likely to be heavily en-grossed in the murder I was investigating, with little time, I hoped, to feel sorry for my-self. Having finally divorced my wife Helga and moved to a flat in Surbiton, everything had been going swimmingly: Sarah and I had really hit it off. And then this.

I couldn't blame her really, try as I might; there's no contest between a detective facing danger at all hours – her view, not mine – and an army officer in a swish uniform who'd take her to glittering balls, point-to-point meet-ings and polo matches. Well, that's the way I saw the army. I just hoped, for Sarah's sake, that he didn't end up in Iraq or some such

God-awful place. I don't think she could stand losing another soldier.

'Let's find something to eat, Dave,' I said.

Detective Constable Nicola Chance had been busy in my absence. During the morning, she'd visited the estate agent who'd handled the sale and purchase of the house in which the Barkers now lived at Chelsea. The vendors were indeed called Mason, as the Barkers had said, and they lived in Putney. Well, that was a relief. They could have moved to Scotland, I suppose.

But my optimism was short-lived. Nicola had already telephoned them and although they confirmed that Patricia Hunter had rented a flat at 19 Saxony Street, she had left some four years ago and they had no idea where she'd gone. But, they had told Nicola, a man by the name of Bruce Phillips had shared the accommodation with Patricia.

And Bruce Phillips was the guy who'd paid her shoplifting fine.

As if that wasn't enough, the result of the DNA database search had come back: there was no match with the seminal fluid found in Patricia Hunter's body.

But there was one glimmer of useful information in the report from the forensic science laboratory. Fibres had been found in the hair of the dead woman. And tests were being carried out at the laboratory to see if the possible origin of those fibres could be narrowed down.

I sent for Detective Inspector Frank Mead, the former Flying Squad officer in charge of the legwork team that made all the enquiries I didn't have time to make.

'We know that Patricia Hunter was calling herself an actress five years ago, Frank,' I began, 'and with any luck she may still be one.'

'If she was one in the first place, Harry,' said Frank. He also knew that 'actress' was often how call girls described themselves. That's when they weren't calling themselves 'models', of course.

I told him about the slight trace of grease-paint that Sarah had found on the ligature with which the girl had been murdered. 'So it's possible that the body *is* that of an actress,' I said.

'Or a prostitute,' said Frank, refusing to give up.

'Exactly so, but we've got to start with the obvious.'

'Like a check on all the theatres in London,' Frank said with a sigh.

'There's only about fifty of them,' I said with similar irony to that used by Sarah only that morning but which, now, seemed like ages ago. 'And get someone to check the toms' register, too. If she was on the game, we might be able to trace someone who knew her. Or has missed her.'

'Right.' Frank had been making notes as I spoke. 'Anything else?'

'Not at the moment.' I told him about the

28

fibres found in the woman's hair. 'There is one thing puzzling me though. Henry Mortlock said that the body had post-mortem grazing on the back.'

'Given that she finished up in the river,' said Frank, looking up from his pocket book, 'she could have been pushed over a bridge. That might have caused the grazing.'

'That's what I was thinking. Get someone to have a word with Thames Division' – I couldn't be bothered with this Marine Support Unit business – 'and see if anyone there can hazard a guess as to where the body might have gone into the river.'

'I thought you'd asked them already.'

'I spoke to them on Wednesday, but we didn't know how long the victim had been dead then. With any luck we'll finish up with a fairly short stretch of the river and not many bridges. And if the grazing was caused by a concrete coping, we can rule out those with metal guard rails, like Waterloo Bridge, Albert Bridge, Tower Bridge and one or two others. At least, I think they've got metal rails. But get someone to check it anyway. With any luck we can reduce it to two or three bridges. That at least might give us a starting point. If this girl really was pushed off a bridge, that is. It's a shot in the dark, I know, but right now we're clutching at straws.'

'I don't see any straws at all, guv,' said Dave and paused. 'But what about dentists?'

'What d'you mean by dentists, Dave? You got a dental problem?'

'Not me, her.'

With exaggerated patience, an unusual trait in my make-up, I said, 'Would you mind explaining that?'

'Why don't we get an odontologist to make a chart of the victim's teeth and send it round to dentists. Might just be that she's had some treatment recently and her dentist could give us a current address.'

'D'you know how many dentists there are in London, Dave?' I asked.

'Got a better idea, sir?' Dave always called me 'sir' when I asked what he regarded as a stupid question.

I had to admit that I couldn't come up with anything that was more feasible than Dave's suggestion. I turned to Frank Mead. 'Does the job still have its own tame dentist, or at least a consultant on its books?'

'I don't know, Harry, but I'll find out. We might get lucky.'

'We need to get something,' I said gloomily.

'I'll get the team started on the theatres, then,' said Frank. 'You never know, we might get *really* lucky.'

'That'll be the day, guv,' said Dave.

Until we started to get the results of the enquiries that had been put in tow, and the outcome of the scientific analyses, there was little point in working over the weekend.

But by Monday, things had begun to happen.

A report from the lab had partially identified the fibre found in the victim's hair. Although it later turned out to be a bum steer, the examining scientist was of the opinion that the fibre was likely to have come from the floor covering in a Ford, Bedford or Renault van.

I tried not to get too excited by this shred of information, but it did point to the possibility that the victim's body had been transported from wherever she had been killed to where she had been pitched into the river.

But then she would have been, wouldn't she? I didn't somehow see a guy carrying the body of a dead nude woman through the streets. Oh, I don't know though: these days anything goes. If he had the unlikely misfortune to meet a patrolling constable he'd probably claim to be taking her to a fancy-dress ball at a nudist colony.

There was only one problem: there were thousands of Ford, Bedford and Renault vans in and around London. And we still didn't know which bridge the woman had been thrown from, assuming we had guessed right that the grazing was caused by a bridge coping anyway.

Later on the Monday, Frank Mead reported that a chart of Patricia Hunter's teeth had been prepared and forwarded to the General Dental Council in Wimpole Street for circulation.

Three

It was at about three o'clock on Monday afternoon that I got the phone call from a DI at Charing Cross.

'I understand you're dealing with the Patricia Hunter job, guv'nor,' he said.

'Yes, I am.'

'Ah!' There was a distinct pause. 'I've just been doing a bit of checking up...'

'Congratulations.'

'I've been on annual leave for a few days, you see.'

'Go on.' I was beginning to get disturbing vibes about this phone call.

'Well, not to put too fine a point on it, guv, there's been a bit of a cock-up.'

'I'm glad nothing's changed in the job,' I said. 'So?'

'This Patricia Hunter was reported missing here last Friday.' The Charing Cross DI sounded unhappy about all this and, as the tale unfolded, it proved that he was entitled to be. 'The clown who took the details forgot to enter it on the PNC. It was only this morning that I heard someone mentioning it. I found the idiot who took the report and put a squib up his arse.'

'Oh, good!' It wasn't the DI's fault. In fact, he had been the one who'd spotted the error. Every report of a missing person should be entered on the Police National Computer database. Someone had indeed cocked up.

'Who was the informant?' I asked.

'A Miss Gail Sutton.'

'Address?'

'She's got a bedsit at thirty-seven Griffin Street – it's off Kingsway somewhere – and she's currently appearing in a musical called...' There was a rustling of paper and I visualized the DI fervently riffling through his notes. 'Yeah, got it. *Scatterbrain* at the Granville.'

'What time will she be there?' This was pure laziness on my part, although I preferred to regard it as economic use of the commissioner's time, the Granville Theatre being closer to my office than Kingsway.

'Hang on a minute.' There were further rustlings. 'Monday to Thursday she gets in at about seven. In the evening that is. Fridays about four and Saturdays at two. Sorry about all this, guv.'

'So will my commander be,' I said, determined not to afford the collective staff of Charing Cross police station too much comfort.

The stage-door keeper at the Granville was seventy at least, either that or he'd had a hard life, and sported a ragged, nicotine-stained walrus moustache.

'Yus?' He looked up from the racing page of that morning's edition of the *Sun* and peered at me through finger-marked, pebble-lensed, vintage spectacles.

'We're police officers,' I said, indicating Dave as I did so. 'We want to see a Miss Gail Sutton.'

'I'll bet you do, guv'nor,' said the stage-door keeper with a cackle. 'Everyone does. Bit of all right, she is. A real beauty. I'll see if I can get hold of her.' He chuckled again. 'Everyone wants to get hold of *her*, and who's to blame 'em, eh?' He moved a mug of tea to one side, ran his finger down a list and made a telephone call. 'She's a smasher,' he added as he waited for an answer.

'I think I get the picture,' I said.

The stage-door keeper hadn't exaggerated. The blonde who appeared some minutes later was tall – probably about five-ten, even without her high heels – and wore a feathered headdress that added a good ten inches to her already impressive height. And she was indeed a beauty.

Beneath her open robe was a figure-hugging basque in red and gold satin above a pair of very long legs that were encased in sheer black nylon.

'I'm Gail Sutton. How can I help you?' she asked in cultured tones, casting an appraising glance at Dave.

'We're police officers, Miss Sutton. Is there somewhere we can talk in private?' There was now a constant stream of chattering people

34

passing through the stage door.

Without a word the girl led us down a short flight of stone steps and into an unused dressing room that was not much larger than a cupboard.

'What's this about?' she asked, turning to face us.

'Patricia Hunter,' I said.

'Oh, at last. I was beginning to wonder if the police were in the slightest bit interested in her disappearance.'

'I'm Detective Chief Inspector Brock of the Serious Crime Group,' I began. 'I'm afraid that Miss Hunter is dead.'

'Oh my God, no!' The girl sat down heavily on a hard wooden chair, the only seat in the small room, and crossed her legs. Outside there was a burst of laughter as more people – members of the cast, I presumed – traipsed down the steps.

'When did you last see her, Miss Sutton?' I asked, having explained the circumstances in which Patricia Hunter's body had been found.

'You don't happen to have a cigarette, do you?' The girl was obviously distressed by the news we had just given her. 'And I wish you'd call me Gail.'

I gave her a Marlboro, and Dave produced his cigarette lighter with all the panache of an unctuous head waiter.

'Thanks.' Gail blew a plume of smoke into the air and dispersed it with a wave of her hand. 'I saw Patricia at about eleven o'clock last Monday evening, after we'd finished the show, but she didn't turn up for either the Tuesday or Wednesday performances. I had a word with Charlie—'

'Charlie?' queried Dave.

'Charlie's the stage-door keeper,' said Gail, 'but he hadn't heard from her. I wondered if she'd been taken ill or something. Anyway, when she didn't turn up for the Thursday-evening performance, I began to get really worried, so I went up to her place—'

'Where is that?' asked Dave.

'Coping Road, Islington. Number thirty-four,' said Gail. 'Anyway, her landlady hadn't seen anything of her either and was a bit worried. So I popped into Charing Cross police station and reported her missing. You see, no one in the theatre had heard from her, and there was no answer when I rang her mobile.' Somewhere outside, a bell rang. 'Ah, overture and beginners,' she said. 'I'm on in ten minutes.'

'What part d'you play?' asked Dave.

Gail gave a scornful laugh. 'I'm in the chorus line, darling,' she said. 'And quite frankly at thirty-five I'm getting a bit too old for it. A show every night, Monday to Thursday, and two on Fridays and Saturdays. Wears a girl out, I can tell you,' she added, forcing a smile in Dave's direction.

'Yeah, I know,' said Dave. 'My wife's a dancer.'

'Really? What's she in?'

'The Royal Ballet,' said Dave.

'Oh, a classical dancer.' There was a hint of envy in the way Gail said it. 'I wanted to go into the ballet, but they said I was too tall. So here I am hoofing it for a living in this silly costume.'

'It's a very nice costume,' said Dave, making that comment an excuse for appraising the girl's legs once more.

'Look, Gail,' I said, interrupting this cosy little chat, 'we really need to talk to you at some length, and now doesn't seem to be the right moment. When can you spare us some time?'

'Could you make it tomorrow morning at about eleven? Would that be OK?'

'Certainly,' I said. 'And I understand you live at thirty-seven Griffin Street.'

'It's only a bedsit,' said Gail, confirming what the Charing Cross DI had told me. 'I go home at the weekends ... what's left of them. I live in Kingston.'

'With your husband?'

Gail gave me a long, penetrating look before replying to what was blatantly an unnecessary question. 'Not any more,' she said disdainfully. 'We divorced about three years ago.' She stood up. 'If you'll excuse me, the show must go on.' Pausing at the door, she said, 'Why don't you come in and see it? Charlie will fix you up with a couple of seats. There are plenty to spare.'

'I'd love to,' I said, 'but unfortunately we don't have the time. We've a murder to investigate.'

★ ★ ★

Dave and I went straight from the Granville to the address that Gail Sutton had given us for our murder victim.

The landlady was a businesslike woman named Mrs Parsons. She was about fifty, and clearly didn't much like the look of us. Until we told her who we were and why we were there.

'Aren't you supposed to have a warrant to search someone's room?' Mrs Parsons posed the question hesitantly when we asked if we could have a look round Patricia Hunter's bedsit.

But Dave knew how to deal with such half-hearted obstruction. 'Not when the occupant's dead,' he said.

'*Dead?* Holy Mary, Mother of God!' Mrs Parsons crossed herself. 'When did this happen?'

'Her body was found in the river last Wednesday evening, Mrs Parsons,' I said. 'She'd been murdered.'

'Oh the poor dear child.' Mrs Parsons's mild Irish accent became a little more pronounced.

At a guess the wallpaper in Patricia Hunter's sparsely furnished room must have been at least ten years old, and was peeling in places, mainly from the damp that was seeping through the walls. The room looked very much as though it was only used for sleeping during the working week. I'm not too familiar with theatrical lodgings, but I

38

imagined it to be fairly typical.

'Found anything, Dave?' I asked, by which I meant anything that was likely to reveal more about Patricia Hunter than we already knew. Which was precious little.

'A notebook with addresses in it, a building-society passbook and some corres, guv.'

'Corres' is police shorthand for any form of correspondence, and these days, I suppose, anything stored on a computer.

'What does it tell us, Dave?'

'The passbook's got about eighteen grand in it, and all the letters are from a couple called Mum and Dad. Probably her parents,' he added with a smirk.

'We'll make a detective of you yet,' I said. 'Where do her parents live?'

'Wimbledon,' said Dave. 'And that's the address in the passbook, too.'

'Eighteen thousand pounds is a lot to have in the bank,' I mused. 'She doesn't get paid that well, surely.'

'Perhaps she's a bit more than a chorus girl,' said Dave.

'Yeah, quite possibly.' Perhaps Frank Mead had been right after all, and she had been a prostitute, if only part-time.

'There's something else,' said Dave, still thumbing through the book he'd found. 'This guy Bruce Phillips has popped up again. There's an address for him here: nine Petersfield Street, Fulham. Flat twelve.'

'I'm looking forward to meeting Mr Phillips,' I said. 'I've a feeling he may be able

39

to assist us in our enquiries.' I glanced at my watch. 'But right now we'd better go and tell Patricia Hunter's parents.' It was not a task I relished, even after upwards of twenty-four years in the job. Her name had been deliberately withheld from the press until we'd found her family, but now we were going to have to break the news to them. Turning back to the landlady, I asked, 'How long had Miss Hunter lived here?'

'It must be a couple of months now,' said Mrs Parsons. 'She was in *Scatterbrain* at the Granville, you know. We get a lot of theatricals here, and I'm glad to have them. They're never any trouble. Too tired, most of the time, poor dears.'

'Did she ever mention a man called Bruce Phillips?'

'Not to me, but like I said, she'd only been here a few months. We hardly had time to chat, what with the hours she worked.'

'Did she have any callers?'

'Not that I know of.'

'D'you know if she went anywhere last weekend?' I asked.

'Well, she didn't stay here, that's for sure. She left for the theatre on Saturday afternoon and I didn't see her again until the Monday morning.'

'Any idea where she went, Mrs Parsons?'

'I think she said she'd been to Brighton, but I don't know where. She mentioned something about having connections down there.'

'There's a Brighton address in this book of

hers, guv,' said Dave. 'Number sixteen Fenwick Road. Well, I imagine it's the address where she stayed. Mr and Mrs Hunter, it says here.' And he tapped the little book.

'I wonder if they're relatives. Either that or they're Patricia Hunter's parents and have moved recently.'

'It'd have to be very recent,' said Dave. 'One of the letters from "Mum and Dad" is dated last month.'

'Even so, Dave, it looks as though we're due a trip to Brighton.'

'Can't we get the local law to do it, guv? After all, it might be a blow-out.'

I gave that some thought, but not for long. 'Good idea. We could go traipsing down there and find they're out. Get Colin Wilberforce to ring the Brighton police and ask them to make an appointment for us to see Mr and Mrs Hunter tomorrow afternoon.'

'Right, guv,' said Dave, and pulled out his mobile.

I turned to Patricia Hunter's landlady. 'Thank you for you help, Mrs Parsons. We may have to see you again, of course. However, in the meantime I'd like to have some of my other officers come here to do a proper search of her room and her belongings, probably first thing tomorrow morning. Will that be all right?'

'Yes, of course.' Mrs Parsons shook her head sadly. 'I still can't believe it,' she said.

Given that the letters Dave had found in

Patricia Hunter's room were dated only a matter of weeks ago, it seemed likely that her parents were living in Wimbledon rather than Brighton. So we went there first, even though it was now quite late in the day, but it was the sort of unpalatable duty that could not be delayed.

Having arranged to meet a family liaison officer at Wimbledon police station, the three of us made our way to the Hunters' house. According to the electoral roll, they were called Robert and Daphne.

'Do you have a daughter called Patricia, Mr Hunter?' I asked, once we were settled in their front room.

'Yes, we do,' said Hunter, a worried expression already on his face. 'What's happened?' But he and his wife knew instinctively why we were there.

'I'm afraid I've got some bad news for you,' I said.

There is no easy or sympathetic way to tell people that their daughter has been murdered, but I did it as quickly and as tactfully as possible.

It's not as if I didn't know how they felt. I shall never forget the day the governor called me into his office to tell me that my four-year-old son Robert had drowned in a neighbour's pond while Helga was at work. And that was the start of the long-drawn-out dispute between Helga and me that had led, eventually, to our divorce.

Daphne Hunter had burst into tears at the

42

news of her daughter's death and was still sobbing uncontrollably. I was glad that the liaison officer was a woman. They're much better than men at coping with that sort of thing.

The FLO took Mrs Hunter upstairs to her bedroom and then went into the kitchen to make tea. It's the copper's universal panacea: if in doubt, make some tea.

But I still had to find out what had happened to Patricia. Beyond what we knew already, that is. Which wasn't a great deal.

'Mr Hunter, can you tell me if your daughter had any boyfriends?' I asked, once he was alone with Dave and me.

'Quite a few, I should imagine.' Hunter had maintained a stoic reserve at the news of his daughter's death. 'She was an attractive girl.'

'What did she do for a living?' I knew that Patricia had been in *Scatterbrain* at the time of her death, but I wondered whether she had pursued another career prior to taking up dancing.

There was a long pause before Hunter answered. 'She was a dancer, Mr Brock. It wasn't a choice of career I approved of, and neither did my wife. We might be old-fashioned, but the theatre seems to me to be a sordid world, and the idea of our daughter being mixed up with those people did worry us. We weren't very keen on her living in Islington, either, but she said it was all that she could afford. You see, Trisha wanted to earn enough to put herself through university. She was a very bright kid at school, got A-levels and all that sort of thing. But I'm a fire-fighter, and even though the missus works on the check-out at a local supermarket, there's still not enough money to pay for higher education. She was determined though, and said she didn't mind what she did if it meant that she could get a degree. She wanted to be a solicitor.'

'It looks as though she was getting near her goal,' I said. 'Her bank book had eighteen thousand pounds in it.'

'Good God!' said Hunter. 'I had no idea. The theatre obviously pays better than I thought.'

'D'you know where she was working ... as a dancer?' I knew, but I wondered if he did.

'No, I'm afraid not, not exactly. It was a West End theatre. At least that's what she told us. We asked if we could come and see the show she was in, but she said it wouldn't be worth it.' Hunter gave a bleak smile. 'She said she was in the back row of the chorus and we wouldn't even see her.' He paused. 'I must admit it made me wonder.'

'Wonder what, Mr Hunter?'

'If she was in the theatre at all.'

'When was this?'

'About a year ago, I think.'

'Have you any idea how long she had been on the stage?'

'About five years, I think, but she never said much about it on the rare occasions we saw her. Always changed the subject, if you know what I mean.'

'How long ago did Patricia leave home, Mr Hunter?'

'It must be all of six years now.'

'Do you happen to know the names of any of her boyfriends?'

'I think she mentioned some chap in one of her letters,' said Hunter. 'I'll see if I can find it.' He stood up and left the room with the slow shambling walk of a man bowed down with grief.

He returned a few moments later, clutching a piece of blue notepaper. 'His name was Bruce Phillips,' he said, 'but she didn't say much more about him than that she'd met him. Daphne – that's the wife – said she thought it sounded serious. You know what women are, always hoping for a wedding so they can buy a new hat. We wrote and asked when we could meet him, but Trisha never replied.'

'Did she mention his address, or how long she'd known him?' I asked.

'No,' said Hunter, 'just the name.'

'One last question. Does the address sixteen Fenwick Road, Brighton, mean anything to you?'

Robert Hunter shook his head immediately. 'Not a thing,' he said. 'Should it?'

'It was listed in your daughter's address book with the names Mr and Mrs Hunter against it.' I looked up. 'Not relatives, then?'

'Not as far as I know,' said Hunter.

And that was it. All that our interview with

Patricia Hunter's father had achieved was to muddy the waters a little more than they were muddied already.

The reply from the Brighton police was waiting for me when I arrived at the office the following morning. There was no Mr and Mrs Hunter living at 16 Fenwick Road, nor had there been for at least the last four years. The address was that of a boarding house that catered for holiday visitors and was run by a couple called Richards.

'I suppose we'll have to go down there at some time,' I said.

'Thought we might,' said Dave. 'Nothing like a day at the seaside to cheer us up.'

'Yes, but first we've an appointment with Gail Sutton.'

Gail Sutton's room was small but very tidy. The bed was one of those contraptions that folds up against the wall, and there was an armchair, a dressing table and a television set. And precious little else.

This morning, the chorus girl was dressed in jeans and a tee shirt. 'Excuse my bare feet,' she said, 'but hoofing in a pair of heels isn't good for them. I like to let them out occasionally.' She pulled down the bed and invited us to sit on it. 'Sorry about the accommodation, but it's really only somewhere to sleep when I've finished at the theatre. As I said, I live in Kingston.'

'I live in Surbiton,' I said.

46

'Oh, whereabouts?'

We exchanged addresses and then got down to business.

'We think that Patricia may have had some connection with Brighton. Did she ever mention Brighton in conversation?'

'No, I don't remember her doing so.'

'D'you know if she had any men friends, Gail?'

'Not that I know of. Of course, we all get the usual pushy lechers who hang around the stage door in dirty raincoats, but a few choice Anglo-Saxon words usually sees them off.' She laughed at the thought. 'And more often than not there's a policeman there at turning-out time to see we're all right.'

'I'll bet there is,' I said. *And to hell with crime.* 'But I was thinking more of a regular boyfriend that Patricia might have had. Did she, for example, ever mention a man called Bruce Phillips?' The guy who had paid Patricia's shoplifting fine five years ago – and had been described to her parents as a boyfriend – was still intriguing me, but relationships tend to come and to go. As I knew only too well. 'Lives in Fulham.'

Gail shook her head slowly. 'I don't recall her mentioning anyone of that name,' she said, 'but perhaps...'

'Perhaps what?'

'Over the last couple of weeks she's been shooting off straight after the show.'

'D'you think she was meeting somebody?'

'Possibly, but if she was, she was unusually

secretive about it. Normally we talk about boyfriends with each other. All the girls do.' Gail shot me an amused glance. 'I suppose you men are the same about girlfriends.'

'When we've got girlfriends to talk *about*,' I said somewhat wistfully.

Dave looked sideways at me, a quizzical expression on his face; I'd have to tell him about Sarah's departure soon, I supposed. But Gail was on it immediately.

'You're not married, then?'

'No, divorced. But to get back to Patricia, you've no idea who this was she may have been meeting?'

'No, I'm sorry. I'd love to be able to help. She was my closest friend.'

'Does that mean you knew her before this show started then?'

'Oh no, but one tends to make friends quickly in this game,' said Gail. 'And lose them just as quickly,' she added, a sad expression on her face.

'What sort of girl was Patricia?' I asked.

Gail didn't hesitate. 'She was a super girl. There were times when I thought she was too innocent to be in the theatre. Very homely sort of kid. Always talking about her parents. In fact she used to visit them quite often.'

That, however, did not accord with what Patricia Hunter's father had said. He had talked of 'the rare occasions when we saw her'.

That our victim was supposedly a homely, parent-loving girl certainly didn't fool Dave.

48

He looked up from his pocket book. 'Was Patricia bisexual, Gail?' he asked.

Gail stared at him in surprise. 'Why on earth should you think that?'

'I don't think it, I'm just asking the question.'

'I'd put money on her being straight,' said Gail, but it was obvious that the possibility had never occurred to her.

I knew why Dave had posed the question: he was wondering if Patricia Hunter had been having an affair with another woman. If so, that might have explained her secretiveness. And if that was the case, she might have been murdered by that other woman. Lesbian murders were not unknown in the annals of crime.

Four

It had gone half past three that afternoon by the time we reached 16 Fenwick Road, Brighton. There was a neon sign over the door, which read 'The Golden Riviera Guest House'.

'Bloody hell!' said Dave. 'Talk about delusions of grandeur.'

John Richards – he ran the place with his wife Barbara, he told us – was a dapper little man in his forties, with a pencil-line moustache and a fold-over hairstyle. He looked as though he'd have been more at home running a hairdressing salon than a boarding house.

'As a matter of fact, we had the police here yesterday,' he announced when we'd told him who we were.

'I know,' I said, 'that's why we're here.' I explained how his establishment featured in our enquiry, and asked if the names Mr and Mrs Hunter, Patricia Hunter or Bruce Phillips meant anything to him.

Richards shook his head. 'As I told the police yesterday, I've never heard of any of them,' he said, as he conducted us into what he described as the lounge, where, at one end, he had created a small bar. It was fussily done: a large mirror behind spirit bottles in optics, coloured glasses on shelves illuminated by spotlights and a flashing neon sign that read 'Every Hour is Happy Hour'. 'Care for a drink, gents?'

'No thanks. Did any young women stay here over the last two or three weeks, Mr Richards?' I asked, bearing in mind that Gail Sutton told us that Patricia Hunter had been secretive about her movements during that time. 'This one would have been about twenty-six. A good-looking brunette.'

'We've had quite a few girls like that staying here,' said Richards, 'but usually with their husbands ... or partners, I suppose I should say. Must be politically correct these days,' he added with an embarrassed laugh.

'This would have been between late on a Saturday and first thing on a Monday. And very likely last Saturday.'

Richards shook his head. 'We only take bookings Saturday to Saturday,' he said. 'One-nighters will usually go to a hotel. Either on the seafront or somewhere in town. There's plenty to choose from.'

'What about young men staying here on their own?'

'Been one or two. I think they come down here from the Smoke intent on picking up a girl in one of the nightclubs, but I tend to discourage bookings from their sort. Nothing but trouble. They're either peddling drugs or they come in late, pissed out of their brains.'

'I'd like to have a look at your register,' said

Dave, opening his pocket book and waggling his pen in anticipation. 'Or is it all on a computer?'

'God, no. I can't cope with those things. Won't keep you a minute.' Seconds later Richards reappeared with a large book.

'You've had three or four single men staying here over the past couple of months,' Dave said accusingly, as he glanced up.

'I told you that. But at the end of the day, we're in this business to make money, you know, and as I said just now, we tend not to encourage singles. They always expect a discount for single-room occupancy.'

Dave scribbled down the names that interested him and then looked up. 'How long have you been here, Mr Richards?'

'About four years now, I suppose. I used to run a newsagent's business in Balham, but I got sick and tired of getting up at four in the morning. And then there were the complaints from people whose papers hadn't been delivered. Half the time the bloody wholesaler's delivery would turn up after the kids who did the paper rounds had gone off, and I finished up having to do it myself. I tell you, there was no fun in it, so me and the missus decided to come down here and set up this place. She was born just along the coast, in Hove.'

'Has it always been a guest house?'

'No, it was a private house when we bought it. Cost us a packet to set it up, but now that we've recouped what we laid out we're into profit.'

'And who were the people you bought it from?' I asked.

Richards furrowed his brow. 'Webster, I think.'

'Not a Mr and Mrs Hunter?'

'No, definitely not. Like I said, the name doesn't mean anything to me. I'm sure it was Webster. A retired bank manager or something of the sort. Went to live in Yorkshire. He was about seventy then, so he's probably dead now. He said something about being browned off with what he called the refugees on social security who were taking over the town.'

First thing next morning, I held a conference with Frank Mead and Dave to mull over what we'd learned so far. It wasn't much.

'The Marine Support Unit wasn't much help, Harry,' said Frank. 'They took a rough guess that Patricia Hunter probably went into the river around Hammersmith, and that she was carried downstream by the current.'

'Can't they be more specific than that?' I asked.

'The problem,' Frank continued, 'is that we know roughly when she died, but not when she went into the river. If you want my opinion, we can forget Hammersmith. It's too iffy.'

'Henry Mortlock reckoned that Patricia Hunter had been dead less than twenty-four hours,' I mused. 'I suppose it's possible that the murderer had her hidden away some-where before he dumped her.'

'You said that Gail Sutton last saw her at eleven o'clock on Monday evening,' volun-teered Frank. 'So the murderer couldn't have had her stacked up for long.'

'*Quot homines, tot sententiae*,' said Dave quietly.

'What the hell does that mean, Poole?' de-manded Frank. He was always irritated by Dave's occasional Latin quotations.

'So many men, so many opinions, guv,' Dave answered.

'Bloody university tossers,' muttered Frank.

Dave Poole had graduated in English at London University, a fact I'd only discovered a year after he'd joined the Serious Crime Group. His grandfather, a doctor, had come over from Jamaica in the fifties and had practised in Bethnal Green. Dave's father, an accountant, had put Dave through university and had been disappointed that his son had become a copper and thus, as Dave himself put it, the black sheep of the family. But I wasn't at all sorry. Dave was one of the best sergeants I'd ever had working with me.

'Anyone else worth following up in the address book you found at Patricia Hunter's place at Coping Road, Dave?' I asked.

'There's Bruce Phillips, the guy who paid Patricia Hunter's shoplifting fine, guv,' said Dave. 'Seems to be popping up everywhere, that guy. And there are one or two others, but it wasn't an index book, just a notebook. So the names and addresses were probably entered in chronological order.'

'Phillips didn't by any chance feature in Richards's register, did he?' I asked.

'What, he of the Golden Riviera Guest House?' asked Dave with a smirk. 'No, guv. The three most recent names in that – for what they're worth – were Craig Pearce, Rikki Thompson and Sam Johnson.'

'I suppose this Sam Johnson didn't stay there with a bloke called Boswell, by any chance?' Frank asked sarcastically, determined to get back at Dave for flaunting his knowledge of Latin.

'Not to my knowledge, sir,' said Dave with a straight face. 'I've put them all on the PNC, guv,' he continued, turning to me, 'but a Bruce Phillips came up. The Australians tried to extradite him for fraud a few years back.'

'What happened?'

'He did a runner. Not been seen since apparently.'

'Frank, perhaps you'd get someone to make enquiries at this Phillips's place in ... where was it, Dave?'

'Number nine Petersfield Street, Fulham. Flat twelve,' replied Dave promptly.

Frank scribbled down the address. 'Good as done,' he said. 'D'you want him brought in? If he's still there, which is extremely unlikely.'

'Not yet. Hang on, though. Dave and I'll do Petersfield Street. You take the three that were listed in the guest-house register at Brighton. Colin Wilberforce has got the addresses in the incident room.'

'Whereabouts are these addresses?' asked Frank.

'One of them is in London, guv,' said Dave, 'one's in Chichester and the other's in Slough.'

'Thanks a bundle,' said Frank.

'I should get the local law to do the ones in Chichester and Slough, Frank,' I said. 'I doubt that they're involved, but if any of them do turn out to be a bit tasty, I'll have a go at them myself.' I glanced at my watch. 'And now, Dave, we'll go and have a chat with the manager of the Granville.'

In my experience, managers of West End theatres are usually rather pompous individuals who parade about in evening dress in the foyer smiling at the patrons just as they are arriving. But disappearing the moment there is a complaint. About the service in the crush bar, the austerity of the seating, the cost of the programmes or the exorbitant price of the ice cream. However, in the case of the Granville, I couldn't have been more wrong.

The woman into whose office Dave and I were shown was about fifty, with immaculate, slightly greying hair, and a smart two-piece suit in navy blue.

'I was hoping to speak to the manager,' I said, unwisely as it turned out. Chauvinist that I am, I assumed that the woman was the manager's secretary.

'I *am* the manager. Elizabeth Price. And you are?'

'Detective Chief Inspector Harry Brock of Scotland Yard, and this is DS Poole, Mrs Price. It is *Mrs* Price, is it?'

'It is indeed. Please sit down. May I offer you some coffee?'

'Thank you.'

Elizabeth Price crossed to a side table. 'I presume you've come about Patricia Hunter.' She spoke over her shoulder as she busied herself pouring coffee from a jug that stood on a heated stand. 'I understand that you were here the day before yesterday and talked about her to another of the chorus girls, Gail Sutton. A tragedy. I'm told she was a good dancer, that girl.' She placed two cups of coffee on our side of the desk and sat down behind it.

'Do you happen to know where her parents live?' I asked. Having already spoken to the Hunters, I knew where they lived, but I was hoping to resolve the apparent enigma of the Mr and Mrs Hunter of Fenwick Road, Brighton, who Patricia had recorded in her address book.

'No, I'm afraid not.' Mrs Price absently stirred her coffee. 'To be perfectly honest, Mr Brock, these girls come and go. The producers of shows like *Scatterbrain* hire the theatre and come with the complete package. We have no part in arranging casting or anything like that.' She paused. 'I could try the producer for you to see if he knows anything

57

about her, but somehow I doubt it.'

'Thank you. That would be helpful.'

While Mrs Price made a telephone call, I gazed around at the framed posters with which the walls were adorned. There had been some well-known shows at the theatre over the years and some well-known actors and actresses in them.

After a short conversation, Mrs Price replaced the receiver. 'I'm sorry, Mr Brock, but he has no idea. To be frank with you, chorus girls are two a penny, and when the producers want a line-up they advertise in *The Stage* and hold auditions. The queue usually stretches halfway down the road outside. Most of the time they don't know the names of the dancers they hire. And even if they do, the girls have probably assumed stage names. If you've been christened Vera Higginbottom, for example, you're unlikely to see it up in lights. These girls all want to be stars, but most of them never make it.'

'No, I suppose not,' I said, digesting this piece of harsh realism.

'Are there any vans here?' Dave asked suddenly.

I knew why he was asking, but Mrs Price looked puzzled by the question.

'Vans? D'you mean the sort that are used for shifting scenery?'

'Any sort.'

'No, there aren't. Moving scenery is the responsibility of the people who put on the show. There are companies that specialize in that sort of thing and when a show closes the producers arrange movement of the scenery. Why, is it important?'

'It could be,' said Dave, not wishing to give too much away.

'And the way this show's going, they'll be turning up to take the scenery away very soon.'

'Is it closing then?'

'Looks like it,' said Mrs Price phlegmatically. 'It's just not getting bums on seats, what with the constant terrorist threat.' She glanced at an old theatre bill advertising a Second World War show entitled *The Yanks Are Coming*, and smiled. 'Contrary to the old song, the Yanks *aren't* coming, not any more. I'll give it another week.'

'We'll have to get a move on then,' said Dave. 'Does your chief electrician happen to be about this morning?'

Mrs Price was clearly having difficulty in following Dave's constantly changing line of questioning, but didn't ask why he wanted to know. Presumably she believed that we knew what we were doing. A refreshing change from the usual armchair detectives who thought they knew more about our job than we did. *And sometimes they did, but we never admitted it.*

'I'll see,' she said, and made another phone call.

A few minutes later the chief electrician appeared in the office. He was wearing a blue boiler suit and his glasses were held together with a piece of sticking plaster across the bridge. 'You wanted me, Mrs Price?'

'Yes, Jim, these gentlemen are from the police. They're making enquiries about Patricia Hunter, the girl who was murdered.' Mrs Price indicated the electrician with a wave of her hand. 'This is Jim Rugg,' she said, turning to me.

Rugg nodded in our direction. 'So how can I help, gents? Terrible business.'

I wasn't sure whether he meant the business Dave and I were in, or the murder of the chorus girl.

Dave opened his briefcase and withdrew a clear plastic bag containing the ligature with which Patricia Hunter had been strangled. 'Have a look at that, Mr Rugg.'

The electrician took the bag and stared closely at the contents. 'What about it?' he asked, looking up.

'Is that sort of wire ever used in the theatre?'

'Could be. It looks like the cable we use for the lighting circuits. There's miles of the stuff running all over the theatre.'

'D'you have a lot of it?'

'We've got drums of it. I keep it in my storeroom. Why, d'you want some?' Rugg asked with a grin.

'Yes, please. Half a metre should do.'

'Half a metre? What you wiring up, then? Half a metre won't get you far.'

'I'm not wiring anything up, Mr Rugg,' said Dave, taking back the exhibit. 'We need it for comparison.'

'Oh, right. I'll nip and get you some.'

'I'll come with you, if I may,' said Dave, and followed the electrician from the room.

'Why on earth does your sergeant need some of that wire, Mr Brock?' asked Mrs Price, surprised yet again by Dave's apparently unrelated demands. Perhaps being in the theatrical business, she thought that all policemen should be as staid and courtly as the principal character in Priestley's *An Inspector Calls.*

'The piece that Sergeant Poole showed Mr Rugg was the wire that Patricia Hunter was strangled with,' I said.

'Good God!' Elizabeth Price gave an involuntary shudder. 'But I thought she was drowned.'

'No. She was certainly found in the river, but she was already dead by the time she went in. As a matter of interest, would your electrician ever have anything to do with greasepaint?'

Mrs Price laughed. 'I doubt it. The electricians are very scathing about the acting profession – it's a trade union thing, I think – and the less they have to do with them the better. But to answer your question, no electrician would have any legitimate reason for having anything to do with greasepaint.' She paused. 'I suppose it's possible they might get some on their hands if they were called to replace a bulb in one of the dressing rooms ... something like that. But it would be accidental. I presume you have a reason for asking.'

'Yes, I do,' I said, without enlightening the theatre manager any further. But I didn't need to.

'Does that mean you have grounds to suspect an electrician of having something to do with that poor girl's death?'

'Not at all,' I said. I thought it unnecessary to tell her that, right now, I was considering it as a possibility. And on the meagre evidence we had so far, a very strong possibility.

'Get your length of flex, Dave?' I asked on the way back to Curtis Green.

'Yes, guv, and it certainly looks like the piece that was round Patricia Hunter's neck. But on the down side, Jim Rugg told me that we'd probably find the same stuff in every theatre in the country. Incidentally, the electrician's storeroom is not kept locked. Anyone could walk in there. I also learned that he's got three assistants working with him at the Granville.'

None of which was a pleasing result. Even in the unlikely event that we found the drum from which our piece of flex had come, we'd only get a mechanical fit if it had been cut directly from what was left.

'Did Rugg know Patricia Hunter?'

'No. He's seen the chorus, obviously – he reckoned there were about twenty or so of them – but says he never had anything to do with them. And, as far as he knew, neither did any of his assistants. He did have occasion to change a few light bulbs around the mirrors in their changing room last week, though. Reckoned it was full of half-naked birds at the time. Some people have all the luck.'

'Nevertheless, I'll get one of Mr Mead's team to have a word with his assistants,' I said. 'In the meantime, grab someone to take your bit of flex across to the lab.'

'Is Sarah dealing with that, guv?'

'Yes.'

Dave paused for a moment or two, as though debating whether to put his next question. 'Is there something wrong between you and Sarah, guv? I mean, if it's none of my business, tell me to belt up.'

'We've split,' I said.

'Sorry to hear that,' said Dave. But that was all he said. The CID is a graveyard of broken marriages and abandoned partnerships.

'The commander wants a word, sir,' said Colin Wilberforce the moment we entered the incident room. I suppose one day the confusing-names squad will change it to 'occurrence room' in the interests of accuracy.

'What about, did he say?'

'No, sir.'

The commander was seated behind his desk. But, there again, where else would he be?

'You wanted me, sir?'

'Ah, Mr Brock...'

The commander always called me 'Mr Brock' rather than 'Harry', in case, I suppose,

I returned the compliment by using his first name. He couldn't have handled that.

'What progress are you making in the Hunter death, Mr Brock?' The commander never called a murder a murder until the jury said it was. After all, it might turn out to be manslaughter. Bit meticulous is the commander. He leaned back in his executive chair and linked his fingers across the waistcoat he invariably wore, winter and summer. I think the waistcoat's a status thing. 'The assistant commissioner was asking,' he added, as though he had no personal interest in the investigation.

I told him that we'd positively identified the dead girl and found out where she'd been living. I also mentioned that she'd been associated with a Bruce Phillips, a fugitive from Australian justice.

'There's an extradition warrant out for him, sir.'

'Why's he not been arrested then, Mr Brock?' asked the commander, as though it was my fault that Phillips was still at large.

'When the Extradition Unit went to knock him off, sir, he'd done a runner.'

The commander frowned at that. 'You mean he'd absconded?'

'Yes, sir,' I said, and only just stopped myself from adding, 'That as well.' The commander's a bit short on humour.

To finish up with, I told him about our visit to the Granville, and threw in a bit of unintelligible mumbo-jumbo about the flex with which Patricia Hunter had been strangled. 'Enquiries are continuing, sir,' I said unnecessarily.

'Yes, good, good.' The commander nodded as though what I had just told him made sense.

Well, it had, of course, but not necessarily to him.

'I'll keep you posted, sir.'

'Of course,' said the commander, in a way that suggested I would be unwise not to do so.

Five

Colin Wilberforce appeared in the doorway of my office.

'Excuse me, sir.'

'Yes, what is it, Colin?'

'While you were with the commander, sir,' he said, 'a Mrs Price rang from the Granville Theatre. She's got some information for you if you'd care to ring back.'

Elizabeth Price certainly had got some information. The first, and comparatively unimportant piece of news, was that *Scatterbrain* was closing on Friday. She sounded almost pleased that her prediction had been correct. The second, and far more useful snippet, was that a man named Peter Crawford had telephoned the theatre enquiring after Patricia Hunter, who, he had said, was his girlfriend.

'What did you say to him, Mrs Price?' I asked.

'I'm afraid I lied. I said that I wasn't responsible for the cast and didn't know the name anyway. I felt a bit guilty at not telling him what had happened, but I didn't want to break the news that his girlfriend was dead, not over the phone. So I took his telephone number and said I'd get someone to call. Did

66

I do the right thing, Mr Brock?'

'You did absolutely the right thing, Mrs Price, and thank you very much. I'll get in touch with him straight away.'

Colin did a subscriber check on Peter Crawford's telephone number, and within minutes came up with the address where he lived.

Peter Crawford's apartment at Burgundy Court, a modern block of flats in Davos Street, Chelsea – not far from Saxony Street where Patricia Hunter had once lived – must have cost an arm and a leg. From which I deduced that Crawford was worth a bob or two. Or he was a villain. But then I'm a cynic.

The suave Crawford was dressed in shirt, slacks and shoes that, judging from their cut and quality, could not possibly have come from a high-street chain store. Inclining his head in bafflement when we introduced ourselves, he invited us into a tastefully furnished sitting room.

'May I offer you gentlemen a drink?'

'No thank you.'

'Do take a seat, then,' said Crawford, indicating a Chesterfield with a sweep of his hand, 'and tell me how I can help you.'

'It's about Patricia Hunter,' I said.

'How did you know that she and I——?'

'The manager of the Granville phoned me to say that you'd been making enquiries about her, Mr Crawford.'

'Well, that's true, but how does that involve

the police?' As Crawford realized how it might possibly have involved us, his expression changed dramatically. 'Oh, God, you don't mean something's happened to her, do you?' It was what, in the theatre, is called a bravura performance. *Perhaps he was an actor. And used greasepaint. And was, therefore, a suspect.*

'I'm afraid so,' I said. 'A week ago, her body was recovered from the Thames. She'd been strangled.'

'But I didn't see anything about that in *The Times*.'

'Her name's not yet been released to the media,' I said.

For a few moments Crawford remained silent, his head forward, chin on chest. Then he made a strange comment. 'I don't think I've ever known anyone who was murdered,' he said.

'How long had you known Miss Hunter?' I asked.

'Only about six or seven weeks, I suppose.'

'And how did you meet?'

There was a moment's hesitation, and then: 'I went to see the show – *Scatterbrain* – and noticed her in the front row of the chorus. I went to see it twice more after that, and then I sent her an invitation to have dinner with me. Bit old-fashioned these days, I suppose, and I didn't think she'd accept. But she did.' Crawford managed a wry smile, and I wondered if he was one of the stage-door, rain-coated, pushy lechers that Gail Sutton had mentioned. 'We went out a few times, not that it was easy with the hours she worked, but we did manage the occasional lunch.'

'And a weekend or two in Brighton?' asked Dave, raising an eyebrow as he took out his pocket book.

Crawford glanced sharply at Dave. Not a hostile glance, but not a friendly one either. 'How did you know that?'

'I didn't,' said Dave, 'but we know that Miss Hunter went down there a few times.'

We didn't know that, of course, but I think it was a safe assumption.

'Yes, as a matter of fact, we did go to Brighton two or three times.'

'And where did you stay?'

'The Grand. It's the big hotel on the front.'

'Yes, I know where it is,' said Dave, hiding his disappointment that Crawford hadn't stayed at the Golden Riviera Guest House.

But looking around Crawford's apartment, that came as no surprise. I couldn't visualize him staying at John Richards's crummy boarding house in Fenwick Road, not with the money he'd so obviously got. And that led to my next question.

'What's your profession, Mr Crawford?'

'Advertising.' Crawford snapped out the answer, almost as if he resented what to him must have seemed like intrusive questioning.

It certainly explained his wealth. He must have been in one of those advertising agencies that charges telephone numbers just to change a company logo. As I've said many

69

times before, I'm in the wrong business.

'Did she ever mention someone called Bruce Phillips?' I asked.

'No,' said Crawford. 'Who's he?'

'I've no idea. Just a name that came up in the course of our enquiries,' I said, and paused. 'When did you last see Miss Hunter?'

Crawford thought about that. 'The weekend before last,' he said eventually.

'And you've had no contact since then?'

'No, but not for the want of trying.'

'Meaning?'

'I tried ringing her mobile. From about Wednesday of last week, I suppose. But there was never any answer, even though I left messages on her voicemail or whatever it's called. Now I know why.'

'Was there some reason why you didn't call at the theatre after the show? Or at her address? I presume you knew where she lived.'

'Yes, of course I did,' said Crawford. 'But I was out of town.'

'Where exactly?'

'Look, is all this really necessary?' Crawford spread his hands and assumed an apologetic expression. It was almost as though he thought we were wasting *our* time rather than his.

'Yes it is, Mr Crawford,' I said. 'I am dealing with the murder of Miss Hunter, and it's necessary for me to ask questions.'

'Yes, of course. I'm sorry. I should have realized. Well, it so happens that I was in Edinburgh, and I can give you the address of

70

the company with whom I was discussing a television advertising campaign. I'm sure the young lady I saw up there would be happy to confirm what I've just told you. And that's why I was ringing Patricia on her mobile, rather than trying to see her in person.'

Frank Mead had not been wasting his time. By the time Dave and I got back to Curtis Green at nine o'clock, he'd already checked two of the three names that appeared in the register of the Golden Riviera Guest House at Brighton.

Local police had confirmed that both Sam Johnson and Rikki Thompson had copper-bottomed alibis that covered them for the period between which Patricia Hunter was last seen alive, and when her body had been found in the Thames. But it appeared that the Londoner, Craig Pearce, had furnished a false home address when he went to Brighton. Certainly the occupants of 117 Minerva Road, Tooting, had never heard of him. Frank had promptly put Pearce's name on the Police National Computer.

Someone who gave a false address always aroused my interest. The reason could usually be traced back to one of two things: a woman or a crime. In this case it could well be both.

However, given the lateness of the hour – as we say in the trade – that could wait another day.

But one should never say things like that.

'Craig Pearce has been nicked, guv,' said

71

Colin Wilberforce, the moment I stepped into the incident room.

'Christ, are you a bloody mind-reader, Colin?'

Colin smiled. 'Wish I was, sir,' he said. 'Anyway, a crowd of yobs was indulging in a bit of a punch-up on a bus in Whitehall, and as luck would have it, there was an area car coming round from Parliament Square. The crew got stuck in but there were only two of them against about ten yobs. The upshot was that most of the tearaways scarpered, but our lads managed to lay hands on Pearce. He's in Charing Cross nick awaiting your pleasure.'

In my early days in the job, I once had an inspector who reckoned that a police station ought to be like a bank: tranquil. It's as well that he didn't live long enough to see Charing Cross nick this evening.

Among the twenty or so prisoners in the custody suite there was the usual collection of drunks – male *and* female – a couple of low-life layabouts whose profession was the sale of cannabis and other assorted narcotics, and a Bosnian refugee who'd been duffed up simply because he was a Bosnian refugee – that's what he'd told the constable who'd arrested him anyway – and whose blood had made a mess of his Pierre Cardin shirt and his expensive suede jacket. But the officer who'd arrested him was charging him with assault on police. So whose blood was it? Not my problem.

72

I fought my way through this amorphous mass to the accompaniment of muttered protests from the few whose native language was English and who thought I was jumping the queue.

A harassed custody sergeant – custody sergeants always look harassed – glanced up. 'Help you?' he asked wearily.

'Detective Chief Inspector Brock, SCG West,' I said, 'and this is DS Poole,' I added, indicating Dave with a jerk of my thumb.

'Yes, sir?'

'I need to talk to a prisoner called Craig Pearce. Nicked in Whitehall. Punch-up on a bus.'

'Yes, sir. Charged with assault and making an affray with persons not in custody. He's banged up in Cell Three. I'll get the gaoler to bring him up.' The custody sergeant put down his pen and bellowed for someone he called GH.

I should explain that GH is the job's internal code for the police station at Hackney, and I wondered what a Hackney officer was doing at Charing Cross, some six miles distant from his home turf. However, when the officer appeared, it was clear why he was called GH: he was suffering from a nasty affliction of acne ... as in 'Ackney. But that's copper's black humour for you.

Craig Pearce was an unsavoury-looking youth with ironmongery adorning his earlobes, his nose, his tongue, his lower lip and probably other parts of his anatomy that, mercifully, were not currently on display. His head had been shaved to leave a four-inch-wide strip of greasy black hair that culminated in a ponytail. In his position I'd've sued my barber with all the certainty of a successful outcome and substantial damages. It is, however, a widely held belief among such human detritus that the further away from courts of law they can stay, the healthier they will remain.

Patricia Hunter had been a pretty brunette and I wondered what the hell she'd seen in this gorilla. If, in fact, she'd seen him at all. He certainly didn't stand comparison with the urbane Peter Crawford whose apartment we'd left an hour ago.

'You were arrested on a bus in Whitehall having been involved in a disturbance,' I began, just to test the water.

'Nothing to do with me,' said Pearce, rehearsing the villain's standard reflex response to any accusation of crime. Had his solicitor been present, he would have said something trite like, 'My client has a complete answer to the charge.'

'Frankly, I couldn't care less,' I said. 'Such minor matters are of no interest to me.'

'You see, Mr Pearce,' chipped in Dave, 'my guv'nor wants to talk to you about a murder.'

'Do what?' Pearce sat up straight with all the alacrity of someone who has just received a substantial electric shock up his arse. He stared, mesmerized, at Dave. 'I ain't done no murder. It was just a bit of a bundle on a bus.

74

The driver was giving us lip, see. Not showing respeck.' I was pleased to see that Dave's intervention had introduced a measure of alarm into Pearce's response. 'I want a brief.'

'Why?' I asked.

''Cos I never done it, that's why.'

'Never did what?'

'I never done no murder.'

Dave frowned at Pearce's use of a double negative.

'Then you won't be needing a mouthpiece, will you?' I said.

The logic of that appeared to elude Craig Pearce.

'Well, I, er...'

'How long have you known Patricia Hunter?'

'Never heard of her.'

'How about the Golden Riviera Guest House at Brighton?'

'What about it?'

'You stayed there some time ago.'

'Free country, innit?' said Pearce, clearly labouring under an age-old delusion.

'Miss Hunter was an actress who stayed there.' There was no proof that she had, but the address had been in her little book. 'So what were you doing in Brighton?'

'Having a weekend down there, wer'n I? Done a few clubs an' that.'

'When you say you did a few clubs, do you mean you robbed them?'

'Leave it out.'

Dave leaned across the table, his face very

close to Pearce's. 'Where were you on the eleventh and twelfth of June?'

A smile spread across Craig Pearce's face. 'In the nick.'

'*What?*' Dave sat back and surveyed the prisoner.

'I was in the Scrubs doing three months for GBH. Mind you, it was a fit-up. Just like this job you're trying to put on me now.'

Which turned out to be true – not the fit-up, of course – and just goes to show that a suspect's criminal record should be examined *before* you waste your time interrogating him.

We went back to Curtis Green and booked off. But not before I'd sent a message to the Lothian and Borders Police asking them to check Peter Crawford's alibi with the company he claimed to have visited in Edinburgh.

The police in Edinburgh had been highly efficient. By half past nine the following morning they had informed us that Crawford had indeed visited the advertising manager of the firm he'd mentioned. But he had been with her *only on Monday*, leaving in good time to catch the 6 o'clock flight to London. If he had been so minded.

Colin turned to his computer and played a brief scherzo on the keys. 'That means that he could have arrived at Heathrow as early as ten past seven, sir,' he said.

'Which would have given him plenty of time to murder Patricia Hunter, guv,' said Dave, as he peeled a banana. His wife Madeleine had told him that bananas were good for him. 'And that puts him well in the frame.'

'Thanks a lot, Dave,' I said, 'but I don't somehow see a wealthy advertising executive murdering an actress.'

'Funnier things have happened, guv,' said Dave, pointedly waving his banana skin in the air before dropping it into a wastepaper basket. I suppose I should have read some symbolism into the little charade of the banana skin.

'Yes...' I mused. 'I think it's time we spoke to Crawford again, Dave,' I said. I was suspicious about the discrepancy between what he'd told us concerning his absence from London – or at least what he'd implied – and what we'd learned from the police in Edinburgh.

'He's there, guv.' Dave had done his usual telephone trick: ringing Crawford and apologizing for having dialled a wrong number. In that way we wouldn't have a wasted journey, nor would we alert him to our impending visit.

Although it was only just past six o'clock when we arrived at Peter Crawford's flat, he was attired in a beautifully-cut dinner jacket when he answered the door.

'Oh, it's you.'

'Yes, Mr Crawford, it's us,' I said. 'We need to have a few words with you.'

'I don't have very long.' Crawford drew back the cuff of his shirt and glanced at his gold Rolex watch. 'I'm due to attend a dinner in the West End very shortly. At the Dorchester, as a matter of fact. It's an advertising convention. May pick up a bit of business.'

Crawford didn't look as though he needed to pick up any more business. He appeared to be doing all right as he was. Certainly if the quality and cut of his dinner jacket was anything to go by.

'It shouldn't take long,' I said.

'That's all right, then. You'd better come in.'

'You told us that you were in Edinburgh during the week commencing Monday the tenth of June, Mr Crawford,' I began.

'That's correct.'

'And where did you stay?'

'I, er...'

'Let me try something else. How *long* were you in Edinburgh?'

'The whole week. Monday until Friday.'

'So where did you stay?'

If Crawford was starting to get rattled by my persistent questioning, he didn't show it. 'Does this have something to do with Patricia Hunter's death?' he asked patiently.

'It's what we call a process of elimination, Mr Crawford.'

But now he did begin to get a little annoyed. 'Really?' It was a sarcastic response. 'Well, I don't see that where I stayed has anything to do with your so-called process of elimination.'

I adopted an attitude of infinite patience, something that always surprised Dave. 'I am

78

naturally suspicious of anyone who declines to tell me where they were at the time of a murder, Mr Crawford. Particularly when that person claims to have been a friend of the victim.'

There was a distinct pause while, I imagine, Crawford 'considered his position'.

'I was staying with my wife.'

'So, you had a girlfriend in London and a wife in Scotland?'

'I wouldn't be the first man to have a mistress,' said Crawford, glancing at his watch again. 'Look, Chief Inspector, I really do have to go.'

'Of course you do, sir. If you just tell me where it was that you stayed with your wife, I'll leave you in peace.'

'But why d'you want to know?'

'Because we have checked with the company you visited and they told us that you were with them for just one day: Monday the tenth of June. If you'd told me that in the first place, I wouldn't have had to come and waste your time again. Or mine.'

Crawford sat down, suddenly. For a moment or two he gazed at the floor, his hands linked between his knees. Then he looked up.

'My wife is a few years older than me, Chief Inspector. She's been suffering from Alzheimer's disease for a while now, and she's in a secure home. I visit her whenever I can, but it's largely a waste of time. She doesn't seem to know who I am any more, or what I'm talking about.'

'I see. And where is this home, Mr Crawford?'

'Edinburgh.' Crawford rose to his feet and walked across to a side table upon which stood a telephone. He scribbled a few lines on a sheet of paper he took from a pad and handed it to me. 'That's the address of the home,' he said. 'I stayed in our house in Edinburgh from Monday night to Friday morning of that week. The address of that's on there too.' He gestured at the piece of paper.

'How old is your wife?' I asked.

'Forty-five.'

'A little young to have Alzheimer's disease, isn't she?'

Crawford raised his head, a suspicion of weariness on his face as if he'd been obliged to explain this many times. 'I can see you know little about the disease,' he said. 'I can assure you that age is no bar to contracting it. And it doesn't matter how intelligent the victim is. My wife had a very high IQ.'

Six

'I suppose it's understandable that he didn't want to admit to having a mistress while his wife was in a secure home in Edinburgh suffering from some incurable disease, Dave,' I said, as we left Crawford's apartment.

'So what are we going to do about it, guv?'

'Ask the Edinburgh police to check on his story. Get Colin to phone them when we get back.'

'He's a bit dodgy, if you ask me.' Dave was always prepared to see the worst in people, particularly those who seemed to make a lot of money out of doing very little. I suppose he's been working with me for too long.

'If he was in the frame, Dave, he'd've made sure he'd got a cast-iron alibi, all sewn up neat and tidy. Not something as woolly as his story was.'

'Yeah, maybe.' Dave was always reluctant to believe what anyone said, especially if they were as supercilious and well-heeled as Crawford. 'So where are we going now?' he asked as he started the engine and slammed the gear lever into drive.

Even though Crawford had told us that he was Patricia Hunter's boyfriend, it didn't necessarily mean he was her *only* boyfriend. And there was still the shadowy Bruce Phillips to track down. Not that I expected easily to find a man who was on the run from the Australian courts.

'Petersfield Street, Fulham, Dave. See what we can learn about Phillips.'

Number 9 Petersfield Street, Fulham, was a block of fairly new luxury service flats. And according to the array of bell pushes next to the intercom there were twelve apartments. But the label for flat 12 no longer bore the names of either Hunter or Phillips. If it ever had. At random, and because I'm inherently lazy, I picked flat 1 on the ground floor. The label said it was occupied by someone called Mace.

The woman who answered the door was in her forties and wearing jeans, a tee shirt and an apron. She examined us suspiciously – Dave Poole in particular – but the look changed to one of curiosity when we told her who we were. And who we were looking for.

'Bruce Phillips?' For a moment or two the woman savoured the name, eventually shaking her head. 'No one of that name here, love,' she said. 'Not as far as I know.'

'Do you happen to know if there's *ever* been anyone of that name here?' I asked. 'We were told that he was living in flat twelve.'

'No, love, sorry. I've never heard of him.'

I played a hunch and tried another tack. 'Do you know if there were any theatricals living here at any time, Mrs Mace? It is *Mrs*

82

Mace, is it?'

'Yes. Toni Mace. It's short for Antonia, but I never really liked the name. That's life, though, isn't it? Your parents give you a name and you're stuck with it.'

'Yes, it's a problem,' I agreed. I'd been stuck with the name Harold, but never used it. 'I asked about theatricals, Mrs Mace.'

'Do call me Toni, love, and you'd better come in. Don't mind the kitchen, do you?' she asked as she led us into an expensively fitted kitchen in which there was a state-of-the-art cooker and an American-style refrigerator. 'Cup of tea? I've just made one.'

'Thank you.' Dave and I sat down on high stools along a breakfast bar. 'I was asking about theatricals,' I said once again.

'Come to think of it, there was a nice young girl here for about a year after we moved in, and I'm sure she was in number twelve. It was one of the top flats anyway, and there's only two on each floor. She could have been an actress, I suppose. Trouble is, we don't see very much of each other here, what with the lift and everything. It's only if you happen to be going out when they're coming in – or vice versa – that you bump into the other people living here.'

'You didn't know her name, I suppose?' I asked hopefully.

'No,' said Toni. 'We do tend to keep ourselves to ourselves.'

'Can you describe this girl?' Dave asked.

'Early twenties, I should think. Brunette.

83

Nice-looking girl. I certainly envied her the figure she had,' she added wistfully. 'She must have been at least a thirty-eight D-cup, and she had a tiny waist and gorgeous legs. Often wore a miniskirt, and so would I have done if I'd had her body.'

The description certainly sounded like Patricia Hunter, but could also have fitted a thousand other women. 'D'you happen to know when she moved out?' I asked.

'No, love, sorry.' Mrs Mace paused for a second or two. 'Come to think of it, though, it could have been a year ago. It must have been that long since I last saw her.' She put mugs of tea in front of us. 'There you are.' She pulled a packet of cigarettes from her apron pocket and lit one. As an afterthought, she offered the packet to Dave and me.

'Did you ever see her with a man?'

'Only the once, and that must have been well over a year ago. Big hunk of a guy.' Toni Mace glanced at Dave. 'About your build, I should think, but with blond hair. Wouldn't have been surprised if he dyed it. Some men are so vain, aren't they?'

'Did you ever speak to this girl?' I asked.

'No more than half a dozen words at most, I should think. And that was only once or twice, just to say hello, or talk about the weather. Funny that, isn't it, the way people always talk about the weather when they can't think of anything else to say?'

'And you've no idea what she did for a living, Mrs Mace?'

'It's Toni, love,' she reminded me as she waved her cigarette smoke towards an extractor fan. 'No, d'you know I never thought to ask. But like I said, she could have been in the theatre. Or a model.' Then, as an apparent afterthought, she asked, 'Why are you interested in her? Has she done something wrong?'

'No, she was murdered. On the eleventh or twelfth of this month.'

'Well I never,' said Toni. 'You never know what's going to happen, do you?'

'One other thing,' said Dave. 'Are these flats owned or rented?'

'We bought ours. Well, us and the building society,' said Toni with a laugh. 'But some are rentals. We've seen all sorts of different people come and go since we've been here. Trouble is, we sometimes get a noisy lot. They don't care who they disturb, and I wouldn't like to see what they do to the flats they rent. Just don't seem to care these days, some young people, what with their noisy parties and God knows what else that they get up to. I can tell you, I've smelled cannabis in the hall on more than one occasion. We've had a go at the ground landlords about it from time to time, but they don't seem to care so long as they get their money.'

'Who are the ground landlords?' I asked.

Toni Mace rummaged about in a drawer next to the cooker and produced a bill. 'That's them,' she said. 'Anyway, that's who we pay our ground rent and maintenance to.'

Dave took a note of the details, and we thanked Toni for the tea.

'D'you think your husband might be able to tell us anything, Toni?' I asked.

'He's dead, love. Died last year. Cancer, it was. Still, his life insurance took care of the mortgage, otherwise I wouldn't still be here.'

We took the lift to the top floor and tried number 12 first, the flat that Patricia Hunter had apparently shared with Bruce Phillips, if the entry in her notebook was true.

But we fared no better there. The woman who answered the door had only just moved in and had never heard of anyone called Patricia Hunter or Bruce Phillips.

The door of number 11 was eventually opened by a white youth whose arm was around a half-naked black girl whose hair was braided into dreadlocks. Both were giggling, and each of them was openly smoking a joint.

The giggling stopped when we mentioned the magic word 'police' and a murder, but as they'd only rented the place a week ago they were unable to take us any nearer finding Phillips.

Dave was all for pursuing the drugs offences, but as we had neither the time nor a warrant, and the government didn't give a toss anyway, we left it. Even these days, murder takes precedence over narcotics. Just.

The next morning, I rang the ground landlord's agent. But he added very little to what we knew already. As far as he could tell from his files, a Bruce Phillips had rented flat 12 – 'Before it was decided to sell them all off,' he volunteered – and had paid the rent regularly. The lease had been terminated at the end of May last year and he didn't know where Phillips had gone. There had never been any complaints about him that the agent was aware of, and he had no idea whether Phillips had shared the accommodation with a woman. And judging by his tired response to my questions, the agent couldn't have cared less if he had done. I floated the name of Patricia Hunter, but that drew a blank as well.

I now considered the enigma that was facing me. The address of the Golden Riviera Guest House had been found in Patricia Hunter's address book, but she had no apparent connection with it. However, we had confirmed that the Petersfield Street address of Bruce Phillips that had been in her book was correct. And presumably Patricia Hunter had lived there with him prior to moving to 34 Coping Road, Islington. But Toni Mace had never heard of Phillips. My problem was going to be finding him, because suddenly he had become a front-runner for Patricia's murder.

Frank Mead dropped into the office. While Dave and I had been amusing ourselves talking to Toni Mace in Fulham, he'd been busy. One of his detective sergeants had interviewed the assistant electricians at the Granville

Theatre, but none of them had even known Patricia Hunter, at least not by name. The officer had also obtained their dates of birth from the obliging Mrs Price, and had searched their names in Criminal Records Office, or whatever it's called these days. But nothing.

'I think we'll have to go further back in Patricia Hunter's address book than we've been already,' I said, clutching at straws and tossing them in Frank's direction. 'There's got to be a connection somewhere. Talk to the guys whose names have been crossed out, Frank.'

'Edward Archer and Nick Lloyd, guv,' said Dave, without even having to think about it. 'Addresses are in the incident room.'

I took Saturday off and left Frank Mead in charge on the strict understanding that he was to call me if anything cropped up that couldn't wait until Monday.

It was no fun being single again. The freedom it brings is offset by having to do everything oneself. If you wanted morning tea, that is. And I couldn't get under way without tea. I had a wonderfully cheerful lady cleaner who came in and 'did' twice a week, so I was able to avoid things like dusting, polishing and vacuuming.

Maybe I should have gone to work after all. But not wanting to sit in my flat alone, watching daytime television, I decided to go into Kingston and catch up on some essential shopping. Like shirts, all but one of which were in the washing machine.

I didn't recognize her at first. Probably because she was wearing sunglasses. I'd noticed her, of course: I tend always to notice tall, shapely blondes. She was wearing jeans – the sort that makes it look as though she'd been poured into them – a sloppy sweater and a baseball cap with her long hair tucked through the gap at the back.

'It's Mr Brock, isn't it?'

'Yes.'

'It's Gail. Gail Sutton.' She laughed and waved a hand in front of my face in a parody of testing my vision.

'Sorry, I was miles away.' *What a brilliant liar I am!* 'How are you?'

'Unemployed.'

'Yes, I heard that *Scatterbrain* had closed, but I thought you called it "resting" in your profession.'

Gail laughed. 'Self-delusion knows no bounds in the theatrical world,' she said. 'Call it what you like, but the money stopped at eleven o'clock last night.'

'I'd better buy you a cup of coffee, then,' I said. 'Now that you're penniless.'

'Are you any nearer finding out who murdered Patricia?' asked Gail, once we were settled in a nearby coffee shop with cups of coffee-flavoured froth in front of us.

'No, but we have found her parents. They live in Wimbledon.'

'Oh God!' Gail paused, cup in mid-air. 'I'll

bet they were upset.'

'Of course they were,' I said rather tersely, but then apologized. 'I'm sorry, but we get hardened to tragedies of that sort in my business.'

Gail shuddered, and I suspected it was from the thought that the psychopath who'd killed Patricia Hunter was still at large. She took a packet of cigarettes from her bag and offered it to me.

I paused briefly and then took one. I'd been trying to give up for ages. Ever since I was at school in fact, when a master caught me having a quick drag behind the bike sheds and told me a horror story about his brother dying from tobacco-induced lung cancer. But I'd never been able to summon the willpower. And Dave was no help.

'D'you think you'll catch him, Mr Brock?'

'It's Harry, and yes I do. No doubt about it.'

My God! Did I just say that?

I glanced at my watch. 'D'you fancy a spot of lunch? I hate to see starving actresses on the streets. Begging's a big problem in London now.'

Gail hesitated and then smiled. 'Well, I er...'

'I'm going to eat somewhere anyway,' I said, 'and I hate eating alone.'

'OK, thanks.'

We found a decent pub and spent a few minutes studying the bar menu.

'Red or white?' I asked.

'Neither, thanks,' she said. 'I've got to drive later on.'

We took our food and a couple of soft drinks out to a terrace facing the river, and settled at a vacant bench beneath a sun canopy. For a few minutes we watched the river traffic of small motor boats crewed by weekend sailors accompanied by middle-aged, overweight women stretched out on cabin roofs, and wearing bikinis in the vain belief that they could get away with it.

'You told me the other day that you're divorced.'

'Yes, and so are you, aren't you?' Gail glanced at me and took a sip of her diet cola.

'Yes, I am,' I said, and left it at that, hoping for some inexplicable reason that she would not probe further.

'So, you're on your own now?'

It was understandable, I suppose, that Gail wanted to be under no illusions about my precise marital status. I guessed that she'd had some unhappy experiences with men who'd turned out to be married. Something I imagined to be the fate of an attractive chorus girl.

'Yes, I'm afraid so.' I didn't think it was a good idea to mention that I had broken up with my long-standing girlfriend only a week ago. 'What about you?'

'The hours of work in the theatre are not exactly conducive to finding a partner.' It was a sour comment and for a moment Gail looked sad. 'Hoofing it every night, and twice on Fridays and Saturdays, doesn't leave much time for socializing.'

'No, I suppose not.' It looked as though this banal conversation was going to continue, so I decided to explore more deeply. 'What happened to your husband?'

Gail shot me one of those looks that said it's none of your damned business, and for a moment or two I thought she wasn't going to answer. But she did. Eventually. 'I was in a revival of Coward's *Private Lives* at Richmond – this was about four years ago – and I went down with some bug. I took some paracetamol, lumbered my understudy and came home early. Surprise, surprise, I found him in bed – *our bed!* – with some nude dancer he'd picked up. Well, she was nude then, anyway,' she added with a wry smile.

'What did he do, your husband?'

'Took off with a flea in his ear, and so did his bedmate. We divorced nine months later.'

I laughed. 'No, I meant what was his profession?'

Gail laughed too. 'Oh, he was a director. That's how I met him. Directing a musical I was in.'

'Just now you said you were in *Private Lives*. Does that mean you're really an actress? Rather than a dancer.'

'I was then, but in this game you have to take what you can get. Fortunately, I was trained as a dancer so I've always got that to fall back on.'

'What are you going to do now?'

'Go home and do some washing and ironing.'

'No, I meant what are you going to do about a job?'

'Oh, I'll find something. Sweet-talk my agent and scour the pages of *The Stage*, I suppose. That's the usual thing. I hope I can find something that lasts a bit longer than *Scatterbrain*.'

'Will you try for an acting part? I should think that's less strenuous than dancing,' I said, as we left the pub.

Gail smiled. 'If I can persuade someone to give me an audition,' she said, but she didn't sound too sanguine about the prospect.

'It's a pity I don't know any casting agents,' I said, smiling. Well, I did know one, but he was doing life in Parkhurst prison. And he hadn't been any good at it anyway. After a suitable pause, I took a chance. 'How about having dinner with me tonight?' I'd said it without thinking and immediately wondered whether it was a good idea.

'No, Harry. Sorry.'

Obviously not a good idea. 'Just a thought,' I said.

'Oh, I'd've loved to have dinner with you, but I'm committed for this evening.'

I might have known it. Despite what she'd said about the difficulty of establishing re-lationships, a stunningly attractive girl like Gail was bound to have an admirer. Or two.

But I was wrong.

'I'm visiting my parents this weekend. Driv-ing up this afternoon, as a matter of fact. They haven't seen much of me lately, mainly because they live in Nottingham, and it's quite a hike up there. But another time, eh?' She ferreted about in her handbag, took out a pen and a small notebook. She scribbled a few lines, tore out the page and handed it to me. 'That's my Kingston phone number,' she said.

We parted outside the pub and I spent a few seconds watching her walk away. And wondering if this could be the start of something more lasting than my relationship with Sarah Dawson.

Seven

On Monday morning we received confirmation from a dentist in Ewell that Patricia Hunter *was* Patricia Hunter, according to her teeth anyway. We'd asked the General Dental Council to circularize the practitioners in London and the Home Counties first, rather than waste their time, and ours, in sending her records all over the country. Although we had identified her before seeking the help of the dental profession, it did provide us with another address for her.

'According to this dentist, sir,' – Colin Wilberforce tapped the printout – 'Patricia Hunter had lived in Epsom at the date of her last treatment, which was some six years ago.'

'Well, I hope he's right,' I said, 'I don't want to waste any more time. Get on to Linda Mitchell, tell her that Dave and I are going to this Epsom address now, and she's to stand by at Epsom police station in case we need her. I'll want fingerprints lifted from the address to make sure it tallies with the body we've got in the mortuary.'

'It's in the Surrey Police area, sir,' cautioned Colin.

'I know it is, Colin, and if they want to get

95

all territorial about it and investigate my murder, they can have it with pleasure. But until then, I'll use our own resources.'

Colin grinned. 'I thought you'd say that, sir.'

'But you'd better send the Surrey lot a message saying that we'll be on their patch.'

'Right, sir.' Colin made a note on his pad. 'Where's Dave?'

'I'm here, guv,' said Dave, entering the incident room with a tray of coffee.

'Good. We're going to Epsom.'

'We've missed the Derby, guv,' said Dave.

'Yes, I'm Eleanor Hunter,' said the woman who'd answered the door. She was a plain woman. Her hair, greying slightly, was severely cut in a short, mannish crop, and she wore trousers and a baggy sweater.

'Are you Patricia's sister?' I asked, after telling her, as sympathetically as I could, that Patricia was dead.

'I am, but she didn't live here any more. We didn't get on.'

'Did she ever visit a dentist in Ewell, Miss Hunter?' I asked, doing my belt-and-braces routine.

'Yes, I believe she did, but that was a long time ago.'

'And presumably she lived here at that time.'

'For a while,' said Patricia's sister, 'but she left about five years ago.'

'I'd like to have some of my people examine

the room she lived in. You see, we need to check it for fingerprints in order to make sure that it is Patricia that was found.' That wasn't the reason, of course. I wanted to see if there were any fingerprints of someone else. Someone else who might have murdered her. Even so, I didn't hold out much hope, not after five years.

'Do whatever you have to. It's upstairs, first on the right.'

Dave went into the street and called up Linda Mitchell on his mobile.

'What happened to Patricia?' asked Eleanor.

It struck me as rather strange that Patricia's sister had waited so long to pose that question.

I explained, as briefly as possible, the circumstances in which the body of Patricia Hunter had been found.

'I'm not surprised,' said Eleanor coldly. 'I warned her that the life she was leading would end in tragedy, but she wouldn't listen.'

'How old was she, Miss Hunter?'

'She'd've been twenty-six now. She was five years younger than me.'

Really? You look more than thirty-one to me.

'What was this lifestyle of hers that you disapproved of?'

'She was in the theatre. Dancing half-naked was contrary to all the Christian principles of our church. Our late parents brought us up in the Methodist faith and that sort of thing was

97

frowned upon.'

'Your *late* parents?' Dave and I had been speaking to Patricia Hunter's parents only last Friday in Wimbledon. Strange that. The Hunters hadn't mentioned that they had another daughter. There was clearly something amiss here, but I wasn't going to raise it at this point. Not until I'd found out more about Eleanor Hunter. So I let her continue.

'Our father died of cancer at quite an early age, and our mother committed suicide shortly afterwards.' Eleanor Hunter spoke in matter-of-fact tones, with no trace of sadness as she recounted a story that I knew damned well was a pack of lies. And I wondered why she was lying. But I wasn't going to challenge her account. Not until I'd checked with a few independent sources. 'I was left to look after Patricia, but she insisted on the theatre as a career and I'm afraid we fell out over it. There was nothing I could do to dissuade her. She was of age, after all. I told her to leave.'

'Did your sister ever talk of any men friends, Miss Hunter?'

'Certainly not,' said Eleanor vehemently. 'She never discussed her private life with me, and I wouldn't have wanted to hear anyway. These stage women lead a dissolute life, you know.' It was obvious that the Christian principles which Eleanor so fervently espoused did not include one of sisterly love.

There was a knock at the door and Dave admitted the crime-scene examiners.

The room that Patricia Hunter had occupied had been cleaned and there was no trace of any of the girl's possessions. But to my surprise, Linda's people did manage to lift one or two fingerprints. And after they had taken a set of elimination prints from Eleanor Hunter we left.

At two o'clock that afternoon I was told that the fingerprints Linda Mitchell had found were those of Patricia Hunter and her sister Eleanor.

Eleanor Hunter had told us very little. She didn't know where Patricia had been living and she didn't know the names of any of the shows she had been appearing in. And what was more, she didn't seem to care about the fate of her sister. But that she had claimed their parents were dead was a bizarre twist.

I set young John Appleby the task of arranging for an urgent search of the General Register Office in Southport to check on the dates of birth of Patricia and Eleanor Hunter. It was possible that, despite Eleanor's claim that Patricia was her sister, they weren't related. Hunter was, after all, a fairly common name. But why should she do it? More to the point, why should she lie about the fate of their parents?

What was important now was to discover what Patricia Hunter had been doing before she joined the chorus line in *Scatterbrain*. We had traced some of the addresses where she had lived, all of which were in the Greater London area, but she could as easily have been with some second-rate repertory company in Sheffield, Truro or Glasgow for some of the time since leaving Epsom. If she had been in the theatre at all before appearing at the Granville. But she'd been found in the Thames at Westminster, and that gave me the probably fallacious hope that it was in London that she'd met the man, if it was a man, who had killed her. And the address in Brighton was still puzzling me.

What I needed now was a photograph of her. Her callous sister Eleanor had told us that she had no pictures of Patricia – which may or may not have been true – and I asked Frank Mead to arrange for searches of the Passport Office, and the Driver and Vehicle Licensing Agency at Swansea.

I was not interested in whether Patricia had been abroad or whether she could drive a car, but putting a post-mortem photograph in the newspapers or on television is counter-productive on two counts. Firstly, it is rarely a good likeness, and secondly, it alerts the killer to the fact that we've found the subject's dead body. However, a passport photograph, accompanied by a brief report saying that she is missing from home, would merely indicate that we don't know where she is. That was the theory, anyway.

Frank, as usual, came up with the goods.

After telling Patricia's parents what we proposed to do, I rang the Head of News at the Yard's Public Affairs Directorate and asked him to arrange publication of the photograph in the London press and on local television stations.

It was about two o'clock the following afternoon when Colin took the phone call.

'A woman called Candy Simpson just rang, sir,' he said. 'She'd seen Patricia Hunter's photograph in the paper. She says she's not missing at all,' he added with a wry grin.

'That's true,' said Dave. 'We know where she is: in the mortuary.' But as he often says, he has a black sense of humour.

'Where is this woman, Colin? Do we have an address?' I asked.

'Another actress, sir,' said Colin with a sly smile as he handed me the message. 'She's got digs in Pender Street, Paddington, but she's appearing in a play at the Alhambra in Holborn. She'll be there from about six o'clock.'

The theatre advertised a play called *The Birthday Party*, and Candy Simpson's name was listed well down among the cast. In fact, it only just made it. The stage-door keeper made a phone call and then showed us to a tiny dressing room with a star on the door. For what that was worth.

The actress, quite unembarrassed at wearing nothing but a G-string, was seated at a dressing table. I reckoned she was in her twenties.

'I hope you don't mind me carrying on, darlings,' she said, talking to our reflections in a mirror around which was a battery of lights, 'but it always takes me ages to get ready.'

'Not at all, Miss Simpson. You carry on.'

'I suppose you want to know where Patricia's gone,' she said, leaning closer to the mirror as she examined the mascara she had just put on.

'We've already found her.'

'Oh, that's good.' Candy Simpson carefully applied lipstick and puckered her lips before pressing them gently with a tissue. 'So you don't really need to talk to me at all, then. But as you're here you may as well sit down.' Without diverting her gaze from the mirror, she indicated a worn sofa with a theatrical flourish of her hand.

'I'm sorry to have to tell you that Patricia Hunter's dead.'

Abandoning all thoughts of preparing for her imminent appearance in *The Birthday Party*, Candy swung round on her chair, her face registering shock. 'Oh no! But the piece in the paper only said that she was missing.'

'It was deliberately misleading,' I said, 'because we didn't want to let her killer know that we'd found her body.'

'Her killer?'

'Yes, she was murdered.'

'How awful. When did this happen?'

'Her body was found in the Thames at Westminster, a week ago last Wednesday. She'd been strangled.'

Candy gave a convulsive shudder. 'I was her understudy, you see. Not that it's a great part, but it was a start. I play the maid and I have to come in and say, "Dinner is served, My Lord." Twice. I suppose you could say she did me a good turn really.'

I wondered why a maid with only one line to speak should have required an understudy. I'd've thought that, in an emergency, anyone could have taken it on. Even one of the usherettes.

'Patricia Hunter was in *Scatterbrain* at the Granville up until her death,' I said.

'What?' Candy stared at me in disbelief. 'I never knew that,' she said.

'So how did you come to get her part?'

'It must have been about three months ago,' said Candy, her concentration now fully on me. 'I thought she'd done what she said she was going to do.'

'And what was that?'

'She'd met this man. Jeremy, he was called.'

'Did you meet him?'

'No, but Patricia was ecstatic about him. A wonderful guy, she said he was.'

'What d'you know about him?'

'Only what Patricia told me. She said he'd got a studio flat in Docklands and a villa in the South of France at a place called...' Candy paused. 'Yes, it was in St Raphaël, or just outside, I think she said. Apparently she and Jeremy were going to get married and move there permanently. She kept on about it. Her idea was to walk out of the play one night without telling anybody and never come back. And that's what I thought she'd done. She was always promising to do it if she ever won the lottery. And I thought she had. Sort of.'

'How long had she known this man, Miss Simpson?'

'I don't really know, but I got the impression that she'd only recently met him. At least, she didn't start talking about him until about a fortnight before she left. I warned her about the risk of getting married so quickly and I told her that she ought to get to know him first.' Candy spread her hands. 'I mean, how can you decide a thing like that when you've only known a guy for a fortnight? But it was probably the money. You know, the sports car, the flat in London and the villa in France. I think he turned her head with all his talk of spending cloudless days soaking up the sun on a French Riviera beach.'

'What was this man's surname?'

'I'm sorry, I don't know. She never told me. I don't think it was a secret, but I never thought to ask.'

'A flat in Docklands, you say? D'you know where?'

'No. Sorry,' said Candy again, and paused. 'D'you think he was the one who murdered her?'

'I don't know, Miss Simpson, but obviously I'll have to talk to him.'

'When did Miss Hunter manage to see this man?' asked Dave. He'd once told me about the problems he'd had when he was courting Madeleine; having a girlfriend who worked

104

most evenings in the theatre made socializing difficult. 'I assume you're on stage every night Monday to Saturday.'

'*And* matinees on Wednesday and Saturday, darling,' said Candy ruefully. Turning briefly to the dressing table, she picked up her watch and glanced at it. 'I think they spent most lunch times together, but it is very difficult. Unless we're resting, of course.' She forced a smile. 'God knows why we do it. It's certainly not the money. The theatre's nothing short of slavery, you know.' She stood up, donned a bra, a short black dress and a frilly cap before tying on a white apron.

'Did Patricia ever go to this flat of Jeremy's?' I asked. 'Or to his place in France?'

'Not that I know of. If she did, she never mentioned it. But I'm pretty sure she didn't go. She was so bubbling over with it all that I'm certain she couldn't have kept it to herself. Mind you, she did shoot off every night, straight after her second entrance.'

'Have you any idea what this guy Jeremy did for a living?' Dave asked.

'No, she never said anything about that. Actually, I thought, from what she said, that he was so rich he didn't have to work.'

'So it's possible that he was spinning her a yarn, and she just believed everything he told her?' I said, taking back the questioning.

Candy nodded slowly. 'I imagine so. Poor little kid. Fancy getting taken in with a story like that.'

'It happens, Miss Simpson,' I said.

'One other thing,' said Dave. 'D'you know where Patricia lived?'

'Yes. She had a flat in Courtney Street. It's just round the corner from here. Number sixty-four, I think.'

Yet another address to be checked out. A last thought occurred to me. 'Did Patricia Hunter ever mention a man called Bruce Phillips?' I asked.

Candy Simpson considered the question for a moment or two. 'No, I don't think so,' she said eventually. 'In fact, I'm sure she didn't.' She took a last look in the mirror and adjusted the frilly cap.

There was a loud knock at the door as we stood up to leave, and a voice shouted, 'Five minutes, Candy!'

'Think there's anything to be read into Riviera, guv?' asked Dave next morning. 'We've got the Golden Riviera Guest House in Brighton, and the Côte d'Azur in the South of France where Jeremy – whoever he is – promised to take Patricia.'

'You're having me on, Dave,' I said. 'If this guy's got as much money as he claimed to have, I don't see him putting up at Richards's boarding house in Brighton. And even if he wasn't rich, he'd have splashed out just to make an impression.'

'D'you know what I think, guv?' said Dave, ferreting about in his shabby nylon briefcase and eventually producing a banana.

'Enlighten me, Dave.'

'I think that Patricia Hunter was a lying little bitch. All this chat about some guy turning up and promising to marry her and cart her off to the South of France is a load of bullshit. I reckon that she was up to something and just didn't want anyone else to know what it was.'

'Yeah, it all sounded too good to be true. One thing's certain, though. If we find Jeremy, and his DNA matches the seminal fluid found in Patricia Hunter's body, I reckon we've got our man.'

'So long as he's got a Ford, Renault or Bedford van,' said Dave, peeling his banana.

'All of which gives me an idea,' I mused. 'But we're going to need more men.'

'Amen to that.'

'I know the body was found at just after eight o'clock on the Wednesday evening, and Henry Mortlock estimated that she'd been dead about twenty-four hours, but common sense tells me that this guy disposed of her during the night. Only a maniac would dump a body in the river in broad daylight.'

'Only a maniac goes about murdering people,' observed Dave laconically.

'And that means that he probably has a legitimate reason for driving a van in the middle of the night,' I continued – ignoring, as I usually did, Dave's dry aside – 'and lives close to the Thames between, say, Hammersmith and Westminster.'

'That's a bloody great "if", guv,' said Dave. 'And a hell of a lot of houses to visit.'

I stood up and put on my jacket. 'I suppose I'll have to see the commander and plead for help.'

'Good luck,' said Dave, 'but why?'

'I think the only thing we can do is to arrange for police to stop all Ford, Bedford and Renault vans operating during the night in that area.'

Dave dropped his banana skin into the wastepaper bin. 'What a very good idea, sir,' he said.

Somewhat hesitantly, I tapped on the commander's door.

'Hello, Harry.'

I was surprised to see, not the commander, but Detective Chief Superintendent Alan Cleaver sitting in the boss's chair.

'I was looking for the commander, guv,' I said.

'On leave, Harry. On a whim he decided to take Mrs Commander off to Paris for a long weekend. I'm acting. What can I do for you?'

I explained, as succinctly as possible, my progress in the murder I was investigating, and my thoughts about setting up roadblocks to check on vans.

'Jesus!' said a surprised Cleaver. 'I didn't realize how complicated that job had become. Just bring me up to speed, will you?'

'Yes, sir. The river police recovered Patricia Hunter from the Thames at Westminster on the twelfth of June, but it's beginning to look as though she was a dark horse. She had various addresses, a sister who didn't give a damn about the girl's welfare, and who told us her parents were dead, despite our having interviewed them two days previously. And then there's a boyfriend called Bruce Phillips who we've yet to trace, mainly, I think, because it's likely he's identical with a Bruce Phillips who's on the run from an Australian extradition warrant. And then there's some mysterious guy called Jeremy. According to another witness, he had promised to spirit our victim away to the south of France for a life of luxury. She was an actress by the way.'

'A bit of a puzzle,' said Cleaver, as usual understating the case.

'And some,' I said. 'All we really know so far is that she'd indulged in sexual intercourse shortly before her death, but there's no match for the semen in the DNA database. The CSEs also found fibres in the woman's hair that appear to come from the matting in a Ford, Renault or Bedford van. And there were some unidentified particles in grazing on her body.'

'And the commander's not given you any extra men?'

'Not one, guv,' I said, sitting down in the commander's plush armchair.

'Right. First of all, more officers.' Cleaver started to make notes on a pad as he spoke. 'And we'll arrange to have Territorial Support Groups doing checks throughout the night.' He glanced at his watch. 'If you can list the areas where you want this done, I'll get on to the Area DACs and set it up for tonight. That OK with you?'

'That'd be fine, guv,' I said.

'Good.' Cleaver leaned back in his chair.

Dave looked up despondently as I entered my office. 'Don't tell me,' he said. 'The answer's no.'

'The answer's yes,' I said.

'Blimey, how d'you swing that, guv?'

'Mr Cleaver's acting commander,' I said. 'He didn't even blink. Now all we've got to do is work out where we want these stops done.'

'I've done it,' said Dave, handing me a sheet of paper. 'And while you've been twisting the guv'nor's arm, I've been thinking.'

'You be careful, Dave,' I said. 'Carry on like that and you might get promoted.'

'It doesn't work that way according to what I've heard,' muttered Dave, and tossed me a cigarette. 'But there is one thing. What about the mysterious Bruce Phillips?'

'What about him?'

'Well, we haven't found him yet. He's not only listed in Patricia Hunter's address book, but when we checked that address, it turned out to be where she had lived herself at one time. What's more, her father reckoned that she mentioned him in a letter as being a boy-friend.'

'But how the hell do we track him down, Dave?'

'There's a fortune-teller who turns up at the fair on Clapham Common every year,' said

Dave drily. 'Incidentally, while you were having an audience with the acting commander, I rang Richards at the Golden Riviera Guest House and got him to go through his books. No couple called Jeremy and Patricia stayed there during the last year.'

'Thanks, Dave. Somehow I didn't think they would have done.'

'So, d'you reckon that this Jeremy and the missing Bruce Phillips could be one and the same?'

I shrugged. 'It's a possibility, Dave.'

Eight

'We've got an answer from the Edinburgh police, sir,' said Colin Wilberforce, appearing in the doorway of my office.

'What do they have to say?'

'First of all they made enquiries at the address in Colinton – it's a suburb of Edinburgh – that Crawford said was his house, but there was no one there. However, the next-door neighbours claimed to have seen a car on his drive a couple of times between Tuesday and Friday of the week he said he was there, but they couldn't remember exactly when. One neighbour mentioned that he'd told them he was visiting someone in a local hospital.'

'Hospital? I thought it was a secure home. That's what Crawford said.'

'Yes, but the local police checked it out, sir, and it's an expensive nursing home that caters for rich people with mental problems. The door's kept locked and visitors are admitted by whoever's on duty at the time. The police up there say that Crawford visited a few times during the week, but they don't know how often. The home doesn't keep a log and so long as a visitor's *bona fide*, they let

112

him in.'

'That rules him out, then,' I said. 'I don't suppose these neighbours of his noted the car number, did they?'

'No, sir. They didn't even know the make.'

'Incidentally, Colin, have we had any follow-up on the grazing found on the victim's back?'

'Yes, sir.' Colin shuffled through the sheaf of papers he was carrying. 'Linda Mitchell's team checked those bridges that have concrete balustrades and there's no match.'

'No match? Well, that blows that theory out of the water.'

'It seems that they recovered some minute specks of dust or concrete from the grazing on the body – something like that – but it doesn't correspond with anything on the bridges they checked. Linda's hazarded a guess that they might have come from the floor of a garage or storeroom. There was also a slight trace of a substance that could be motor oil. The lab's doing further checks now.'

'Interesting. Perhaps she was strangled in a garage somewhere, conveyed in a van, and then dumped.'

'Or,' said Dave, 'she was conveyed in a van that had traces of this dust and oil in it.'

As usual, Dave had found fault with my all-too-easy assumption.

On Thursday morning, I found Colin Wilber-force at his desk sorting through a pile of report sheets.

'What have you got there, Colin?' I asked.

'Results of the TSG's stop-and-search operation last night, sir.'

'Any good?'

Colin grinned. 'Matter of opinion,' he said. 'Altogether the TSG units stopped some thirty-seven Ford, Renault and Bedford vans. All the drivers appeared to have a legitimate reason for driving about in the middle of the night. There were electricians, computer repair men, postmen, night-delivery guys and office-cleaning people. Oh, and a few plumbers.'

'Got the plumbers' telephone numbers?' asked Dave.

'D'you fancy a plumber for this topping then, Dave?' asked Colin.

'No,' said Dave, 'but there's something wrong with my bloody drains.'

Colin Wilberforce had reduced the bundle of reports of the TSG 'stops' to what he called a computerized database – whatever the hell that meant – but the results were disappointing. There was not a single driver whose name was Jeremy. Or, for that matter, Bruce Phillips either. But that was no surprise. Not that any of it meant much: the man with whom Patricia Hunter had been so besotted may not have given her his real name. And if he was indeed her murderer, who would blame him? Apart from which, if he was as rich as Candy Simpson said Patricia Hunter had told her he was, he wouldn't be driving

114

about in a van in the middle of the night. Unless...

'Only one thing for it, Frank,' I said to DI Mead. 'Every one of these people has to be checked out. Find out where they were on the nights of the murders and see if they had anything to do with theatres or were even regular theatre-goers.'

Frank was busy making notes. 'I'll run them through Criminal Records Office too,' he said, glancing up from his pocket book. He couldn't be bothered either with the constant name changes with which the job seems to be beset these days.

I don't know why he bothered to say that: a CRO search is standard procedure. Perhaps it was his way of telling me not to try teaching my grandmother to suck eggs.

I grinned and held up my hands in an attitude of surrender. 'Yeah, OK, Frank.' I turned to Dave. 'Dave, see if the lab has had second thoughts about the fibres found on the victim. It's possible that they've refined their conclusions to exclude some makes of van.'

'Right, guv.' Dave tapped his teeth with his pen. 'Of course, what would be really helpful right now would be to have another murder that took place last night. Then we could double-check Mr Mead's list of van drivers. Never know, might get a match.'

'Shut up, Poole,' said Frank.

I was still puzzling over how we could track down the mysterious Bruce Phillips. The

London telephone directory was no help: there were hundreds of people called Phillips, and only a very stupid fugitive would publish his name in a telephone directory. I just hoped that something would turn up to point me in the right direction.

And it did, sooner than I'd expected. Nearly.

'Later this afternoon, we'll take a look at Patricia Hunter's flat in Courtney Street, Dave.'

'Yeah, sure. By the way, Appleby got the results of the search of the General Register Office at Southport. There's no trace of an Eleanor Hunter being born thirty-one years ago. But the people up there did confirm Robert and Daphne Hunter as Patricia's parents.'

'In that case, we'll talk to Eleanor again. Right now. I wonder what the hell's she's playing at.'

We drove to Epsom, determined to unravel the mystery of Eleanor Hunter and what she'd told us about the 'death' of her parents.

'When we were here last, Miss Hunter, you told us that your parents had died some years ago.'

'That's correct.'

'In that case, how d'you explain the fact that I spoke to them last Friday?'

For some moments, Eleanor Hunter remained silent.

'Miss Hunter?'

116

When eventually she spoke there was disdain in her voice. 'I don't see that any of this is your business,' she said.

'Perhaps you'll let me be the judge of that,' I said.

There was a further silence before the woman spoke again. 'We had a relationship,' she said curtly.

'Who did?'

'Patricia and me.'

'What sort of relationship?' I asked, having deduced from Eleanor Hunter's masculine appearance what form that relationship would have taken.

'A lesbian relationship,' Eleanor said defiantly, raising her chin slightly and staring me in the eye. 'And then Patricia ruined it all. She found some man and went off with him. After all I'd done for her too. I'd looked after that girl, doted on her. I loved her. And how did she repay me? She went with a man.' The expression on her face was one of bitter hatred, and I wondered if we'd just found another suspect for Patricia Hunter's murder.

'So this story you told my chief inspector about the death of her parents was all nonsense, was it?' asked Dave.

'I said *our* parents. But it was my parents who'd died.'

'Why did you tell me that they were Patricia's parents then?'

'I don't know. I just said it on the spur of the moment,' said Eleanor, her eyes glittering.

'You do appreciate, I hope, that obstructing the police in a murder enquiry is a very serious matter.' But as I said it, I had a nasty thought that Eleanor may just enjoy a few months in the women's prison at Holloway. Not that I anticipated the Crown Prosecution Service stirring themselves sufficiently to bring a case against her.

'I don't care,' said Eleanor. 'That bitch deserved everything she got. I told her that no good would come of associating with men. They always let you down, and it looks as though one of them killed her. Well, serve her right, I say.'

'And is your name Hunter?'

'No, it's Carson.'

'Why did you change it to Hunter?'

'I didn't. I adopted it. Despite what you may think, neighbours still look down their noses at two women living together and sharing a bed, so we pretended to be sisters.' For no good reason, Eleanor laughed. 'The neighbours are a terrible trial,' she said. 'Got nothing better to do than mind other people's business.'

'You have wasted a great deal of my time,' I said sternly. 'And time is of the essence in a murder enquiry.'

'That's your problem,' said Eleanor, still refusing to be cowed by my earlier threat.

'What was the name of this man that Patricia went off with, Miss Carson?'

'I've no idea.'

'I think you have.'

118

There was a long pause before Eleanor Carson spoke again. 'It was someone called Bruce Phillips,' she said. 'The silly little bitch said she was going to marry him,' she added, and scoffed at the thought.

I couldn't work out whether Patricia Hunter's former lover was acting out of spite – it certainly seemed that way – but for the moment I decided to leave it. Apart from logging her in the back of my mind as a suspect.

'Go via Epsom nick, Dave,' I said as we drove away from Eleanor Carson's house. 'You never know, we might learn something there.'

The station officer at Epsom, a grizzled, grey-haired sergeant, laughed outright when we mentioned Eleanor's name.

'Mad as a hatter, sir,' he said. 'On average we get called there by her neighbours about once a month. The last time was at two o'clock on a Sunday morning. Dear Eleanor was standing in her back garden, stark naked, holding a paraffin lamp aloft and singing hymns at the top of her voice. It seems that "Onward Christian Soldiers" was her favourite. She really ought to be sectioned. Not that we haven't tried,' he added with a sigh.

'I don't wonder Patricia cleared off,' said Dave.

We drove direct from Epsom police station to Holborn.

Number 64 Courtney Street, Holborn, was an old Victorian house that had been converted into flats. Next to the front door was the usual entryphone system, but no names were posted alongside the bell pushes and the door was open anyway. So much for security.

There was a table in the entrance hall on which was a pile of letters. I sorted through it but it was only junk mail for someone called James Meredith who resided in Flat 2.

I rang the bell of the ground-floor flat.

The man who answered the door inspected us closely. I suppose that, in common with most Central London residents, he had been plagued by market researchers and door-to-door salespersons flogging anything from religion to subscriptions for magazines that were destined to go bankrupt before you'd received all the copies you'd paid for. Or even the first one.

'Yes?' he said in a tired voice, and adopted the stance of a man fully prepared to throw us into the street the moment we mentioned money, or suggested that the Lord was his salvation. Or worse still, both.

'I understand a woman called Patricia Hunter lived here...' I began.

'Not any more,' said the man, and started to close the door.

Dave put a hand against it and pushed. 'Police,' he said.

The door opened again. 'So?'

'We are investigating Patricia Hunter's murder,' I said.

'Bloody hell!' The man opened the door wide and stared at us, slack-jawed. 'When did that happen then?' There was the slightest trace of an accent, East-European maybe, possibly Polish at a guess. So what? We're all in the European Union now.

'Perhaps we should come in, Mr, er...?'

'Lang, Erik Lang,' he said. Which may or may not have been his real name. 'Erik with a K.'

'When did you last see Miss Hunter?' I asked as we followed him into a cluttered sitting-room-cum-office.

Lang thought about that before answering. 'When she moved out,' he said. 'That must have been a couple of months ago, I suppose.'

'Did you know her well?'

'Not really. We'd exchange a few words if we met in the hall, or when she came in to pay the rent. Nothing more. We tend to keep ourselves to ourselves here.' Just what Toni Mace had said. Strange how one can live in a crowded city and never really get to know anyone else.

'I take it that you're the landlord.'

'Yes.'

'And do you actually own the property?'

'Yes, I do, but what's that got to do with—?'

'When did she move in, Mr Lang?'

I think Lang grasped that I didn't intend to be messed about. 'Just a tick,' he said and crossed to the window sill. Picking up a cashbook of some sort, he thumbed through a couple of pages. 'Just before last Christmas.'

'And was the tenancy in her name?' asked Dave, his pocket book already out.

'Yes, er ... well, no. I don't know.'

'Well, which is it: yes, no, or don't know?' asked Dave in the manner of someone conducting a public opinion poll.

Lang paused, presumably because he was contravening some part of the various Rent Acts, the Finance Act, the plethora of VAT regulations or one of the multifarious European Union regulations that these days emanate from Brussels. And was wondering whether we were about to do him for it. *I should care, when I've a murder to clear up.*

'There was nothing formal. No written agreement or anything like that. It was a man who rang up first off. He said he was arranging a flat for his girlfriend. He mentioned something about her being in show business and didn't have the time to look around. But she was the one who paid the rent.'

'And his name?' demanded Dave.

'Ah, you've got me there,' said Lang.

'It is important, if you can remember, Mr Lang,' I said.

'Oh, just a minute. Come to think of it, I do have it here somewhere.' Lang pulled down the flap of a bureau and took out a desk diary. 'Yes, here we are. He rang to make an appointment and I jotted his name down.'

'And what was his name?' Dave asked with a sigh of impatience.

'Bruce Phillips,' said Lang.

'Did he leave a contact number, by any chance?' Dave gave no indication that the name was of vital importance. 'Or an address?' he added hopefully.

'No,' said Lang. 'I never thought to ask him.'

'And did he actually come here?' I asked.

'No. He said he was making the appointment for Miss Hunter, and it was her that turned up.'

'Did you ever see a man going up to her flat, Mr Lang?' asked Dave.

'No.'

'Who's occupying the flat now?' I asked.

'No one. I had a man in there for two weeks, but he moved out again the day before yesterday.'

'It's empty then?'

'Yes.'

'I'd like to have a look round.'

'Sure. I'll get the key.'

To say that it was small would be exaggerating: a bed, a tiny kitchen area, and a shower, all squeezed into a converted loft space. In places the slant of the roof made it difficult to stand upright. Unless you were about four-feet-two tall. I was not surprised that the last tenant had stayed for only a couple of weeks. It made me wonder what had brought Patricia Hunter from the comparative luxury of the flat at Petersfield Street to something that was little more than a flop.

Dave and I spent a few fruitless minutes looking round, but there was nothing of interest to us, and certainly nothing that would advance our investigation.

As we returned to the ground floor to give

the key back to Lang, I noticed that James Meredith's junk mail had vanished from the hall table. Good, he was in. With any luck, he'd have been nosier than the landlord.

And he had.

We told Meredith who we were and he almost dragged us into his flat. Perhaps the poor guy was lonely or just adored policemen. The first I could believe; the second I doubted. 'Come in,' he said warmly, 'and join me in a drink.' Brooking no refusal, he produced a bottle of whisky and three glasses from a tall cupboard fashioned from some exotic tropical wood. 'It's nice, isn't it?' he said, running his hand lovingly over the carved surface. 'It's ethnic.'

I didn't bother to point out that everything was ethnic to a greater or lesser degree, and hoped that Dave wouldn't come out with one of his thumbnail lectures on the misuse of the English language.

'I've had a bloody awful day at the office,' Meredith continued, handing Dave and me a glass of Scotch, 'so I thought to myself, sod it, and knocked off early. Still, nothing to what you chaps have to put up with, I imagine,' he added ruefully.

'What do you do in this office of yours?' Dave asked.

'I'm an accountant,' said Meredith, looking even more apologetic. 'Bloody computers all day long.'

'Patricia Hunter,' I said before Dave could make one of his sarcastic comments about accountants.

'Girl who used to live upstairs, you mean? Moved out a while back. I was sorry to see her go.'

'I'm afraid Miss Hunter's been murdered, Mr Meredith,' I said. 'That's why we're here.'

A look of stunned disbelief appeared on Meredith's face. 'Oh God, surely not!' He shook his head like a boxer who'd just received a debilitating uppercut, took a sip of whisky and remained silent for some moments. 'Christ! You just don't know what's around the corner, do you?' he said eventually. 'She was some looker, that girl. She was an actress, you know. Not surprising really. Like I said, she was a good-looking girl.'

I'd seen some quite ugly actresses over the years, but didn't think it was worth mentioning.

'How well did you get to know her?'

'I think it's fair to say I got to know her very well.' Meredith grinned and drained his whisky. 'As a matter of fact, I chatted her up shortly after she arrived and we hit it off straight away. She came down here for a drink from time to time, and I took her out to dinner on the few occasions she wasn't working. It wasn't all that easy, you see, what with her being on the stage and working late. Sometimes she was so tired that she'd stay overnight at the theatre. Apparently they've got bedrooms there, so she said. But I don't know much about the theatre.'

Dave shot me a glance that said it was

bloody obvious Meredith didn't know anything about the theatre. But Dave did, and he knew that what Patricia Hunter had told our helpful accountant was nonsense. The nights she claimed to have been staying at the Granville, or wherever, were more than likely spent in a client's bed.

'But it was getting serious,' the naïve Meredith went on. 'After she'd been here for about four months, I made a tentative suggestion that she should move in with me, never thinking that she'd say yes. But she jumped at it, and we agreed to shift her stuff down to my flat on the following Sunday.' He let out a sigh of exasperation. 'And that's when it all went pear-shaped.'

'What happened?' I asked.

Meredith stood up and poured himself another whisky. 'Another one?' he asked, pointing at our glasses.

'No thanks.'

'Well, I met her in the hall on the Friday morning and she was with this guy,' Meredith continued. 'I didn't have a clue who he was. I thought maybe he was someone from the theatre who'd come by to collect something. You know, like a script.' Dave glanced at the ceiling. 'Anyway, I said something like "Hello, darling" and asked her if she was all set for Sunday's move, but she cut me dead. Never said a word.'

'Did you speak to her about it later?'

'Too right,' said Meredith. 'I went up to her flat and asked her what the hell it was all about.'

'And what did she say?'

'Well, for a start she didn't let me in, and she said she didn't want to talk about it. I asked her if she'd met someone else, but she said no. I just got a complete blank. And she couldn't close the door fast enough. As a matter of fact she seemed frightened even to be talking to me. And the very next day she moved out.'

'Did she tell you where she was going? Or leave a phone number?'

'No, nothing. I never saw her again. In fact, I didn't even know she'd gone. I went upstairs to her flat but there was no answer. I had a word with Erik Lang and he said she'd gone, vamoosed, but he didn't know where.'

'What sort of impression did you get of this man you saw, Mr Meredith?' I asked. 'Did the two of them look as though they were well acquainted?'

'Hard to say really. I only saw him that one time and that was very brief.'

'What did he look like, this guy?' Dave asked, pocket book and pen once more at the ready.

Meredith looked out of the window, as if trying to visualize the man he'd seen with Patricia Hunter. 'About five-ten or eleven, I suppose. Heavily built.' He glanced at Dave. 'Bit like you except that he had blond hair. That's about it really.'

'Did he speak with an Australian accent?' Dave asked.

'I don't know. He didn't say anything, just glowered. Why? D'you think an Australian killed her?'

Dave ignored Meredith's query and glanced at me. 'E-fit, guv?'

'What?' Given that Dave had graduated in English at London University, I often wished he'd get into the habit of speaking the language he'd spent three years studying.

'I think it may be a good idea if we got Mr Meredith to create a computer-aided likeness of the man he saw with Miss Hunter ... sir.'

'Why the hell didn't you say so?' I said. 'Good idea.' I turned to Meredith. 'Would you be prepared to come to a nearby police station and have a go at making up a picture of the man you saw?'

'Sure. When?'

'How about now?' I gave Dave a questioning look. 'What d'you reckon, Dave?'

'Got the car outside. Let's do it.'

But after a session lasting over an hour, aided by a very patient E-fit operator, the image that Meredith finally produced could have fitted a thousand men. Oh well, it was worth a try.

Nine

'This man Phillips is beginning to annoy me, Dave,' I said, over a pint in the Red Lion in Whitehall. 'There wasn't a Bruce Phillips on that list of stops the TSG did last night, was there?'

'Come on, guv, you know there wasn't. You checked it.'

'I was hoping I might have missed it,' I said gloomily, 'but he wouldn't have been on the list, not with the luck we've been having with this damned enquiry. And if he's still about, he's almost bound to have changed his name by now.'

'I doubt it,' said Dave. 'It strikes me he's an arrogant bastard. He must know he's wanted on an extradition warrant, but he still goes around using his own name. It pops up all over the place. Everywhere we look.' He ordered two more pints before continuing his theorizing. 'And I reckon he must have known Patricia Hunter for some time, guv.'

'Yeah, that's bugging me too. When was it that Eleanor Carson said Patricia left her for Bruce Phillips?'

'Five years ago, if we can believe anything that Eleanor told us, particularly after what that skipper at Epsom said about her. But Patricia could have known him even longer. We don't know when she put his name in her address book, but her old man said she'd mentioned Phillips in a recent letter as a boyfriend, *and* he rented the flat for her at Courtney Street.' Pausing long enough to give me a cigarette, Dave added, 'I suppose we could do the rounds of the theatres with that E-fit that Meredith did.'

'What, fifty-odd theatres and at least two hundred people, cast and staff, in each? Waste of time, Dave. Anyway, I doubt that he got it anything like our man. Just trying to be helpful. And can you imagine the result? It would be a whole load of "maybes" followed by hours of fruitless legwork.' I had long been of the opinion that E-fits were successful in a ratio of about one to every thousand.

'Yeah, I suppose you're right, guv.' Dave stared dolefully into his beer as though hopeful of finding the answer there. 'But what about the business of her going away with this Jeremy guy?'

'I've got reservations about that too, Dave. I think she was just spinning Candy Simpson a line. Like you said, boasting she'd got a rich boyfriend when Candy hadn't. Go home, Dave. We've done enough for one day.'

'And we haven't achieved a damned thing,' said Dave gloomily.

'Buy you a drink, gents?' said a voice.

I turned. Standing behind me was an odious creep known universally as Fat Danny, crime reporter of the worst tabloid in Fleet Street. And that, believe me, is an accolade for which there is much competition. Danny was overweight, and his pudding face was permanently greasy. And he had a tendency to wave his podgy little hands about the whole time he was talking. He had a reputation – envied by several other crime reporters – for being able not only to sniff out the most salacious of crimes, but also to track down the officers investigating it. Not that that was difficult, given that the Red Lion was the nearest pub to Curtis Green.

'Sure, Danny, we'll take a couple of pints of best off you.'

'So, Mr Brock, how's the Patricia Hunter job going?' asked Danny once he'd got a round in.

'Nowhere right now,' I said.

'But you must have some leads, surely?'

'One or two, but none that I can tell you about.'

'Your secret's safe with me, Mr Brock, you know that.'

'You given up journalism to become a Trappist monk then?' put in Dave.

'You know what I mean, Mr Brock,' said Danny, ignoring Dave and tapping the side of his nose with a forefinger. 'Non-attributable and all that. But a little bird told me that you had teams of uniforms out last night stopping vans. That something to do with this Hunter job, was it?'

'Maybe.'

'It's a good story. Glamorous showgirl brutally murdered and found floating in the river right opposite the Houses of Parliament. It's what front pages were made for. And a bit of publicity wouldn't do you any harm. Might even get you promoted. Oh, come on, Mr Brock, give me a break.'

'OK. We think the body of Patricia Hunter was conveyed in a van from where she was murdered to where she was dumped in the river.'

'And whereabouts *was* she dumped?' asked Danny optimistically.

'If you can tell me that, Danny, I'll make sure you get a letter of thanks signed personally by the commissioner.'

'Terrific, but seriously, haven't you got any suspects lined up?'

'Not one, Danny.'

'Leave it out, Mr Brock, I've got to write something.'

'Try your resignation,' said Dave.

It's one of life's paradoxes that even when you tell a journalist the truth, he still doesn't believe you.

It was almost seven o'clock. Having checked with Gavin Creasey, the night-duty incident-room sergeant, that there was nothing demanding my immediate attention, I went into my office and rang Gail Sutton.

'Hello?' The voice was hesitant and didn't sound like the chorus girl I'd met at the Granville and with whom I'd later had lunch

132

in Kingston. I wondered if she shared her house with another girl.

'Is Gail there, please?'

'Who's that?'

'Harry Brock.'

'Oh, Harry, it's you.' There was relief in her voice, and I suddenly realized that the death of her friend, and her own association with the same theatre, might well have caused a woman living alone to feel vulnerable and not a little scared.

'I've got an idea.'

'What's that?'

'How about you jump on a train at Surbiton and come to Waterloo? It's only sixteen minutes. I'll meet you and take you to dinner. *And* I'll take you home afterwards. How about it?'

'That would be wonderful, Harry. Where are we going?'

'I know this great restaurant that does a wonderful steak and kidney pudding,' I said.

There was a distinct pause, and then, 'Have you ever noticed my figure, Harry?' Gail asked.

I laughed. 'What sort of question's that, for God's sake? Of course I've noticed it.'

'Well, it doesn't stay like that on a diet of steak and kidney pudding. I'm not in the running for playing one of the Ugly Sisters yet.'

'This place does fish as well, or whatever takes your fancy.'

'That's all right, then.'

'Have you got a mobile?'

'Yes, of course.'

'Right. Once you're on the train give me a ring and I'll be there to meet you.' And I gave her the number of my own mobile.

The concourse at Waterloo station was still thronged with bustling crowds of workers on their way home, even though it was nearing eight o'clock. Several trains that had stopped at Surbiton were due to arrive about now and I positioned myself near the indicator board in an attempt to spot Gail.

For a moment or two my attention was riveted on an elegant blonde in a silver-grey trouser suit gliding between the mass of self-centred travellers – a mass that, nevertheless, seemed automatically to part as she neared them – when suddenly I realized that it *was* Gail.

'Hi! Hope you haven't been waiting long.'

'No, I only just got here,' I lied and took her arm, convincing myself that this was a necessary precaution against her being knocked down by the panic-stricken runners obsessed with catching a train that had probably already left. 'You look great.'

'Gawd bless yer, sir,' she chided in bantering, mock-Cockney tones that ably demonstrated the range of her acting ability. 'Where are we going?'

'You'll see,' I said, steering her towards the taxi rank outside the station.

When we arrived at Rules Restaurant in

Maiden Lane, the cab driver, his eyes on Gail but talking to me, said, 'Enjoy your game, guv'nor.'

'What's this about a game?' Gail asked, giving me a suspicious glance as the taxi pulled away. 'What did he mean by that?'

I laughed. 'Nothing sinister,' I said. 'This restaurant specializes in game. You know, venison, pheasant, quail. That sort of thing.'

'Oh, that's all right then,' said Gail, flashing me a sexy smile.

As the restaurant manager conducted us to our table, an inordinate number of male eyes seemed to lose interest in their food, and a man on the far side of the ornate room gave Gail a discreet wave. He probably hoped that I wouldn't notice. But I did. Jealousy was already beginning to set in.

'An admirer of yours?' I asked.

'One of many,' she replied airily with a wave of her hand. 'A starving chorus girl can't afford to turn down free meals.'

I was sufficient of a cynic to wonder what she had offered in return. 'Have you found another job yet?' I asked, once I had ordered a carafe of white wine as a preamble to studying the menu.

'To tell you the truth, I haven't been looking. Anyway it was only last Friday that *Scatterbrain* closed. So I'm resting for a bit. Literally, I mean, rather than in the theatrical sense.'

I assumed that the fear of what she believed to be a psychopath with a taste for murdering showgirls, and who was running loose in the capital, had played some part in Gail's decision to steer clear of the stage for a while.

And as if confirming that view, she asked, once again, 'Are you any nearer to discovering who killed Patricia yet, Harry?'

'No, I'm afraid not. But we have found out that she lived at three different addresses recently. And she had a boyfriend called Peter Crawford, one called Bruce Phillips and another called Jeremy. Did she ever mention any of them?'

'I'm sorry, no. Patricia never mentioned boyfriends. Just a minute though.' Gail paused to take a sip of wine. 'Jeremy. Yes, come to think of it, she did mention a Jeremy.'

'Surname?' I prompted.

'Payne. That was it. Jeremy Payne. Funny that. You can know someone for quite a while and never find out much about them. Not that that seems to be a problem for you,' she continued with a smile. 'You've already found out that I've been divorced for three years, and why. But I don't know a thing about you.' She gave me a questioning glance.

'All right, you've got me,' I said, and laughed. I went on to tell her about meeting Helga Büchner, a German physiotherapist at Westminster Hospital who had treated me professionally – at first anyway – after I'd been involved in a ruckus with a crowd of yobs in Whitehall. I'd been a young uniformed PC at the time and Helga and I had embarked on a whirlwind romance. Two months later we were married. The cynics at the nick, the women police in particular, had scoffed and said it wouldn't last, and they were right: it didn't. Mind you, sixteen years of marriage isn't bad by today's batting average. Looking back, the only thing I really got out of it was to have learned fluent German. And that was in the interests of interpreting the snide asides about me that habitually passed between Helga and her harridan of a mother.

'How long ago?' asked Gail. She touched the arm of a passing waiter. 'D'you think you could get me a bottle of still water, darling?' she purred. 'Evian, or something of the sort.'

'Of course, madam.' The waiter was clearly besotted by his gorgeous customer, and scurried away to do her bidding.

'How long ago what?' I asked.

'How long ago was the divorce?'

'Oh, about a year, but it had started to fall apart well before that. Helga insisted on carrying on working, even after Robert was born.'

Gail raised her eyebrows. 'Oh, you've got a son, have you?' She didn't sound too happy at that. Perhaps her plans for the future were working more rapidly than were mine.

'Not any more. He was drowned in a friend's pond. Helga had left him with her while she went to work. He was only four.'

There were no words of condolence from Gail, she just nodded. Her devoted waiter arrived with a bottle of water and, briefly touching his hand, she gave him a captivating smile and mouthed a word of thanks. Looking at me again, and picking her words with obvious care, she said, 'That, I should think, is enough to destroy any marriage.'

That suited me. I couldn't stand false sentiment, and, in any event, the accident had happened years ago.

'What about you? Are you happy working in the theatre?'

'Are you happy in the police force?' she countered.

'It's what I do,' I said. 'I'm stuck with it, and I wouldn't know what else to do.'

'Exactly,' said Gail, somewhat ambiguously.

'Did Patricia ever mention anything about sixteen Fenwick Road, Brighton?'

She looked a little surprised at the sudden change in subject. 'Not that I can recall. Is it important?'

'It may be,' I said.

Gail considered my question for a moment or two longer. 'No, definitely not. Why?'

'It's a bit strange really. That Brighton address was in her address book together with the names of a Mr and Mrs Hunter, but when we went there it turned out to be a boarding house. The guy who runs the place had never heard of Patricia. Anyway, as I told you, we tracked down her parents to an address in Wimbledon.'

'Perhaps she got the Brighton address wrong. Did you try the houses on either side?'

Don't you just love it when a rank amateur tells you how to do your job? And gets it right.

'No,' I said thoughtfully. 'Have you ever considered the police as a career?'

Gail laughed. 'I don't like the uniform. Mind you, if ever I'm forced into doing strippagrams, I might learn to like it.'

'I don't like the uniform either,' I said, trying to force from my mind the vision of Gail performing a strippagram routine. 'That's why I became a detective.'

The first course arrived, and we reverted to discussing mundane matters.

'Have you always been in the theatre, Gail?'

'Yes. Eighteen years now. My parents wanted me to be a doctor, but I'm afraid that wasn't my scene. I left school at sixteen and did a year at dance school. I'd always had this heady ambition to be an actress, but I had to start in the chorus before I was able to land a few walk-on parts. After that I managed to get some speaking roles – even got one or two television parts – but now I'm back hoofing again. Or was. Still, you have to take what you can get.'

'Are you happy with your lot?' I asked.

'Case of having to be really. It's nowhere near as glamorous a profession as some people think. And on top of everything else, I've a suspicion that my ex put the bubble in for me. I certainly had a longish run of unsuccessful auditions after we split. Bit spiteful was Gerald.'

'Are your parents still alive?'

'You know they are. Don't you remember me telling you that I was going to see them last Saturday? They live in Nottingham.' Gail sounded as though she was beginning to doubt my abilities as a detective. 'My father's a property developer. Done very well, too, which is why I don't have to worry much about working. I'm an only child and he dotes on me. *And* he sends me an allowance when I'm "resting". Anyway, I got the house out of the divorce settlement, so I'm coping quite well.'

In other words, mind your own business.

And I did. For the rest of the meal we talked pleasantries.

'Would you like something else?' I asked when Gail's adoring waiter returned to hover with the dessert menu.

'No thanks, just coffee. I can't afford to put on weight.'

The man who had been seated on the other side of the restaurant waved as he left.

Gail waved back. ''Bye, darling,' she said loudly, and a few heads turned. Her admirer looked as though he wished he'd crept out. Particularly as I waved too.

'This guy Jeremy Payne,' I said, reverting to our previous conversation. 'Did Patricia say anything about him?'

'Only that he was very rich.'

'Nothing about where he lived?'

'No.'

'Did she mention a flat in Docklands or a villa in the South of France?'

'No, she certainly didn't.' Gail laughed. 'If she had I'd've had him off her. Men like that are few and far between.'

I know she'd laughed, but her comment was not exactly encouraging to a detective chief inspector for whom promotion was a distant and probably vain hope.

We travelled back to Surbiton together, and I saw her to the door of her house in Kingston. It was a three-storied townhouse tucked away in a quiet little mews, and I wondered if Gail's property developer father had bought it for his daughter and her ex-husband as a wedding present.

'Thank you for dinner, Harry,' she said. 'I really did enjoy it.' And holding both of my hands in hers, gave me a chaste kiss on the cheek. Just like my mother used to when she sent me off to school.

There wasn't much to cheer me up on Friday morning.

'What about the fibres, Dave? Have we got anything back on that?'

'Ah, the fibres, yes,' said Dave, and flicked back through his 'action' book. 'I rang the lab and the guy I spoke to agreed that on closer analysis, the fibres could only have come from a Ford van, rather than a Bedford or a Renault.'

'Hooray!' I said sarcastically. 'Progress at last.' I glanced at my watch. 'Time for the morning briefing.'

The incident room was crowded, not only with my own team, but with the additional officers that the acting commander had managed to steal from somewhere.

'I'll just run over the story so far,' I began. 'We've got a dead woman: Patricia Hunter, found in the Thames opposite the Houses of Parliament.' I indicated the photograph of the victim with a wave of the hand. 'We found an address book at the flat she lived in last – that's the one at Coping Road, Islington – but I think we can safely discount the names and addresses that we found in it, with the exception of Bruce Phillips.'

'Who's he, guv'nor?' asked a sergeant from among the ranks of Cleaver's reinforcements.

'Apart from fancying him for this job, he's wanted by the Australian police for fraud, if it's the same Phillips. There's an Interpol red-corner circular out for him, but when proceedings were started at Bow Street, he disappeared,' I said.

'Don't blame him, guv'nor,' said a voice in the audience.

'According to Patricia's little book,' I continued, 'he had an address in Petersfield Street, Fulham, an address that she probably shared with Phillips. But he'd long gone when we checked there, and none of the present residents had heard of him. He did however arrange the viewing of a flat on Patricia Hunter's behalf at sixty-four Courtney Street, Holborn, and she'd lived there for about six months before moving on to her last address at Coping Road, Islington.' I nodded towards Dave. 'DS Poole will fill you in on a few other details.'

'A guy called Meredith, one of Patricia's neighbours at Courtney Street, saw a man who could have been Phillips,' Dave began, 'but we're not sure it was him. However, Meredith was almost certainly screwing Miss Hunter on a regular basis and she'd agreed to move into his flat. However he was stupid enough to mention it to her when he met her in the hall with this mystery man. The next thing that happened was – abracadabra – she'd moved out and left no forwarding address.'

'Any ideas as to why, Skip?' asked a DC.

'The inference is that she was scared stiff of the guy Meredith saw her with,' said Dave. 'We got Meredith to do an E-fit but it's worse than useless. And just to complicate the whole business, when we interviewed Patricia Hunter's parents in Wimbledon, her old man said she'd written saying that Bruce Phillips was her boyfriend. But again, he hadn't seen Phillips in the flesh. And finally, we tracked down someone at an Epsom address who purported to be Patricia's sister, a woman called Eleanor Hunter. She told us that her parents – and therefore Patricia's – had both died some years ago, despite the fact that we'd interviewed them only two days previously. But that's turned out to be a bum steer. Patricia and Eleanor, whose real name is Carson, were having a lesbian relationship before Patricia took off in favour of a man who she told Eleanor was called Bruce Phillips. However, we later learned from the police at Epsom that Eleanor's a screwball with a predilection for singing hymns in the nude in her back garden at two in the morning. There, that's simple enough for you, isn't it? I may ask questions later.'

'What about the Brighton address that Patricia Hunter had in her book?' asked a woman detective.

'We drew a blank there,' said Dave. 'It turned out to be the Golden Riviera Guest House, run by a couple called Richards. They'd never heard of Mr and Mrs Hunter, Patricia Hunter or Bruce Phillips.'

'Which reminds me,' I said, remembering what Gail Sutton had suggested. 'Frank, get someone to ask the Brighton police to check a few of the houses on either side of sixteen Fenwick Road. It's just possible that Patricia Hunter wrote down the wrong house number.'

Frank nodded as he wrote on his clipboard. 'Leave it to me, I'll get someone to do it.'

'Just to summarize the rest of it,' I continued, 'the victim was a chorus girl. She had recently indulged in sexual intercourse but the lab couldn't match the semen to their DNA database. And the ligature used to strangle the Hunter girl was possibly from a type of electrical cable used in the theatre.'

'Theatre as in song and dance, not as in surgical operations,' said Dave in an aside, and got a laugh.

'And finally,' I said, 'the grazing on her body revealed traces of dust and oil that may

144

be linked to the floor of a garage somewhere. And the fibres found in the dead woman's hair indicated that she might have been transported in a Ford van. The night before last, the TSG did a number of stops in the central London area, but we're no further forward ... at this stage.' I glanced at Frank Mead.

'Still checking them out, Harry. Let you know the results ASAP.'

'Don't forget this guy Jeremy,' Dave whispered.

'Ah yes. We think his name's Jeremy Payne. An actress at the Alhambra theatre – her name's Candy Simpson – told us that Patricia Hunter had said that she was going to marry a guy called Jeremy who'd promised to whisk her off to a life of luxury in the south of France. This guy apparently told Patricia he had pots of money, a flat in Docklands and a villa in St Raphaël.'

One of the women detectives scoffed. 'Stupid little cow,' she muttered.

'About three months before her body was found,' I continued, 'she walked out of the play she was then appearing in, apparently to depart for ever.'

'Well, she got that right,' said the same woman detective.

'The priorities are, therefore, to find Bruce Phillips and to get any more information we can on this mysterious, and ostensibly monied, guy called Jeremy Payne. Any questions?'

There were no questions.

* * *

It was getting on for lunch time when Tom Challis, one of Frank Mead's sergeants, came into my office.

'Got a moment, guv?'

'What's on your mind, Tom?'

Challis handed me a small slip of paper. 'A receipt, guv. Found in Patricia Hunter's room at Coping Road.'

'What about it?' I asked. Apart from the fact that it had been screwed up and then smoothed out again, it looked like any other credit-card receipt.

'It goes out to a shop in Jermyn Street, and it's for a man's shirt. A fifty-five-quid shirt, at that.'

'Well, I suppose it's possible that Patricia Hunter bought it for a boyfriend, Tom.'

Challis shook his head. 'No she didn't, guv. I've checked with the credit-card company, and the account's in the name of a Geoffrey Forman of thirteen Ridgely Road, Barnes. Thought it was worth a mention.'

'Indeed it was, Tom. Where exactly was this receipt found?'

'In her dressing-table drawer along with all her other bits and pieces. You'll notice it had been screwed up. Maybe he dropped it and she put it away in case it was important.'

'It is,' I said, 'and he probably doesn't know he's lost it.' This was beginning to look like the first break we'd had since the whole enquiry had started with the recovery of Patricia Hunter's body from the Thames. 'I

146

suppose the credit-card people didn't tell you what this guy Forman did for a living, Tom, did they?'

'No, guv, and I didn't think to ask. I can get back to them, if you like. But from what I've learned over the years, they don't keep their records up to date, not so far as occupation is concerned anyway. Usually people don't bother to notify of a change of job, not unless it's likely to improve their credit rating. Incidentally, I ran him through CRO, but there's nothing on him. Not on the details we've got so far, anyway. The only Geoffrey Forman I found was a forty-five-year-old East End villain currently doing a handful for a blagging.'

'Well, there's only one thing for it. Dave and I will pay Mr Forman a visit. Is Dave in the incident room?'

'Yes, guv.'

'Good. Ask him to come in.'

Dave sauntered into my office a few minutes later. 'Tom Challis has been shooting his mouth off that he's just solved this job for us, guv,' he said. Challis was the type of brash detective who didn't appeal to Dave.

I laughed. 'He might just have done,' I said, and repeated to Dave what Challis had told me. 'Tom Challis might just have hit on the solution.'

Dave frowned. 'I shouldn't hold your breath, guv,' he said.

And he was right to be cynical. Over the years, detectives have many promising leads that, after hours of painstaking and time-consuming enquiries, turn out to be useless. But we had to try. After all, right now there was nothing else.

Ten

Given that most people in the world seem to knock off at about three on a Friday afternoon – coppers excepted, of course – I decided that Dave and I would make for Barnes.

Number 13 Ridgely Road was a large detached house, the type that estate agents were once fond of describing as a suburban villa. *And it was no more than half a mile from the River Thames.* But I've been excited by coincidences of that sort too often in the past to get excited now.

The woman who answered the door was an elegant brunette who, I guessed, was about thirty. Her hair was straight to just below shoulder length, and she was wearing a low-cut cream-silk dress and high heels.

'Yes?' The glance was one of interest rather than the concern with which two strange men on the doorstep are usually greeted.

'Mrs Forman?'

'No.'

Well, that was a good start. Will nothing go right with this damned enquiry?

'I understood that Mr Geoffrey Forman lived here,' I said. 'We're police officers.'

'Oh!' The woman glanced briefly beyond

my right shoulder at the Alfa Romeo parked in front of her house. Perhaps she thought our visit was to do with some traffic offence. 'How do I know you're policemen?' she asked with an apologetic smile.

Wise woman. Dave and I produced our warrant cards and she seemed satisfied.

'I'm Donna Lodge,' she said. 'Geoff's my partner, but he's not here at the moment. In fact he's abroad on business.'

'I see.' That was unfortunate, to say the least. 'Can you tell me when he's likely to be back?'

'Not exactly. He travels a lot, you see.' As an apparent afterthought, Donna invited us into the front room of the house. 'May I ask what it's about?' With a gesture of her hand, she indicated that we should sit down, and then seated herself in an armchair opposite us, crossing her legs and carefully arranging the skirt of her dress. A woman perfectly at ease.

This is always the tricky part of any investigation. If I mentioned the receipt that had been found in Patricia Hunter's room – the one that DS Challis had traced to Forman – Donna Lodge might just blow a gasket. And, for an encore, collapse in a fit of the vapours. And ask her partner some very searching questions when eventually he walked through the door.

But I could do without all that. I smiled, disarmingly I hoped, and embarked on the sort of bewildering mumbo-jumbo intended to disguise the true reasons for my enquiry. If

Forman was the murderer, the last thing I wanted was his partner warning him that the police were taking an active interest in a dead actress called Patricia Hunter.

'It's a rather complicated case, Ms Lodge, and I won't weary you with the finer details. That said, it's quite likely, at the end of the day, that it'll all come to nothing. But we have to go through the motions, so to speak.' I then launched into the standard fallback lie. 'However, in short, a business card with Mr Forman's name and address on it was found at the scene of an office-breaking where a number of computers were stolen. But the police are obliged to eliminate all the innocent parties. Of which, I'm sure, he is one.' There was a flaw in this little piece of fiction however: a business card would have had a business address on it, not a home address. I just hoped that Forman's partner wouldn't notice.

'What my chief inspector means, Ms Lodge,' said Dave, contributing to the smoke-screen, 'is that in the unlikely event that we have enough to warrant sending a report to the Crown Prosecution Service, they'll ask all sorts of silly questions, like why didn't you check out that address, and if we don't have the answers, the whole thing gets delayed while we go out and do what we should have done in the first place. Even so, I don't think it'll come to anything.'

'I see.'

But judging from the bemused expression

on Ms Lodge's face, she didn't see at all. And that suited me fine.

'Have you any idea when he may return?' I asked again, but in such an offhand way that it gave the impression that I didn't care very much.

'Not really, no. As I said just now, he travels a great deal, and at the moment he's in Germany. In Düsseldorf, as a matter of fact.'

'Mmm!' I nodded sagely. 'What does he travel in exactly?'

Beside me, my English-language purist of a sergeant gave a discreet cough. Had I posed the question to him in that form, he would have said 'an aeroplane', and added 'sir'. But Ms Lodge knew what I meant.

'It's something to do with computers. I don't understand a thing about them. Half the time I haven't a clue what he's talking about when he does come home.'

'I know how you feel. The world of computers is a mystery to me as well,' I said with a smile. 'But that would probably explain it. No doubt he visits offices all the time, and it would be natural for them to have his name and address.' I dug myself in a bit deeper, but I thought I'd mention it before Ms Lodge did. Or worse, Mr Forman. 'That's strange though. Presumably he has an office somewhere, and the card would have had that address on it rather than this one.'

'Not necessarily. He works from home, you see.'

'Ah, that would explain it,' I said, breathing

a sigh of relief. I stood up and produced one of my own cards, hoping that she was unaware that the Serious Crime Group didn't investigate tuppenny-ha'penny office-breakings. 'It'll probably be a waste of his time and mine, but perhaps you'd ask him to give me a ring when he does get home, Ms Lodge. There's no rush,' I added, praying that Mr Forman would not take that proviso too literally. If this guy was Patricia Hunter's killer, the sooner we got hold of him the better, just in case he was thinking of striking again.

Donna Lodge took the card and examined it. 'Yes, of course,' she said, 'but I've no idea when that will be.'

'Does he have a mobile phone?' asked Dave casually.

'I think so, but I don't know what the number is. Geoff's very particular about not using it while he's driving. It's this new law, you know.' Donna paused. 'But then you would know, wouldn't you?' she said with another apologetic smile.

There was little point in mentioning that the law was far from new. But if he was our murderer – and *was* tempted to strike again – he wouldn't want to get pulled by our traffic brethren for using his mobile if he'd got a body in the boot. Smart fellow.

And so we had to leave it there. Being an inveterate collector of such things, Dave took a note of the Alfa Romeo's index number, and we returned to Curtis Green.

Dave wandered into my office with two cups of coffee. 'A rep doesn't work at the weekends,' he said thoughtfully. 'I wouldn't mind betting Forman's over the side, probably with some gorgeous German bird in Düsseldorf,' he added, and nicked one of my cigarettes.

I resisted the temptation to expound on the dangers of becoming involved with German women, gorgeous or otherwise. 'Well, unless there's some innocent explanation for one of his receipts being in Patricia Hunter's room, Dave, I think it's safe to assume that he's screwing around. And if he's in the habit of taking out actresses—'

'In more ways than one,' observed Dave drily. 'But a lot of married guys have it off with other birds. They don't necessarily top 'em though.'

'I suppose we'll just have to wait for him to come home to roost,' was my only contribution.

'If he does,' muttered Dave gloomily. 'There is a bit of toot there, you know, guv,' he continued. 'That house must be worth at least three-quarters of a million, and the Alfa Romeo – which incidentally is registered in Donna Lodge's name – is only a year old. As for the dress she was wearing, well, Madeleine would die for it.'

'There must be more money in flogging computers than I thought,' I said.

'If he is actually selling them, guv. He may be one of those consultants who goes around advising firms on computer systems. And charging them the earth for telling them to buy expensive installations that they don't really need. And then getting a kickback from the computer company that supplies them.'

'On the other hand, maybe it's Donna who's got the money,' I said.

'In which case, he'd be raving mad to push his luck by having it off with another bird. But there again, Madeleine's always telling me that men are complete idiots. She reckons the average male spends more time on buying a new car than he does on picking a wife.'

'Sounds to me as though your Madeleine's a shrewd woman, Dave.'

'You can say that again,' said Dave, and rapidly changed the subject. 'So what's next, guv?'

'If Donna owns the Alfa Romeo, Geoffrey Forman must have a car of his own. See if the DVLA at Swansea can come up with anything.'

Dave made a note and then glanced up. 'He's probably got a company car,' he said. 'And that'll be in the company's name. Or even a leasing company.'

'You're such a comfort to me, Dave,' I said, 'but Donna Lodge said he works from home.'

'Still might be working for someone else,' Dave said. 'Incidentally, I had a look at one of the job's Ford vans this morning.'

'What the hell's that got to do with the price of fish?'

'There's no floor covering in the back. It's

just bare metal.'

'So what, Dave? Could be that some cost-cutting bean counter at the Yard is saving us some money by ordering vans without carpet.'

'I don't think so, but if that's the case, the lab boys might have given us a bum steer, and the fibres found on our victim came from somewhere else.'

'You'd better check that out, Dave,' I said. If he was right, and the lab was wrong, it might have given us a better chance of narrowing down our list of suspects. But if the fibres didn't come from a Ford van, we'd wasted our time, and that of the TSGs that did the night-time stops in Central London last Wednesday. Nevertheless, I was still absolutely certain that the body of our victim must have been moved by night.

Any thoughts of an early night, a forlorn hope anyway in a murder enquiry, were shattered by Frank Mead's arrival in my office.

'I've just had an interesting conversation with a DI on the Sussex Vice Squad in Lewes, Harry.'

'Why Lewes?'

'They cover the whole county but work out of HQ, which is at Lewes, and my query about sixteen Fenwick Road eventually filtered through to them.'

I sat up and took notice. 'Yes, go on.'

'As we know, sixteen Fenwick Road meant nothing to the Sussex lads or to us, but *sixty-*

one Fenwick Road rang a bell with the Vice Squad down there.'

'Is that a coincidence or a mistake, or d'you think Patricia Hunter deliberately transposed the numbers in her address book, Frank?'

'Or it's nothing to do with her at all,' said Frank. 'However, about three months ago the Vice Squad received some information that sixty-one Fenwick Road was a wholesale knocking shop. They kept obo for about a fortnight, during which time they clocked a number of women entering the premises, usually in the late morning or early afternoon. These women were not seen to leave again until much later, well gone midnight in most cases, and sometimes even the following day. But it was the clientele that interested our Sussex brethren.'

'In what way?' I asked.

'They all appeared to be well-heeled. The boys and girls down there collected car numbers and checked them out. There were one or two from the Brighton area, but most of the punters came down from London or the leafy suburbs thereof, some even in chauffeur-driven cars, would you believe.'

'Did they spin this knocking shop, guv?' asked Dave.

'With a vengeance, and on a night when the place was heaving. They found a load of kinky gear, naked guys tied up and getting whipped by naked birds and all sorts of other perversions apparently. What's more, the DI who I spoke to reckoned that a few of the punters were in *Who's Who.*'

'Oh dear!' said Dave. 'I'll bet a few hours of fun there will have cost 'em a fortune.'

'It did,' said Frank. 'But apparently they could afford it.'

'So what's the bottom line?' I asked.

'The place was shut down, obviously,' said Frank, 'and the *madame* who was running the place was done for keeping a brothel and living on the immoral earnings, *et cetera, et cetera.* But the local law were pretty sure that she was just a front put up to take the flak, and that there was someone else behind it: a Mister Big. Probably from the Smoke. They made exhaustive enquiries but, needless to say, no one was talking.

'That said, however, one of the girls let slip to one of the women officers that an Australian occasionally came down, threw his weight about and enjoyed a freebie whenever he wanted it with whoever he wanted. And this tom reckoned he ran the show. But someone obviously got to her, because, when it came to making a written statement, she clammed up and said she must have been misquoted.'

'I think we could hazard a guess as to who the Australian was, guv,' said Dave, and, deciding it was time to consume an orange, plucked one from his briefcase.

'But no mention of Phillips or Patricia Hunter,' I said. 'Or, for that matter, a Jeremy Payne?'

'No, but the Vice Squad only found four

women in the place when they raided it.'

'Only four?'

'Yeah. Apparently there was a secret room that didn't get turned over because they didn't know it was there, not until it was too late. Most of the other girls – the Vice lads reckoned there were six working there at any one time, and ten on Fridays and Saturdays – shot in there and laid low until the Old Bill had gone.' Frank laughed. 'Unfortunately the aforementioned well-heeled punters didn't know this room existed. As a result the trouserless ones were obliged to assist police with their enquiries, until later being released without charge.'

'How very unfortunate,' I murmured.

'Of the four toms who were captured, only one, a girl called Barbara Clark, lived in London,' said Frank. 'At fifteen Westacre Close, Wandsworth. The other three were local. But all of good quality, so I was told.'

'Well, there goes our Friday evening,' I said, glancing at Dave. 'It's too much of a coincidence that Patricia Hunter had sixteen Fenwick Road in her address book, and that the Sussex Old Bill turned over number sixty-one as a brothel. *And* that there's word of an Australian being bandied about. Did the Vice Squad down there collect the names of these punters, Frank?'

'Makes interesting reading,' said Frank, handing me a list. 'A Crown Court judge, a clergyman—'

'Presumably he was in the missionary

159

position when they found him,' said Dave quietly.

'And half a dozen assorted entrepreneurs,' continued Frank, ignoring Dave's aside. 'Apparently one of the punters was heard complaining to the madam that it was supposed to be a discreet set-up. Didn't help much though, she was in handcuffs at the time; the job's, not hers.' He gave a short, cynical laugh.

I ran my eye down the list. 'There are only three of these who live in London: the judge, the clergyman and one of the businessmen. And given that Patricia Hunter was found floating in the Thames at Westminster, we may as well start with them.'

'Definitely a good idea to have a go at the judge,' said Dave. 'Never know when we might need an iffy warrant at some time in the future.'

'You're nothing if not an opportunist, Dave,' I said. 'But why not? He sits in London. But he can wait a bit. First we'll see Ms Clark.'

It was a small, modern town house in a part of Wandsworth that undoubtedly attracted high property prices and, therefore, proved that the sex business must be profitable. Very profitable. But then I always knew that.

I rang the bell, even though the chances of finding a prostitute at home on a Friday evening – or any other evening for that matter – are remote. But this particular evening we were in luck. Which made a change.

'Miss Clark?' I enquired when a young woman opened the door an inch or two on the chain.

'Have you got an appointment?' asked the girl, her expression registering surprise that there were two of us.

'Didn't know we needed one,' said Dave, displaying his warrant card.

'Oh, bloody hell!' The girl closed the door sufficient to disconnect the chain and then opened it fully. 'You'd better come in, I suppose,' she said with a sigh, and led the way upstairs to a comfortably furnished sitting room.

She was a good-looking girl in her twenties, well-dressed, her hair neatly arranged, her make-up discreet. In fact one would not immediately have taken her for a prostitute. Perhaps the Sussex Vice Squad had got it wrong and Miss Clark had been in the Fenwick Road brothel merely to provide ancillary services as a manicurist. There again, maybe not.

'I'm told that you were one of the prostitutes found at sixty-one Fenwick Road, Brighton, when it was raided by police about two months ago, Miss Clark.' I saw no reason to pussyfoot about.

'And of what possible interest is that to you? What I do for a living occasionally interests the police, and may be frowned upon by our virtuous society, except for those members of it who take advantage of my body, of course.

161

But it's not an offence because in my case there's no soliciting involved.'

'I am aware of that, Miss Clark,' I said. I had to admit to being somewhat taken aback by Barbara Clark's confidence. She may have been a prostitute, but she was well spoken, appeared to be well educated and was conversant with the law affecting her 'profession'.

'In that case, what is it you want?' She drew back the sleeve of her jacket and glanced at the gold watch adorning her wrist. 'I do have an appointment shortly,' she said, 'and I don't like to keep my clients waiting.'

Time to bring this rather superior young lady down to earth, I thought.

'I am investigating the murder of a woman called Patricia Hunter,' I said. 'No doubt you have read about it in the paper.'

'Oh!' Barbara Clark sat down, rather suddenly.

'I can see that the name means something to you.'

'Yes, it does. I knew her.'

'And what about Bruce Phillips?'

'Who?' Despite the girl's implied denial, it was obvious that the name had had some effect upon her. She tensed visibly and glanced away from me. Reaching across to an occasional table, she took a cigarette from an open packet, lit it and drew on it heavily enough to make the tip glow fiercely.

'I think you do, Miss Clark,' I continued. 'And I want to talk to him because I think he knew Patricia Hunter. And I'm hoping that

162

you may be able to help me find him.'

Barbara looked up at me, but the confidence had ebbed and there was now a very frightened young girl bunched up in the armchair. 'I don't know anything about him,' she said in less than convincing tones.

'But you knew Patricia Hunter, you said.'

'Yes.' The reply came out in a whisper.

'How did you meet her?'

'We were both working in Brighton, at Fenwick Road. We'd usually meet up here and drive down together.'

'In your car?'

'Yes, in my car.'

'How often was this?'

'Twice a week. Wednesdays and Saturdays. Other girls worked other shifts, so there was a service from three in the afternoon to three in the morning.'

'Why travel all the way to Brighton twice a week? Is the London end of your profession that overcrowded now?'

'For the money, of course.' The woman's response was dismissive, as though her reasoning was quite logical. 'The set-up down there provided an anything-goes service, and we girls were paid two thousand pounds for a twelve-hour shift. That was four K a week ... tax-free.'

I did a quick bit of mental arithmetic. If that was the going rate for the Fenwick Road working girls, the punters must have been forking out small fortunes.

'When did you last see Patricia Hunter,

Barbara?' By now Dave and I had sat down on the sofa facing the woman.

She stubbed out her half-finished cigarette and screwed it hard into the ashtray, almost as if it had offended her.

'I last saw her about two months ago when the fuzz busted the place in Brighton. I was unlucky. When your lot came charging in, I was upstairs with some slob of a clergyman on top of me and couldn't move. But Patricia told me afterwards that she'd been on the ground floor. She was riding her guy, so she was able to dismount and escape to the bolt-hole. Then she waited until the fuss was over and the captains and the kings had departed. But I haven't seen her since then. I don't know where she went.'

'D'you know the name of the guy who was having it off with Patricia?' I asked.

'I don't even know the name of the clergyman who was screwing me,' said Barbara. 'Names were never used unless one of the johns asked for a private meeting at his home or a hotel somewhere, then he'd give us his phone number.'

'Did any of them make an arrangement of that sort with Patricia?'

'Not as far as I know, no.'

'What the hell's a girl like you doing tom-ming?' asked Dave, slowly shaking his head.

'Earning money,' said Barbara. 'I've got a degree in business studies, but the best job I could get when I came down from university was clerking in a building society. It would have taken forever to pay off my student loan on the wages they offered. I can earn more in a night now than I would have done in a month there.' Her explanation was delivered in matter-of-fact tones, and she didn't seem at all embarrassed at explaining her economic strategy. And that, it seemed, was the rationale that had dictated her choice of career.

'Bruce Phillips,' I said, just when Barbara Clark thought I'd forgotten about him.

'I know nothing about any Bruce Phillips,' she said again. But the mere mention of his name had clearly unnerved her and her hand shook as she reached for another cigarette.

'Let's not play games, Barbara. When Fenwick Road was raided, one of the girls told a policewoman that an Australian guy would turn up there from time to time and take his pick of the girls. Were you the girl who told the policewoman that?'

'No.'

'Were you one of the girls that this mysterious Australian fancied?' asked Dave.

'Might have been, I suppose.'

'Does that mean he had the pleasure of your services?'

'He might have done,' said Barbara. 'You tend not to look at faces in my job. It's usually a case of bang-bang and thank you ma'am. Some of the johns were quite old guys and five minutes was a bloody marathon for them.'

'Is that another way of saying you can't give us a description of this Australian?' Dave asked. 'Or won't.'

'Precisely so,' said Barbara.

'Have you seen him again?' I persisted, sensing that she knew who we were talking about. 'Here in London for instance?'

'No. And I'm not sure that I've entertained an Aussie anyway. I'm not very good at accents. I did have a South African doctor once. That any help?'

'This is serious, Barbara,' I said, and decided to show my hand. 'It's quite possible that this Bruce Phillips, who is an Australian, murdered Patricia Hunter, and it's imperative that we find him soon.'

'Before he takes it into his head to murder any of the other girls who work for him,' said Dave casually.

Barbara looked at me, then at Dave, and then back at me. 'That sounds like a very good reason for keeping my mouth shut, doesn't it, guys? Even if I knew the man. Which I don't.' But she couldn't disguise the fact that her face had drained of colour.

'Why did he beat you up?' asked Dave suddenly.

The question coming out of context caught Barbara off guard. 'How did you know that?' she blurted out, before realizing that she'd been tricked by an experienced detective well-versed in interrogation techniques.

'So you do know this Australian after all,' I said.

Barbara Clark parried my accusation with an explanation. 'I suppose it was my fault

166

really. One of my clients at Brighton really hurt me quite badly – a bloody sadist he was – so I grabbed his balls and twisted until he screamed. That put him off his stroke.' Barbara's demure appearance and cultured tones conflicted strangely with her description of the revenge she had meted out to her assailant. 'I was out of order really. After all, that's what I was there for. Anyway he complained to the woman running the place. She told this Australian and he slapped me around. Said this john had paid good money to do whatever he wanted to do to me.'

'How long were you off work after that?' Dave asked.

'A couple of weeks,' said Barbara miserably.

'And was this shadowy Australian who beat you up called Bruce Phillips by any chance?'

'I don't know.'

'Or Geoffrey Forman?'

'I've never heard of anyone called Geoffrey Forman.'

It appeared that Barbara Clark was still too terrified to admit that the Australian was Phillips. But I was sure she knew that he was. I tried another tack.

'Since the Brighton caper came to an end, you've been working in London, haven't you?'

'Yes.'

'And Bruce Phillips is your pimp, isn't he?'

'I don't know what you mean.'

'I'm sure a girl like you doesn't hang around Shepherd Market, Barbara, so you

167

must get your bookings somewhere. And I don't somehow see you advertising in telephone boxes.'

'I don't know how it happens, but I get phone calls from time to time telling me to go to some john's apartment, or a hotel.'The girl was struggling now, desperately trying to avoid revealing the identity of a man who obviously put her in fear, but at once digging herself in deeper each time she opened her mouth.

'So how d'you get paid, Barbara?' Dave asked.

There was a moment's hesitation and then the girl said, 'I take credit cards.'

'And how d'you pay your pimp?'

'I don't know what you're talking about. I've said too much already and I'm not saying any more.'

'We found Patricia Hunter's address book. In it was written: Mr and Mrs Hunter, sixteen Fenwick Road. Any idea what that was all about?'

'Yes. Patricia told me that she could never remember addresses and wrote it down in case she ever had to go down there on her own. She switched the house number round and wrote her parents' name against it.' For the first time since we'd arrived at her house, the elegant young tom smiled. 'She couldn't very well write "the cathouse where I work" next to it, could she?'

Rather than drink in a Wandsworth pub, we

drove back to Curtis Green, parked the car and strolled along to the Red Lion.

'What d'you reckon, Dave?' I asked, once the essential business of buying the beer had been accomplished.

'She's scared out of her wits, guv. I'm surprised that she said as much as she did. It looks very much as though Phillips is her pimp, which means she wasn't telling the truth about getting paid by credit card.'

'No, I reckon Phillips gets the payment and then takes his cut before paying the girl. But how and where does he do it, I wonder?'

'I don't think he'd be daft enough to use a bank account,' said Dave, taking the top off his beer. 'Too easy to trace.'

'If we ever lay hands on him,' I said, 'and can prove he murdered Patricia Hunter, he won't be too worried about living on the immoral earnings. But the business about Patricia writing down the Fenwick Road address perhaps explains why there were other addresses in her book. Each time she got a booking she jotted it down in case she forgot.'

'Evenin', gents,' said the unmistakeable voice of Fat Danny.

'Bugger off,' said Dave.

Eleven

By Monday morning, Dave had all the answers to the queries about the fibres, but those answers were not particularly helpful. In fact, they proved to be downright *unhelpful*, even though they were the result of an innocent mistake.

'It seems I was right, guv,' he began. 'I had another word with the lab and they were full of apologies.'

'You mean they've cocked it up,' I said and sat down in one of the chairs in the incident room ready to be depressed.

'Apparently they gave the analysis of the fibres to some keen young scientist just out of university to cut his teeth on,' Dave continued. 'It seems he made a comparison with a stock control sample at the lab ... and got it wrong.'

'Bloody marvellous,' I said. 'So what's the answer?'

'They had a senior scientist go over the evidence again and he said that the fibres came from a rug or carpet, not one that would be found in a van.'

'I don't know whether that's a help or not,' I mused.

'And,' Dave continued, intent on further depressing me, 'it would appear to be a fairly common sort.'

'Would be,' I said, the depression beginning to take root. 'So what are they doing about it?'

'They're doing a rush job to see if they can narrow it down.'

'I should bloody well hope so,' I said.

'Is there a problem, Mr Brock?'

Just what I needed. The commander back from his sojourn in the French capital and desperate to interfere.

'Did you have a good time in Paris, sir?' I asked.

The commander frowned. 'How did you know I'd gone to Paris?' he asked suspiciously.

'I'm a detective, sir,' I said.

From the expression on his face, the commander didn't much care for that smart remark. 'You mentioned a problem, I believe, Mr Brock.'

I explained about the laboratory's inaccurate identification of the fibres.

The commander frowned again. 'That's just not good enough,' he said crossly. 'I'll speak to the director about it. Here we are dealing with a complex murder and they get amateurs doing the work.'

Well, he should know all about amateurs interfering in murder enquiries.

'Yes, sir,' I said.

'It looks very much to me as though they're

171

not maximizing focused deployment,' the commander mumbled, selecting a bit of meaningless jargon from his ragbag of Police College psychobabble. He muttered a few more unintelligible phrases and finally took sanctuary in his office.

'The DVLA came up with a BMW registered to Geoffrey Forman at the Barnes address, guv,' said Dave, once normality had been restored to the office. 'Colin's put it on the PNC. Oh, and by the way, Tom Challis got back to the credit-card people. They've got Forman down as a consultant, which covers a multitude of sins, but they have no record of which company he worked for. Of course, he may be in business on his own account.'

'And that doesn't vary much from what we were told by Donna Lodge,' I said. 'Assuming she was telling us the truth.'

'It was you who sort of suggested that he was a computer consultant, guv, and she might just have gone along with it. Could hardly say he was running a brothel, could she?'

Dave was right, of course, but I was not prepared to admit it. Fortunately, Dave changed the subject.

'It was in Patricia Hunter's Coping Road room that the receipt was found, wasn't it, guv?' he asked.

'Yes.'

'I wonder if she ever mentioned Geoffrey Forman to that gorgeous bird we chatted up at the Granville. Gail Sutton, wasn't it?

172

Some figure.'

I let it go. Dave didn't know that I was actively pursuing the delectable Gail. 'We didn't know about a guy called Geoffrey Forman when I spoke to her last,' I said, 'but I'll mention it to her. In fact, I'll pop in and see her on my way home tonight. She doesn't live far from me.'

Dave gave me a long, hard stare. 'Yeah, good thinking, guv,' he said eventually, and grinned.

'And this morning, we might just put the same question to Patricia Hunter's landlady at Coping Road...' I paused to ferret around among the papers on my desk, searching for the name.

'Mrs Parsons,' said Dave.

'That's the one. It's possible that Patricia Hunter mentioned him to her.'

'If he's our man,' said Dave. 'I wonder if he's also known as Bruce Phillips,' he added, echoing what I'd been thinking for some time.

I swung round in my chair and asked Colin Wilberforce if Geoffrey Forman had telephoned over the weekend.

'No, sir,' said Colin, which came as no surprise.

'I'm beginning to think nasty thoughts about this Forman guy, Dave,' I said.

'And the elegant Donna Lodge isn't all that she'd like you to think, either, guv,' said Dave.

'Oh?'

'She was convicted of shoplifting in Oxford

Street five years ago.' Dave paused, presumably for effect. 'And guess who paid her fine.'

'Not Bruce Phillips?'

'Got it in one,' said Dave. 'The same guy who paid Patricia Hunter's fine.'

'Why didn't that show up on the CRO search you did on Friday?' I knew that if it had been there, Dave would have spotted it. 'Wasn't it on her antecedents?' I guessed that some sloppy DC had skimped on his paperwork.

'No, but this morning I had a word with a pal of mine on the Extradition Unit in SO6. He'd got more details than are recorded in CRO.'

'And presumably this pal of yours still doesn't know where Bruce Phillips is.'

'No, guv,' said Dave and chuckled. 'But he said to let him know if we found him, and he'd be grateful.'

'I'll bet he would,' I said. 'Incidentally, what exactly do the Australian police want this guy for?'

'Long-firm fraud. The usual thing: he set up shop after shop, ordered loads of gear that he paid for in cash until they trusted him with credit. Then he put in a few more orders, slowly increasing the amount of the order and then did a flit with the goods. Without paying for the last order. Apparently he went from state to state. Took a long time for them to catch up with him and each time they did, he'd gone. That's when the Commonwealth Police took an interest in him.'

'When was all this, Dave?'

'The Australians reckon he was at it for about a year to eighteen months, but he disappeared off their screens about six years ago.'

'So it wasn't very long after he arrived here from Australia that Patricia Hunter and Donna Lodge were both done for shoplifting. Both were nicked at about the same time, and each time Phillips paid their fines. Sounds like he was running a hoist ring.'

'I reckon,' said Dave.

'And is he an Australian national?'

'Yes, born in Sydney.'

'One thing's for sure, Dave,' I said. 'We'll need to have another word or two with Ms Lodge, but first we'll have another chat with Mrs Parsons about Patricia Hunter.

'She'd sometimes sit in the kitchen and have a cup of tea with me,' said Mrs Parsons, 'but I never heard her say anything about boy-friends. I don't think she had much time for that sort of thing.'

'Did a man ever call here for her?' I asked. 'I know I asked you before, but...'

'I wasn't thinking straight that first evening you came round, Mr Brock, what with the shock of poor Pat's death and all,' said Mrs Parsons, 'but now you come to mention it, there was one occasion. He didn't call here, he came in with her, and they went straight up to her room.'

'And you didn't mind that?' I asked.

'Why should I, dear?' said Mrs Parsons. 'If they're going to get up to naughties they might as well do it here.'

Which was a very refreshing outlook, and certainly one that differed sharply from the attitude of section-house sergeants and the harridans in charge of nurses' homes when I was courting Helga. Believe me, St James's Park can be very cold at times.

'D'you remember what he looked like, this man?' asked Dave.

'Very ordinary as I recollect. I do remember that he was wearing jeans and a tatty old sweater though, and I thought Patricia deserved better than a scruff like him. She was always well turned out, that poor girl.'

'How tall was he?' persisted Dave, determined to get as much as he could from the late Patricia Hunter's landlady.

'About your height, dear. What are you, about six foot?'

'Yes.' Dave wrote that snippet of information in his pocket book. 'What colour was his hair?'

'Brown, I think. Or it might have been fair. I don't really remember.'

'Moustache, beard?'

'I don't think so. Maybe. No, I'm not sure.'

Dave gave up on trying to get a decent description. 'Were they carrying anything?'

I wondered why Dave asked that, but then I recalled that the receipt found in Patricia's room had been for a man's shirt and was in Geoffrey Forman's name.

'Yes, they had a few carrier bags with them. I think Pat said something about their having been shopping in the West End that morning. It was a Saturday.'

Shopping, eh? Perhaps shop*lifting* would have been a better description.

'How did you come to see them, Mrs Parsons?' I asked.

'I wasn't being nosey,' the landlady replied defensively.

I smiled and held up a hand. 'I was hoping you *were*,' I said. 'I'm trying to find this poor girl's killer.'

That placated the woman. 'As a matter of fact, I was putting the empty milk bottles out on the step. If you forget, you suddenly find you've got a dozen of them cluttering up the kitchen.'

'It's a problem,' I agreed, even though I bought my milk from the supermarket. And often forgot. I've quite got used to black tea. 'So that's when you saw them, was it?'

'Yes. Just as I opened the front door, Pat was on the step looking in her handbag for her key.'

'Did she introduce this man to you?'

'No. She just said something like "Hello, Mrs P", and went on upstairs.' A sudden frightening thought occurred to Mrs Parsons. 'Glory be, you don't think it was him who murdered her, do you?' she asked, putting a hand to her mouth.

'Right now, Mrs Parsons,' I said, 'I don't know who killed her.'

'Did this man speak at all?' asked Dave, joining in again. He was obviously hoping for confirmation of an Australian accent.

'No, he just smiled, and the two of them went on upstairs. He stayed for about an hour and then went again.'

I didn't ask Mrs Parsons how she knew when he'd gone. I presumed she was putting out more milk bottles.

Donna Lodge did not seem at all surprised to see us again.

'I'm afraid Geoffrey still hasn't come home,' she said with yet another of her apologetic smiles. 'But he did ring me over the weekend. He said that he'll probably be away for another week.' Barefooted, she was attired in a pair of ragged-ended denim shorts and a tee-shirt, and her hair was gathered back into a ponytail.

'As a matter of fact, it's you we've come to see, Ms Lodge,' I said.

'Oh, well, I don't know how I can help you, but you'd better come in.'

'Bruce Phillips,' I said, adopting a full frontal approach once we had been shown, somewhat reluctantly I suspected, into the sitting room.

Donna Lodge's expression didn't change at all, unless you counted the raised eyebrow of puzzlement that suddenly greeted the Australian's name. 'Who?'

'Bruce Phillips. Does that name mean anything to you, Ms Lodge?'

178

'No, I can't say that it does. Is this some-thing to do with the burglary you mentioned when you were here the other day?'

'No.'

'Well, what then?'

'When you were convicted of shoplifting four years ago, Bruce Phillips paid your fine, Ms Lodge.' I sat back and waited for the reaction to my no-frills accusation.

'That was all a terrible mistake. I'd picked up some underwear from one department and then wandered around the shop to where the dresses were. But I didn't find anything I liked. I walked out of the shop, completely forgetting that I'd still got the underwear in my hand. I tried to explain that it was a lapse of memory, but they didn't believe me, and neither did the magistrate. I was fined four hundred pounds.'

The magistrate must have been hellishly benevolent that morning, because her version of what had happened didn't accord with the record of her conviction. According to the arresting officers, she'd been found in posses-sion of considerably more than just under-wear. Like the two expensive dresses, the three sets of silk underwear and a bikini. And it was all in a bag strapped around her waist under her coat so that she looked as though she was pregnant. It was an old hoister's trick.

'And Bruce Phillips paid the fine,' I said.

'Certainly not. I paid it myself. I told you just now, I've never heard of a Bruce Phillips.' Donna began to assume the attitude of the wronged innocent. 'Look, if this doesn't have anything to do with the burglary you came about the other day, why are you asking all these questions about my unfortunate mistake?'

'Because we are interested in finding Bruce Phillips in connection with another matter,' said Dave. 'According to our records, he is shown as having paid your fine. We thought, therefore, that you might be able to tell us where he was.'

It wasn't on her records of course, and it was just possible that Dave's mate in the Extradition Unit had got it wrong.

'I'll say it again,' Donna said crossly, 'I've never heard of him, so I'm unlikely to be able to tell you where he is, am I?'

'In that case, I'm sorry to have bothered you, Ms Lodge. There's obviously been some mistake.' I decided that to mention Patricia Hunter's name would not be a good idea. At least, not at this stage. 'Perhaps you'd get Mr Forman to telephone me as soon as he gets back.'

'Certainly, but I've no idea when that will be.'

'I'm sure she's involved somehow, guv,' said Dave as we drove away from Ridgely Road and made for Curtis Green.

'And sufficiently well briefed, probably by Phillips, to be one jump ahead of us all the time,' I said. 'I reckon that Geoffrey Forman and Donna Lodge could be in this together.

180

It's possible that they both knew Patricia Hunter and something gave them cause to murder her. But God knows what, or how we're going to prove it.'

'And I wouldn't be at all surprised if Forman and Bruce Phillips weren't one and the same,' Dave said for about the tenth time. 'I'd love to hear what she's saying to him on the phone right now. What's the chance of getting an intercept put on?'

'We'd never get the Home Secretary to sign a warrant to tap her phone, Dave, not on the evidence we've got so far.'

'No, I suppose not.' Dave braked sharply and cursed an errant cyclist who appeared to think that traffic law didn't apply to him. 'An obo then?'

'We don't have the manpower for an observation,' I said. 'We're supposed to solve murders single-handed these days, or hadn't you heard?'

I decided it was time to have a chat about Bruce Phillips with Dave's pal on the Extradition Unit.

'Yes, we've got a photograph of him, guv. For what it's worth.' The detective sergeant dealing with Phillips's case was called Don Lacey. 'D'you want a copy?'

'Yes, please. What was the last address you had for this guy?'

Lacey poked about in a filing cabinet and produced both the photograph and a docket. 'He was living at flat twelve, nine Petersfield

Street, Fulham, guv, but when we went there to nick him he'd done a runner.'

'Who did you speak to there?' I asked. I glanced at the blurred head-and-shoulders photograph of Phillips that looked as though it had been taken by a surveillance team. It was the face of a man who I guessed to be in his late twenties or early thirties, and who had long hair, a bushy beard and heavy horn-rimmed spectacles. All of which was no bloody help at all. I'd seen dozens of men who looked like him in the custody suite of a police station. Usually after a drugs raid.

Lacey thumbed through his file. 'A woman called Donna Lodge,' he said. 'But she told us that Phillips had left a couple of days previously and she didn't know where he'd gone. And we haven't seen hair nor hide of him since.'

'Well, I'm buggered,' I said. 'We've just left her and she denied all knowledge of Bruce Phillips. She was convincing enough to make me wonder whether there'd been a cock-up with the paperwork.'

'Don't blame her,' said Lacey. 'Where was this?'

'Number thirteen Ridgely Road, Barnes,' said Dave.

Lacey made a note on his file.

'Where did this photograph come from?' I asked.

'Australian police. He's forty years old now,' said Lacey, and gave me Phillips's date of birth. 'They admitted that it's a bit of an old photograph, and probably wasn't a very good likeness even then, if you can see any likeness at all. It's a racing certainty that he's changed his appearance since it was taken.'

'Did you make any enquiries elsewhere at the Petersfield Street flats, Don?'

'We had a chat with the neighbours at number eleven – it's just across the hall from number twelve – but they hadn't seen anything of Phillips for a week or so. In fact, they didn't even know his name. So it might not have been him anyway. I showed them the photograph, but they couldn't ID him from it. Not surprising really. The only man they'd regularly seen coming out of flat twelve was clean-shaven and apparently with twenty-twenty vision.' Lacey paused to give an expressive shrug. 'Something else that was interesting though, those same neighbours reckoned that they'd seen other men calling at the flat from time to time. Sometimes in the afternoon, sometimes in the evening.'

'Was there any mention of a woman called Patricia Hunter at that flat?'

'No, guv. I was told that there was another woman living there, a blonde who more or less fits the description of the Hunter girl, apart from the hair colour, which doesn't mean a thing. But she wasn't there when we busted the place. And Donna Lodge claimed that she was there on her own, and had been since Phillips left. Patricia Hunter's name didn't mean anything to me until Dave told me you were investigating her murder. D'you reckon she was mixed up with this Phillips guy?'

'I'm bloody sure of it. We knew that Bruce Phillips had paid Patricia Hunter's shoplifting fine, but it was you telling Dave that he'd also paid Donna Lodge's fine that linked the three of them together.' And I went on to tell Lacey about the receipt in Forman's name that had been found at Patricia Hunter's last address.

'Sounds as though Phillips was running a hoisting ring, guv. You know, a professional shoplifting scam.'

'Yes, I do know what a hoisting ring is,' I said, somewhat tersely, 'but that doesn't explain the comings and goings of men at the flat. Unless they were part of his ring. Or were fencing the property stolen by his girls.'

Lacey laughed. 'I reckon it was a high-class knocking shop. I passed the details over to the uniform branch, but by the time they got around to it, Donna had gone as well. We checked back but the flat was occupied by someone else. There was no forwarding address and when we made enquiries of the post office, there was no redirection order either. But from what you say, we now know where Donna Lodge is, and maybe Bruce Phillips isn't far away.'

'Don't put money on it, Skip,' I said. And that proved to be right.

'Harry! What are you doing here?' asked Gail when I arrived at her house.

'I wondered if you fancied a drink. There's

a reasonably decent pub not far from here.'

'Why don't you come in and have one here?'

'Thanks,' I said and followed her upstairs to a sitting room on the first floor that ran the full width of the house, a house not unlike the one in which Barbara Clark lived at Wandsworth. There were two brown leather sofas facing each other with a low coffee table between them. An expensive hi-fi stood in one corner and a wide-screen television in another.

'You seem to be doing all right for a struggling, out-of-work chorus girl,' I said.

'I get by,' said Gail. 'Whisky, gin, vodka, brandy?' She stood with her hand hovering over a selection of bottles on a sofa table.

'Whisky would be fine, thanks.'

'Ice or water?'

'Neither, thanks.'

She handed me a crystal tumbler containing a good inch of Scotch, and poured a gin and tonic for herself. 'Excuse me while I get myself some ice.' She returned from the kitchen and sat on the sofa opposite the one in which I was sitting. Raising her glass in brief salute, she asked, 'And to what do I owe the pleasure of this visit, Harry?'

'I wondered if Patricia Hunter had ever mentioned a computer consultant called Geoffrey Forman,' I said. 'Lives in Barnes.'

'No, she never spoke to me about any of her boyfriends, apart from Jeremy Payne, but as I said the other day, the name Geoffrey doesn't

185

mean anything. Why?'

'We found a receipt in her room. It was on this guy's credit-card account.'

Gail shook her head. 'No, sorry, Harry. Doesn't ring any bells. Still, it's nice to see you.'

I decided against telling Gail about Patricia Hunter's other career in the Brighton brothel – at least, not yet – and for the next hour, we chatted about all sorts of mundane things until, eventually, I glanced at my watch and stood up.

'Well, I must be going,' I said.

'I suppose so,' said Gail.

Oh well, better luck next time, Brock.

Twelve

'I suppose we'll have to go back and see Donna Lodge again, guv,' said Dave.

'Yes, but I've a shrewd suspicion that we may just find the cupboard's bare,' I said, repeating, more or less, what I'd told DS Lacey the previous day. 'If only we'd known that your mate had been to Petersfield Street and spoken to Donna Lodge, we'd've had more to front her with.'

'How about a search warrant and spin the drum, guv?' said Dave.

I looked doubtful. 'Maybe,' I said, 'but I wouldn't mind betting that we'd find nothing. It might come to that though.'

'D'you think there *is* a tie-up between Patricia Hunter's murder and Phillips, Forman and Lodge?' asked Dave. 'Or even the mysterious Jeremy Payne?'

'I don't know, but Forman's certainly got some questions to answer when we find him.'

'But if he's really Phillips, he may be back in Oz already,' said Dave.

'In that case, we'll do the obvious,' I said. 'Colin, ring Steve Granger at the Australian High Commission and ask him if he's going to be in this morning, because I need to see

187

him urgently.'

Colin Wilberforce swung round and grabbed the phone. 'Yes, sir.'

'Yes, I remember this one, Harry,' said Inspector Steve Granger, the Australian Commonwealth Police officer who was seconded to his country's High Commission, 'but once your chaps said he'd shot through, we put the file on the back burner. Have you got some more info on this no-hoper then?'

I told Granger of our particular interest in Phillips and asked whether it was possible that he was now back in Australia.

'Wouldn't be at all surprised. I think if I knew you guys were after me, Harry, I'd shoot through too. But of course he couldn't possibly have got past the airport controls without your guys picking him up, could he?' Granger laughed.

'That was a low blow, Steve,' I said. We both knew that arresting a wanted villain at the airport was a hit-and-miss affair. Both here and in Australia. The irony was that if you nicked one, you'd miss the next one because you were too busy doing the paperwork on the first one.

The Aussie copper laughed again and made a phone call. After a few minutes of exchanging insults with the police officer he was talking to, presumably at the headquarters of the Commonwealth Police, he replaced the receiver. 'It's half past seven in the evening in Canberra,' he said. 'The duty inspector doesn't know anything about Phillips, but he'll leave a message for the bunco squad and they'll let me know.' He paused. 'D'you really think this guy's mixed up in this murder then?'

I shrugged. 'I don't know, Steve, but when we do get hold of him, he's certainly got some questions to answer. Apart from the extradition, I mean.'

'I've had a thought, Dave,' I said, as we left Australia House in the Strand.

'Good heavens, sir,' said Dave.

'It's just possible that this Jeremy Payne guy visited the theatre, and that's where he first met Patricia Hunter. Or at least saw her.'

'How does that help, guv?'

'If he made a booking, the theatre might just have a record of it.'

'The Alhambra's not far from here.'

We grabbed a taxi and ten minutes later were being shown into the manager's office.

'How can I help you, gentlemen?' The manager was called Stroud.

I explained about the murder of Patricia Hunter and Stroud made the usual sympathetic noises before adding, 'Yes, I remember her. She was in the play that's running now.'

'We're interested in tracing a man who befriended her, Mr Stroud, and it's possible that he reserved a seat for the show.'

'Name?' Stroud put on a pair of horn-rimmed glasses and looked important.

'Jeremy Payne.'

'One moment.' Stroud reached for the telephone and tapped out a number. He relayed the name and waited. 'They'll ring me back,' he said.

For the next few minutes we engaged in desultory conversation. The phone rang.

'Stroud.' The manager listened and made a few notes on his notepad. 'It seems he was a regular customer,' he said as he replaced the receiver. 'But I can't give you an address for Mr Payne. All I have is a credit-card number. But it seems he saw the play about three or four times.'

'Thank you for your assistance, Mr Stroud,' I said. I knew that with a credit-card number we stood a good chance of tracing Jeremy Payne.

We found a sandwich shop for a quick 'on the hoof' lunch, and made our way to Barnes.

There was no answer at 13 Ridgely Road, and no sign of Donna Lodge's Alfa Romeo.

The best we could extract from anyone was a next-door neighbour's opinion that our quarry had gone away. 'I just happened to notice her putting suitcases in her car this morning,' said the woman. I got the impression that she would *just happen* to notice everything her neighbours did. Thank God!

'Have you seen Mr Forman lately?' I asked. 'Mr Forman?'

'He's the man who lives with Ms Lodge.'

'*Lives* with? Good heavens, you mean they're not married?' That revelation clearly put Forman's neighbour on our side, for what good it did. 'No, I haven't seen him lately.'

Dave produced the photograph of Phillips that we'd obtained from Lacey. 'Is this Mr Forman?' he asked.

The neighbour studied the poor print and then shook her head, 'Oh no,' she said. 'Mr Forman doesn't have a beard and he doesn't wear glasses.'

'We blew it, Dave,' I said as we drove away from Ridgely Road. 'It was all right when we spun her that fanny about Forman and the office-breaking, but the minute we mentioned Phillips, she made the connection and took off.'

'So what do we do now, guv?' asked Dave.

'Time we started pulling in some favours from a few snouts,' I said, without much hope of finding anyone in the criminal underworld who knew the whereabouts of Bruce Phillips. Or who would be prepared to share that information with us if they did know. Those who populate the shadowy fringes of West End villainy are reluctant to inform on killers, just in case they get topped themselves for opening their mouths.

When we returned to Curtis Green, I gave Frank Mead the job of sending out the members of his team to make enquiries around the West End to see if any of their informants had heard anything of Bruce Phillips. Although I had no great expectation that they would come up with anything, I was wrong.

However, there were other things to do.

'I think we may just catch that naughty judge who was caught with his trousers down at Brighton, Dave,' I said, and reached for the phone. 'Before he packs it in for the day.'

It wasn't difficult to track down the court at which the judge was presiding, and I rang to make an appointment.

'His Honour usually rises at four thirty,' said the judge's adenoidal clerk. 'But he won't be going home. He's dining at his inn of court this evening.'

I glanced at my watch. 'I should be able to make it by then,' I said.

'May I tell His Honour what it's about? Of course, if it's a warrant—'

'No, it's not. You may tell the judge that I'm investigating a serious criminal matter and I think he may be able to assist me in my enquiries.' I didn't deem it politic to mention that, when it came to it, I might just need a warrant *for* the judge, not from him.

The judge, a youngish fellow – probably in his late forties – had abandoned his wig, gown and jacket and was sitting in his shirtsleeves smoking a pipe.

'My clerk tells me that I may be able to help you with some criminal matter, Chief Inspector,' he said after I had introduced myself and Dave. 'I must say I'm intrigued.'

'Fenwick Road, Brighton, sir. Number sixty-one to be precise.'

'Oh Christ!' said the judge and leaned forward, a concerned look on his face. 'What about it?'

'I understand that you have visited the establishment in the past and were there the night it was raided by police. That would have been just over two months ago.'

'Yes, I was there.' The judge sat back and spent several seconds fiddling with his pipe before he got around to relighting it. I assumed that he was giving himself time to think. 'I take it, Chief Inspector,' he continued, raising an eyebrow, 'that none of this will be made public?' It sounded more like a threat than a question.

'I see no reason why it should, sir.'

'So how can I help you?'

'Did you ever engage the services of a young lady called Patricia Hunter?'

'No, I don't think so.'

Dave produced the photograph of Patricia and handed it to the judge.

'That's her, sir.'

The judge examined the print carefully. 'Ah yes, I do remember her,' the judge said. 'That's the girl who called herself Dolores. She and I were, um...'

'Were engaged in intimate conversation, sir?'

'Exactly.' His Honour placed the photograph in the centre of his desk and once more leaned back in his chair. 'Don't tell me that those idiots in Brighton are thinking of launching a prosecution, surely.'

'I doubt it, sir,' I said. 'Apart from the woman who ran the place, and who was prosecuted for keeping a brothel' – the judge winced at my accurate description – 'I don't see that either the prostitutes or their clients have committed any offences.'

'Quite so, Chief Inspector, quite so. I was just about to say the same thing myself.' The judge adopted an air of bewilderment. The sort of expression I imagine he assumed when counsel embarked on a line of questioning that was leading nowhere. 'But what is your interest? I take it that you're Metropolitan officers.'

'We are indeed, sir, and my interest is that I am investigating the murder of that young lady.' I gestured at the photograph on the judge's desk.

'Hell's bells and buckets of blood!' exclaimed the judge. 'When was this?'

'Her body was recovered from the Thames opposite the Houses of Parliament at about eight o'clock during the evening of Wednesday the twelfth of June this year.'

'Thank God for that.'

'I beg your pardon, sir?' It seemed an extraordinarily inapposite statement for him to make.

'Don't misunderstand me, Chief Inspector.' The judge smiled and ran a hand over his desktop. 'I didn't mean to sound callous. It's most regrettable when a young woman like that meets an untimely end. No, what I meant was that I was in St Malo, in Brittany. Sailed across in my boat, d'you see? On Friday the thirty-first of May. Stayed there for

194

three weeks.'

'With your wife, sir?' asked Dave.

'Er, yes. With my wife, Sergeant.'

'While you were at Fenwick Road, sir, did you by any chance come across an Australian?' I asked. 'Or, for that matter, hear anyone talking about such a person?'

'Not that I recall. Why?'

'We believe that an Australian named Bruce Phillips was behind the Fenwick Road set-up.'

'And you think he may be connected with this girl's murder?'

'That I don't know, sir, but there is an extradition warrant out for his arrest. He's wanted in Australia for long-firm fraud.'

The judge looked a little sick and paused for a moment or two, doubtless considering the implications not only of having been caught out visiting a brothel, but now learning that it may have been owned by a wanted criminal. 'Well, I wish you luck, Chief Inspector.' He stood up, signalling an end to our interview. But as we reached the door, he spoke again. 'Perhaps you'd afford me the courtesy of advising me when you've arrested this man, Chief Inspector.'

'If you wish, sir.'

'Good. In the circumstances it would be most improper if he were to be arraigned before me. I'm sure you understand.'

'Oh, I do indeed, sir,' I said, and smiled.

We left the judge to enjoy dinner at his inn of court, if he still had an appetite.

'What d'you reckon, guv?' asked Dave. 'He seems kosher enough.'

'You know me, Dave, I never trust anyone. Particularly lawyers. If his yacht was tied up in St Malo for three weeks, the harbour master there will have noted it. And no doubt the French customs will have known it was there too. We'll check. Just in case he's telling lies.'

'Wouldn't be the first time a judge has done that,' said Dave.

We drove south of the river and eventually found the rectory where our fornicating clergyman lived. 'I suppose this clergyman is the one who prevented Barbara Clark from escaping to the bolthole,' I said as I rang the doorbell.

The door was answered by a woman who announced that she was the clergyman's wife. Which made her husband an *adulterous* fornicating clergyman.

We were shown into the study and were joined shortly afterwards by a man of about forty wearing, unsurprisingly, a clerical collar. But that jarred somewhat with the cricket sweater and jeans.

'Sorry to keep you,' he said. 'I've been gardening.'

I suppose the clerical collar was so that the weeds would know he was a man of the cloth.

'I'm Detective Chief Inspector Brock of New Scotland Yard,' I began, 'and this is—'

But I got no further.

196

'A young man in trouble?' said the clergyman, beaming benevolently at Dave.

'Not at the moment,' I said. 'He's my assistant, Detective Sergeant Poole.'

'Ah!' The parson took off his spectacles and polished them with his handkerchief before replacing them carefully. 'Do sit down, gentlemen.'

'Just because I'm black, doesn't necessarily make me a villain,' said Dave with a beatific smile. He was accustomed to being typecast, but never let anyone get away with it.

'No, quite so. How may I help you then?'

'I understand that you're familiar with sixty-one Fenwick Road, Brighton, padre?' I said.

The clergyman adjusted his glasses and glanced at each of us in turn before returning his gaze to me. 'I'm not sure that I know that address. I don't often have time to get to the seaside. Being a busy rector doesn't give one a great deal of time for holidays. Is it a boarding house?'

'More of a bawdy house,' said Dave, 'and when the Sussex Vice Squad raided it about two months ago, one of the names they took was yours.'

'Oh dear!'

'And one of the other names they took was that of Barbara Clark, a prostitute known to be working there. We were told by the Sussex Police that you and she were *each* unfrocked at the time and were—'

The clergyman held up a hand. 'I know, I

know,' he said, 'and ever since that awful night I've prayed for forgiveness.'

'That's all right, then,' said Dave.

'Our interest is in this young woman,' I said, as Dave, right on cue, handed the parson the photograph of Patricia Hunter. 'She was also a prostitute working at sixty-one Fenwick Road the night of the police raid. Have you ever seen her before, or had sexual relations with her?'

'No.' It had taken the clergyman but a brief glance to disavow any knowledge of the girl known in Brighton, and elsewhere, as Dolores. 'Why d'you ask?'

'Because she's been murdered.'

The clergyman closed his eyes and intertwined his fingers in an attitude of supplication. 'Oh the poor dear child,' he intoned in sepulchral tones.

We asked the usual questions, but our errant parson knew nothing of any Australians, had never heard the name Bruce Phillips, and further assured us that he would never sin again.

It was nearing eight o'clock by the time we drew into the Hampstead road where Tim Oliver lived. 'I'm getting heartily sick of this, Dave,' I said.

'Never know, guv, this might be the one,' said Dave hopefully. But I don't think he believed it any more than I did. But you've got to try.

It was a large house and as we arrived, a

green Bentley saloon pulled on to the drive. A liveried chauffeur jumped out and opened the rear door of the car.

'Mr Oliver?' I asked as the well-fed and well-dressed man reached his front door.

'Yes?' Oliver stared nervously at Dave, as though fearing he was about to be robbed. As Dave often said, he tended to have that effect on people.

'We're police officers, sir. We'd like to have a word with you.'

'Oh? What about?' Oliver put his key in the door, opened it and shouted, 'I'm home, darling.'

'Fenwick Road, Brighton.'

'Oh, that.' Oliver embraced a woman dressed in a green jumper and a tweed skirt. 'Hello, darling.'

'You're early,' said the woman, and glanced at Dave and me. 'Oh no, you haven't brought more of your people for dinner, Tim. It's really too bad. Why didn't you ring me?'

'They're not stopping, dear. Just a couple of policemen wanting to talk to me.'

'Oh, that's all right then. I'll leave you to it.'

Oliver conducted us into a wood-panelled study. There was a desk, a couple of leather armchairs and the obligatory computer set on a custom-built workstation in the corner of the room. Next to it were copies of the *Daily Telegraph* and the *Financial Times*.

'Have a pew,' he said, pointing at the armchairs. 'Now, what's all this about Fenwick Road?' he asked, seating himself behind the desk. 'Care for a drink?'

'No thanks.'

Oliver reached across to a small table and transferred a whisky decanter and a glass to his desk. He poured himself a substantial measure, and took a sip. 'Fire away.'

'Dolores,' I said.

Oliver grinned. 'Ah, Dolores, yes. Good-looking girl, that one.'

'How well did you know her, Mr Oliver?'

'Only carnally, old boy. But why the questions?'

'She was murdered on or about the twelfth of June.'

'Christ! Really?' Oliver took another gulp of whisky.

'When did you last see her?'

Oliver laughed. 'I thought they only asked that in second-rate television shows. Well now, let me see.' He paused. 'A couple of times after the Brighton fiasco, I suppose.'

'Where?'

'West End hotels. Can't remember the names of them, but I could look it up on my credit-card account.'

This man was an enigma. He had a wife who was well preserved for her age, which was probably about fifty, but here he was talking quite openly about his trysts with a prostitute.

'Doesn't your wife mind?' I asked.

'Not a bit, old boy.' Oliver lowered his voice. 'Well, that said, of course, she doesn't know, but I think she may suspect. You know what women are like, never miss a trick. But I don't think she'd care very much even if she did find out. All that sort of thing's over between us. If ever she happened across one of the bills, I'd tell her it wasn't me. Probably spin her some yarn about an arrangement I'd made – and paid for – for some of our visiting Japanese clients. And in a few cases that would be true. The old Japs love to get their leg over when they're in England, you know.'

'Is this the woman you knew as Dolores?' Dave asked as he handed over the print.

Oliver glanced at it. 'Yes, that's her. What a bloody waste. Murdered you say?'

'Yes. Her real name was Patricia Hunter. Did you know that?'

Oliver shook his head. 'No, she was only ever known as Dolores to me.' He returned the print. 'As a matter of fact, she was the girl I was having it off with when your chaps busted in. Dolores was on top of me at the time, but she leaped off and ran. God knows where she went, but when the chief copper got us all lined up and started taking names and addresses, she wasn't anywhere to be seen. I'm afraid the Brighton boys in blue quite ruined a jolly good evening. No sense of humour, that's their problem. And I didn't get my money back either.'

'Bruce Phillips?'

'Who?'

'An Australian,' I said. 'The police in Sussex believe he was the man who was really running the place down there.'

'Don't know the name, old boy, but there was certainly an Australian knocking about when the law came steaming in. But I don't know where he went. He wasn't in the line-up of us naughty boys.'

That was interesting. Barbara Clark had vehemently denied the presence of a mysterious Australian at Fenwick Road the night of the police raid, but it was clear from her demeanour that she would have been too terrified to mention him even if he had been there. She'd certainly done her best to avoid knowing anything about him, apart from mentioning that a man who could have been him had given her a beating. On the other hand, that may have been a coincidence; she may not have seen Phillips. But even if Patricia Hunter had told Barbara Clark that he'd been in the bolthole after the raid was over, she didn't repeat it. However, on her previous form, she may have been too scared to tell us even that much.

'These meetings with Dolores in West End hotels, Mr Oliver. How did you make the arrangements to meet her?'

'About a week before the Brighton raid, I asked her if she was open to a bit of private business, and she jumped at it,' said Oliver. 'And I was pleased too. It worked out much cheaper without a middleman. Not that I minded forking out, but you've got to shop around, haven't you?'

'What time of the day did these meetings take place?'

'The afternoons, of course. I know what I said about my wife not being concerned, but there's no need to antagonize her, eh what?'

'How did you pay Dolores, Mr Oliver?'

'She took credit cards, old boy. Had this wonderful little portable machine in her briefcase. And she was very careful to get her money before we started the fun and games. Shrewd little cookie, that one.'

'Any idea of the name of the payee, Mr Oliver?'

'Not a clue. I know what I said about madam' – he cocked a thumb in the general direction of where he imagined his wife to be – 'but I always shred my bills as soon as I've paid them. To tell you the truth, I never noticed what her account was called.'

'Do you have any connection with the theatre, Mr Oliver?'

'Go there occasionally. The lady wife enjoys the odd evening out, you know.'

'That wasn't quite what I meant,' I said. 'Have you ever been involved in the management or production side?'

'Good God no. Much too risky. Unless you happen to be Andrew Lloyd Webber, of course.'

'Amateur dramatics, then?'

Oliver laughed. 'You must be joking. It's as much as I can do to stand up and say something at the AGM of my company.'

'And what does your company do, Mr Oliver?'

'Import and export. Why?'

I countered his question with one of my own. 'Where were you between the tenth and twelfth of June, Mr Oliver?'

Oliver laughed again. 'You've been watching too much TV, old boy. Now, where was I between those dates?' He glanced at the ceiling for a moment and then looked down again. 'I don't know. If you care to give my secretary a ring at my office sometime, she'll have a look in my diary. But I can't remember offhand.'

And that, I thought, would give you adequate time to make a few false entries.

But, I wondered, could it be that this man was Patricia Hunter's killer? He was rich, confident, and a womanizer. Perhaps we'd been misled into thinking that the Australian fugitive was the one who'd murdered the prostitute known as Dolores, when all along...

Thirteen

Dave and I returned to Curtis Green and mulled over what we had learned. Which wasn't very much. The judge and the clergyman were non-starters in my book, although I still intended to check the judge's story about being in Brittany at the time Patricia Hunter was murdered. But even so, a Crown Court judge? Be reasonable. Although, there again...

Tim Oliver however was a different ball game altogether. For a start he was much too glib and much too open about his sessions with the murdered Patricia Hunter. And he had skilfully avoided giving me a direct answer to my question concerning his whereabouts when she had been murdered.

The other aspect, of course, was that Oliver was undoubtedly affluent. All the trappings were there: a magnificent house, a chauffeur-driven Bentley, and if he had any more suits like the one he was wearing, his tailor must be a rich man too. But if his wife learned of his shenanigans with a prostitute, despite Oliver claiming that she didn't care, she might just take it into her head to seek a divorce. And that could cost him a lot of money. It was possible, therefore, that Patricia Hunter might have been blackmailing him. And blackmail is a very good motive for murder.

Suddenly Mr Tim Oliver had risen to a point very close to the top of my list of suspects.

The next morning, Colin Wilberforce announced that he'd had a call from the Australian High Commission.

'Inspector Granger said that an email from Canberra came in during the night, sir. The Commonwealth Police have no knowledge of Bruce Phillips returning to Australia. But according to this' – he gestured with the printout – 'they say it doesn't mean he hasn't. And they pointed out that Australia is a big place, sir,' he added with a grin.

'Very helpful,' I said. 'Just look how long it took them to find Ned Kelly.'

Just before eleven, Nicola Chance, a vivacious Spanish-speaking detective constable who could charm the birds off the trees, bounced into my office. Despite her slender build, she knew how to take care of herself. There was a story that when she was still in uniform, on duty in Trafalgar Square on a New Year's Eve, a drunken sailor had approached her and asked for a date. But he'd made the terrible mistake of grabbing hold of her and trying to give her a kiss. In a blur of judo movements the sailor had described a parabola through the air and finished up with a broken arm. I'd often wondered how he'd explained that injury to his shipmates in Portsmouth, when eventually he arrived back there. The beak had weighed him off for assault on police and, given that he was technically absent without leave by then, directed he be handed over to the shore patrol.

'I think I've got something, sir,' she said.

'Not measles, is it?'

'No, sir.' Nicola smiled. She'd been on the team long enough to have grown accustomed to my sense of humour. 'Last evening I dropped into the Kookaburra. It's a nightclub in—'

'It's also an Australian laughing jackass,' I said. 'I suppose I should read something into that.'

Nicola smiled again. 'Well, it's certainly frequented by the Australian community. I got talking to one of the hostesses, a girl called Lisa, who knows Bruce Phillips. And she reckoned she'd seen him in the club quite recently.'

'How recently is quite recently?'

'A week ago, sir. Wednesday the twenty-sixth to be exact.'

'How did she come to know him, Nicola?'

'She used to work for him apparently.'

'What, as a tom?' I was sure now that Phillips was the Australian whose involvement in the Fenwick Road brothel Barbara Clark had been at pains to deny.

'No, she was part of his hoisting gang. She said that he had about four or five girls, of which she was one, working the Oxford Street, Regent Street and Knightsbridge shops. It was quite a sophisticated operation by all accounts.'

'Any idea why they packed it in? Presuming they have, of course.'

'According to Lisa, the shoplifting squads at West End Central, Marylebone and Kensington nicks got wise to what was happening and homed in on them enough to make it an unhealthy pursuit. So Phillips's little team moved out of Central London. They had a brief fling at the Bluewater Centre, the big shopping complex at Greenhithe in Kent, but they were chased out of there and tried their hand at Brent Cross. It seems that the job's intelligence system worked well though, and the local police in those places had been warned that they were coming.'

'Did this Lisa of yours say whether she'd spoken to Phillips, Nicola?'

'Only briefly. He asked her if she wanted to work for him again.'

'Doing what?' I asked, but I'd guessed.

Nicola smiled again. 'He offered to set her up in a flat so that she could provide a "service" for carefully selected, affluent clients.'

'I don't suppose he told her where this place was.'

'No, sir, but Lisa told him to get lost. She said he was a nasty bastard and wouldn't shrink from beating them up if they stepped out of line. She didn't want anything else to do with him. End of story.'

'Had she seen him in there before? Recently, I mean.'

'She said not, sir, but that doesn't mean he isn't a frequent visitor. Lisa doesn't work every night and he could've been in at times when she wasn't on duty.'

'Was she ever done for shoplifting?'

'Yes, twice, sir. And each time Phillips paid her fine. But Lisa said that the last time she was up before the beak, she was threatened with imprisonment if she offended again.'

'So she decided to go on the game as a safer option, I suppose.'

'What, being a hostess in a nightclub, sir? Perish the thought.' Nicola gave me a mock frown. 'But she did mention that two of the other girls on his little scam carried on working for him. As high-class call girls.'

'Any names?'

'Yes, sir, Donna Lodge and Patricia Hunter.'

But, surprise, surprise, that was no surprise.

I rang Granger at Australia House. 'You can tell your guys to stop looking for Bruce Phillips, Steve,' I said. 'He was sighted in London a week ago.'

'No worries,' said Granger. 'Let me know when you've baled him up,' he added with a chuckle, 'and we'll have what's left.'

The news that Phillips was still in London created as many problems as it solved. It was now crucial that we find him. In my book, his association with the 'actress' Patricia Hunter, and his reputation for using violence, put him in the front rank of suspects for her murder. And despite Donna Lodge's neighbour's certainty that the photograph of the bearded, bespectacled Phillips that we'd shown her was not the clean-shaven, keen-sighted Geoffrey Forman, I still wondered if they were one and the same.

I sent for Frank Mead.

'Frank, I've got a lousy assignment for a couple of your guys, ideally a man and a woman.' I was joking, of course. It was the sort of assignment that every detective loves.

'Yeah, go on, Harry.'

'Nicola Chance has got a snout at the Kookaburra nightclub called Lisa, a hostess. And Lisa saw Bruce Phillips in there a week ago. Get a couple of our people to sit around in the place until he shows up. I'll get Nicola to brief Lisa to point him out if he turns up.'

'And if he does?' asked Frank.

'Tell them to nick him. He's wanted for extradition. And with any luck the murder of Patricia Hunter.' But then I had second thoughts. 'On the other hand, it might be better if they housed him. He's too smart a bastard to hold his hands up to murder, so we'll need the sort of evidence that may be found at wherever he's living now. But whatever happens, tell them not to lose him.'

'Right, Harry.' Mead paused at the door. 'By the way, all the checks on the stops the

TSG did the other night were blowouts.'

'Of course they were, Frank,' I said.

I sent for DS Challis and told him to get back to Forman's credit-card company and find out where and when he'd been using his plastic since buying a shirt, the receipt for which had been found in Patricia Hunter's bedsit at Coping Road. And if he'd recently notified them of a change of address. I was hoping that he'd used his card in the Kookaburra Club on the night that Nicola's informant saw Phillips there.

That's the beauty of this modern world in which we live: it's very difficult to do anything without leaving a trail.

Mind you, if Forman was as cunning as I was beginning to believe he was, there was no telling what devious steps he might have taken to avoid being tracked down.

It didn't take long. One quick phone call and Challis was back with the answers.

'The company still has Forman's Barnes address shown for him, guv,' said Challis, 'and he's got a variable direct debit with his bank so that the account is settled every month.'

'So he doesn't have to go home to check his credit-card bill,' I mused.

'Since buying his shirt, Forman's visited a couple of restaurants in London...' Challis looked up and grinned. 'They were top-line restaurants and the amounts involved seem to indicate that he wasn't dining alone. And on the twenty-sixth of June, guv, he spent fifty-odd quid in the Kookaburra Club in—'

'Got the bastard,' I said, hitting the top of my desk with the flat of my hand. And instantly regretting it: it hurt. 'That's the same night that Nicola Chance's snout saw Phillips in the K Club. I'm bloody sure that Forman is Phillips.'

'Beginning to look that way, guv,' said Challis.

'Any record of Forman having used his card in Germany recently, Tom? Düsseldorf in particular.'

Challis looked down at his notes. 'No, sir, nothing.'

'If Forman's the womanizer I think he is, he couldn't possibly go to Germany without spending a few Euros, especially in a nightclub,' I said. 'Of which, in Düsseldorf, there are many.'

'Looks like he didn't go, guv,' said Challis, who was fully conversant with the twists and turns of the case.

'Well, if Phillips is Forman, we know that he didn't.' And then something else occurred to me. 'Do a check with the passport office, Tom, and see if Forman's got a passport.'

'If Forman is Phillips, he might have done a *Day of the Jackal* job,' said Challis, referring to the scam whereby villains had been known to obtain a passport in the name of a dead child who would have been about their age had they lived.

'I don't think so, Tom. I seem to recall

something about them having put a stop to that.' Mind you, it takes years to put a brake on the lumbering Home Office administrative machine. And Phillips wouldn't have used his Australian passport in case he got picked up at a port or airport because there was an extradition warrant out for him. 'Incidentally, Tom, while you're in the credit-card mood, see what you can do with this.' I gave him the details of Jeremy Payne's credit card, which we had obtained from the manager of the Alhambra. I had far from excluded Patricia Hunter's rich boyfriend from my enquiries.

Having armed DCs John Appleby and Sheila Armitage with the Australian police photograph of Phillips, for what good that was likely to be, Frank Mead had detailed them to mount the observation at the Kookaburra Club. But I had no great hope that it would produce a result. Despite what Lisa had told Nicola Chance about not wanting anything else to do with Phillips, there was always the possibility that she'd lied. For all we knew, she could have been on the phone to him the moment Nicola left the club.

The two officers had also been given a copy of Donna Lodge's criminal-record photograph on the off-chance that she might show up at the club too. But perhaps I was relying too much on my hunch that Forman and Phillips were one and the same, stronger though that hunch was becoming by the hour.

I considered again Dave's suggestion of obtaining a warrant to search 13 Ridgely Road, Barnes, but I doubted that I could convince a district judge that there was enough evidence to justify it. Yet. After all, I didn't *know* that Forman was Phillips, even though I strongly suspected it. But perhaps that would be enough.

At five o'clock, Dave swanned into my office, a conspiratorial expression on his face.

'I've got some freebies, guv. Madeleine's dancing in *Les Sylphides* tonight. I wondered if you and—' He broke off. 'Ah, I'd forgotten. Sorry.'

'Keep it to yourself, Dave, but I've been seeing Gail Sutton recently.'

Dave grinned. 'Good for you, guv. Well, if you and she fancy a bit of culture tonight, the offer's there.'

'Yeah, why not? I'll give her a bell.'

'OK, guv, let me know. Kick-off's seven thirty at the Royal Opera House.'

Once Dave had left my office, I rang Gail. 'Dave Poole's got some free tickets for *Les Sylphides* tonight,' I said. 'D'you fancy seeing it?'

There was a lengthy pause while, I imagine, Gail was working out how to let me down lightly.

'Harry, I work in the theatre, and to be honest, the last thing I want to do right now is to get togged up, travel to London and *go* to the theatre. D'you mind awfully if I say no?'

'Sorry,' I said, 'never gave it a thought. How about dinner then, locally somewhere?'

There was another pause. Then, 'I've got a better idea. Why don't you come round here and I'll cook you dinner?'

'You're on,' I said. 'What time?'

'As soon as you can make it.'

I got to Gail's house at about eight thirty. She was holding a bottle of champagne when she opened her front door.

'I never open champagne when there's a man around to do it for me,' she said, handing me the bottle before leading the way upstairs to the living room.

'I take it you often open it yourself then,' I quipped.

She gave me a playful punch. 'Hardly ever,' she said.

Living on my own, I tended either to eat out or grab a takeaway. Neither of which did me much good. And when I attempted to cook something for myself it was usually a disaster. Consequently, to have someone prepare a home-cooked meal for me was a real luxury.

We started with smoked salmon, a dill sauce and brown bread. Then came chicken breasts on pasta with a tarragon sauce and green salad. All of which was accompanied by a splendid bottle of Pinot Grigio.

'Would you like some cheese, Harry?' Gail asked. 'I don't eat puddings and I haven't got anything in.'

I shook my head. 'No thanks, that was absolutely superb. You must have done a crash dive on the supermarket to get all that in.' It would have taken me about a week's planning to produce a meal of the sort she had just served. Not that I would have tried.

'No, I had it all in,' said Gail, 'except for the wine. Would you like a brandy?'

'That would be good.'

'It's on the side table in the sitting room. Help yourself and I'll make some coffee.'

Over coffee and brandy we talked about things we had done, some interesting, some dull, and places we had visited and the holidays we had enjoyed. In my case, not many. When I was married to Helga, our holidays consisted of visiting her parents in Cologne. Not to be recommended. They were boring little people and they'd never forgiven Helga for marrying me. On two counts: I was English *and* a copper.

'Good God!' I said, glancing at my watch. 'It's almost midnight. I must be going.'

'Do you have to?' asked Gail.

The next morning, a downcast DC Appleby reported that he and Sheila Armitage had spent the evening in the Kookaburra Club.

'You're not looking too happy, John.' I said. 'Didn't you have any joy?'

'Yes and no, sir,' said Appleby. 'We spotted Phillips—'

'How? He's not still sporting a beard and

glasses, surely?'

'No, sir, but when he came in, Lisa, one of the hostesses, said, "Hello, Bruce." He was quite angry about it and told her to keep her voice down and never to use his name.'

'Why are you so fed up then?'

'We lost him, sir.' Appleby looked even more miserable. 'When he left the club, Sheila Armitage and I followed him, but I reckon he's on the alert for surveillance all the time. He walked casually down the street, stopping occasionally to look in shop windows. But the minute he spotted a taxi, he hailed it and jumped in. There wasn't another cab in sight, otherwise we'd've had a go at following him.'

'Did these windows he looked in have glass that was at an angle to the footway?' asked Dave. 'The sort of shops that have a deeply recessed doorway?'

Appleby thought about that for a moment or two. 'Yes, come to think of it, they did, Skip.'

It was the oldest trick in the book: stopping ostensibly to look in shop windows but using the glass as a mirror to see if you're being followed. 'Don't worry, John,' I said. I was disappointed, naturally, but the young DCs had done their best. 'He'll come again. D'you think he sussed you?'

'I'm pretty sure he didn't, sir.'

'Good. Well, get back there again tonight and see if you have better luck.'

'There was one other thing, sir. Donna

Lodge was there. Sheila ID'd her from the CRO photograph. But we didn't try to house her, because Mr Mead said you were more interested in finding out where Phillips was going.'

'Was she indeed?' I was not so much surprised as pleased. 'Don't worry about that, but did she and Phillips make contact?'

'Only briefly, sir. Donna came in some time after Phillips and sat on a stool at the bar. When Phillips went up to order a drink, he slid an envelope to her. He never said anything, just slid the envelope along the bar and then walked away and sat down with his drink.'

'Did she open the envelope, John?'

'No, sir. She folded it in half and put it in her handbag. Then she finished her drink and left.'

'Looks as though she's still on the game,' I mused.

'She didn't pick up anyone in the club, sir,' said Appleby defensively, presumably wondering if he'd missed something he shouldn't have missed.

'I'm not surprised. I don't think that's her scene. I reckon she's at the top end of the market. Phillips is probably pimping for her, collecting the money and paying her at the club. If Donna turns up when you go back tonight, follow her rather than Phillips. If he *is* pimping for her, he'll come again.'

Despite what Appleby had said, it looked very much as though Phillips had sussed him and Sheila Armitage as being in the job, and had taken evasive action. After all, he was, according to the Australian police, an accomplished villain. On the other hand, he might have been the sort of hardened criminal who employed counter-surveillance tactics *all* the time. Just in case. That too would account for his not talking to Donna Lodge, even though she claimed they were living together. If, of course, Phillips was Forman.

And from what DS Lacey of the Extradition Unit had said about questioning Donna Lodge when he called at Petersfield Street, it was obvious that she must have warned him of our interest. Particularly after we'd paid her a second visit in Barnes. And that must have been why she'd done a flit. What interested me now was to find out where she'd been living since leaving Ridgely Road. And that, I hoped, would be discovered by Appleby and Armitage.

'One other thing, John. Donna Lodge owns an Alfa Romeo. When you get back to the incident room, ask Sergeant Wilberforce to have the number put on the PNC. I'm particularly interested to find out if it's parked up anywhere.'

I brought Frank Mead up to speed on what Appleby had learned the previous evening, and for a moment he sat in thoughtful silence.

'When I was on the Flying Squad, Harry,' he said eventually, 'there was an Australian sergeant called Ebdon.'

'What about him?' I asked.

'It's not a him, it's a her,' said Frank. 'Kate Ebdon. She came to the Squad from Leman Street in the East End. Some years ago now. She's got flame-red hair and usually dresses in a man's shirt and jeans.'

'She's not butch, is she?'

Frank laughed. 'No way. And there are several guys on the Squad who could testify to that. But more to the point, she's Australian.'

'So what are you suggesting?'

'If we could borrow her, she may just be able to get alongside Phillips in the Kookaburra Club, being an Australian, I mean. You never know, it may just short-circuit our enquiry.'

'Well, right now we could use any help we can get. I'll have a word with the governor of the Flying Squad.'

'I hope you know what you're doing, Harry,' said the operational head of the Squad when I rang him and explained why I wanted to borrow his Australian sergeant. And he laughed.

'Why d'you say that, guv?'

'She's a bloody firebrand, that one. Mind you, if you don't mind her hitting your suspect, she should be all right.'

'She'll fit in, guv.' I crossed my fingers and asked if I could borrow her.

At two o'clock that afternoon, Detective Sergeant Kate Ebdon reported for duty. A shapely thirty-five-year-old, she was dressed, as Frank had said she would be, in jeans and a man's white shirt. And her long red hair was tied back with a green velvet ribbon.

'I understand I'm to be attached to you for a while, guv'nor,' she said, gazing around my tiny office before plonking herself, uninvited, in the sole armchair.

'We've got a problem, Kate,' I began, and went on to tell her the situation with Phillips. 'By the way, this is DS Dave Poole,' I added, indicating Dave.

Kate Ebdon afforded Dave a quick smile. 'G'day, mate,' she said. I got the impression she was hamming up her Australian accent, probably because her boss had told her why I wanted her assistance.

'If you can get to know this Phillips, it may help us to tie him in with this murder of Patricia Hunter,' I continued. 'But you'll have to tread carefully. If he makes an admission of murder, which is most unlikely, bear in mind that he may not repeat it once he's in custody and under caution. And a one-to-one confession to someone he doesn't know is a police officer won't count for anything.' I was well aware that cases had foundered in the past where an admission had been made under similar circumstances.

'Yeah, that'd be right,' said Kate with a humourless laugh. 'Protect the villain and to hell with the victim. That's the name of the game,' she added, expressing a view of the law common among coppers.

'What I want you to do, if you can, is to find out as much as you can about his background,' I continued. 'Where he's living, who he's running with. Well, I don't have to tell you. It's more of an intelligence-gathering exercise.'

'Where's he from, guv?' Kate seemed a bit put out that I didn't want her to feel his collar.

'Sydney. At least according to the Australian High Commission.'

'That's a bit of luck,' said Kate. 'So am I. Who d'you talk to at Australia House?'

'Inspector Granger.'

'Oh, right. Steve's a mate of mine. OK if I have another word with him and get all the info? If he's getting his stuff from Canberra, it's probably years out of date.' It was obvious that Kate had no very high opinion of the Commonwealth Police.

'We've got all they have on record, but he's promised to let me have anything else that turns up.'

Kate nodded. 'Right,' she said. 'I was having a chat with the skipper in the incident room—'

'Colin Wilberforce.'

'Yeah, that's the guy. He was telling me there's an extradition warrant out for Phillips. If he's showing up at the Kookaburra Club, why don't we just nick him?'

'It's not that simple,' I said. 'We could have

222

him away any time we liked – now we know he's in the UK – but he's a professional villain and he's not going to cough to a murder. If we arrest him, he'll be sent back to Australia and our murder will be left on the books. We've got to get more evidence against him if we don't want that to happen.'

'So the idea is for me to hang around the K Club and get to know him, right?'

'Yes. D'you know where the K Club is?'

'Sure. Been in there a few times. It's where a lot of the Aussie expats hang out.'

'I should warn you, though. We think he's running a stable of toms. Don't get recruited.'

Kate let out a raucous laugh. 'No probs, guv. He'll get a knee in his balls if he tries to come on to me.'

And even after so short an acquaintance with Detective Sergeant Ebdon, I was in no doubt about that.

Fourteen

The next morning, DC Appleby reported to my office at about nine o'clock.

'Last night was a blowout, sir. Neither Phillips nor Donna Lodge showed up at the K Club.'

'In that case, John, leave it until next Wednesday. It could be that he only turns up once a week for the specific purpose of paying Donna.'

'But he might have other girls working for him, sir, and he wouldn't take the risk of paying them all on the same night.'

I pondered that proposition; Appleby could be right. 'It's possible, John, but I'm putting another officer in there in the meantime. I don't want Phillips to get used to seeing you.'

Appleby looked somewhat crestfallen at that, as though I'd somehow impugned his professional ability.

'Nothing personal, John,' I said, 'but I've borrowed a sergeant from the Flying Squad. She's Australian, and the idea is for her to get alongside Phillips, if that's who he is, and see if she can gain his confidence.'

'Is that the red-haired girl in the incident room, sir?'

'Yes, it is, John, and tread warily. She might be tempted to have a nice young man like you for breakfast.'

Appleby frowned. 'But I'm married, sir,' he said.

'So you are,' I said thoughtfully, 'but I'm not sure that would make any difference to Sergeant Ebdon.'

'Now that we know Forman met Donna in the K Club, guv,' said Dave, after a worried Appleby had left the office, 'I reckon we've got grounds for searching his Ridgely Road address in Barnes.'

'Maybe.' But I was still unsure.

'It stands to reason,' Dave persisted. 'When this guy came into the K Club, Lisa, the so-called hostess, called him Bruce and he got all arsey about it. And the same night Forman puts fifty-odd pounds on his credit card. All in the K Club. That's too much of a coincidence.'

'Most people have a computer these days,' I said.

'Are you changing the subject?' asked Dave, tossing me a cigarette.

'No, but it may be a good idea to get a circuit judge's warrant. I wouldn't like to find something incriminating on their computer – if they've got one – only to have it ruled out as inadmissible in court.'

'Oh, we're going to court now, are we, sir?' enquired Dave sarcastically.

'I hope so, but if this guy keeps personal records on a computer – like his bank details, for example – it could turn out to be evidence.' I was floundering a bit here, but the moguls at the Crown Prosecution Service can get all bitchy if you don't get it absolutely right. To say nothing of assorted judges and barristers.

'On the other hand,' commented Dave, 'we might just find our friend Phillips there.'

'We should be so lucky.'

The circuit judge at Middlesex Crown Court had studied my 'information' with a measure of scepticism, but after a few steps of legal tap-dancing on my part, and the fact that Phillips was wanted for extradition, he finally, and somewhat reluctantly I suspect, granted me a search warrant.

'When are we going to do this, guv?' Dave asked as we left the court.

'As soon as we can assemble Linda Mitchell and her team of crime-scene examiners,' I said. 'I'd like to go in and out without either Forman or Donna Lodge knowing that we've been there.'

'Can't do that, guv. Section sixteen of the Police and Criminal Evidence Act says that if there's no one there, you've got to leave a copy of the search warrant in a prominent place.'

'Define "prominent", Dave,' I said. That had him.

Apart from a mellifluous version of the West-minster chimes, there was no response when

226

I rang the doorbell of 13 Ridgely Road, Barnes. And that suited me fine.

One of Linda Mitchell's CSEs spent a few moments working on the lock and we were in.

A quick tour of the house confirmed what I had suspected. Since last Tuesday, the day that Donna Lodge had departed, according to her nosey neighbour, the place appeared not to have been lived in. Whatever other failings Donna Lodge may have had, slovenliness was not among them: she had left the house in pristine condition. The bed was made, the kitchen spotless and devoid of dirty crockery, and the cushions had been plumped up on the sofa and armchairs in the sitting room. It was almost as if she and Forman had no intention of returning.

But they had left a computer in the study.

'Do we know whether this house is owned or rented by Donna, Dave?' I asked. In view of the basics, like furniture, it had all the marks of a rented property.

'No, we don't, guv, and it takes a hell of a lot of phone calls to find out. The local council are no help: they just send the council-tax demand to whoever's occupying the place. We could try a Land Registry search, but that would take forever and a day. And what would it tell us anyway?'

'It might tell us if they were coming back. We could try the helpful neighbour.'

'I'd put money on them never coming near the place again,' said Dave. 'Looks like we frightened them off.'

I had to agree with Dave. It had been a mistake to turn up here last Monday asking questions about Bruce Phillips.

'D'you want to have a go at the computer in the study, Dave?' I suggested.

'One of Linda's guys is a computer expert, guv. It'd be better if we let him play with it.'

The CSE who knew about computers was called Dennis. 'You wanted me, Mr Brock?'

'Yes, Dennis, see what you can do with the computer. Dave tells me that it'll probably need a password, so I'm not holding out too much hope.'

Dennis scoffed. 'Passwords only stop amateurs getting in,' he said scornfully.

We followed him into the study. He sat down in front of the computer and gazed at it briefly. Interlinking his fingers and stretching them like a pianist about to play Rachmaninov's Third, he began. It didn't take long.

'There's the first one that might be of interest.' Dennis sat back with a satisfied expression on his face. 'Have a look.' He leaned sideways so that I could see the email on the screen: *Donna – meet Nick Lloyd tonight at his h/a eight p.m. for an all-nighter.* It was timed at 1610 hours on Tuesday the second of July, but was unsigned.

But we knew from having called at Ridgely Road at one o'clock on that day that Donna had already left. Poor old Nick Lloyd must have spent the evening watching television. And waiting. And hoping.

'Lloyd was one of the names in Patricia Hunter's address book, guv,' Dave said mildly.

'Bloody hell, so it was,' I said. 'That email says that Donna was supposed to meet him at his home address. Where is it?'

Dave thumbed through his pocket book. 'Tanley Road, Richmond, guv.' He looked up. 'Mr Mead checked it out. This Lloyd guy said he'd never heard of Patricia Hunter, had no idea how his name had got into her address book, and had a rock-solid alibi for the night of her murder.'

'So he's a liar,' I said.

'I wonder if Edward Archer was also one of Donna's clients,' said Dave. 'His address was in Patricia's little book too.'

But before I had time to comment on that, Dennis gave a shout of triumph. 'This you'll like,' he said. 'I've found a website.' He felt it necessary to explain, which was just as well; I hadn't a clue what he was talking about. 'I switched to the internet and it's been programmed to go straight to this...'

The website was an advertisement for prostitutes. And among ten photographs of naked women in provocative poses was one of Donna Lodge. Alongside her picture was the name Fleur and details of her vital statistics.

'Fleur, eh? Looks like her leaves have fallen off,' commented Dave in an aside. 'But a nice little stable of fillies nevertheless.' He looked closer at the screen. 'And guess whose picture is called Kimberley, guv.' He looked up and grinned. 'Judging by this, I'd've said she was more than a thirty-six B-cup.'

I looked at the nude Dave was pointing at. It was Barbara Clark. 'So she did know who Forman was,' I said.

'Bloody tramps,' said Linda, who had joined our little group of professional voyeurs. It was the only time I'd heard her swear.

'How do they make contact, Dennis?' I asked.

'There's an email address, Mr Brock, but I'll put money on it going out to a web-based mail account.'

'Meaning?' I hate all this computer-speak.

'It means that the email address goes out to the guy who makes the arrangements for these girls. He can pick up the messages from any computer in the world, so he could even be in another country. Then he'll relay the message to the chosen girl and off she'll go.' Dennis turned in his chair and gave a lascivious grin.

I was now damned sure that Phillips was on the other end of that email address, and we knew he *was* in the country. However, the website had been kept up to date and there was no photograph of Patricia Hunter, alias Dolores. Assuming, of course, that she had been posted on the website in the first place.

'It could mean that Nick Lloyd was innocent...' I began. Dave scoffed. 'Innocent' was not a word he used very much. 'When Mr Mead saw him, he denied all knowledge of Patricia Hunter,' I continued, 'but he might have got some reaction if he'd known, at the time, that her trade name was Dolores, like Donna Lodge calls herself Fleur and Barbara Clark is Kimberley. It was the judge who first told us that the Hunter girl was Dolores.'

Linda Mitchell's team lifted a few fingerprints from various parts of the house, but our cursory search revealed nothing else of interest. The wardrobe was devoid of clothing and there was nothing of a personal nature. It confirmed my original thought: that Donna Lodge had gone for good. But where, I wondered?

And it was me who'd shot himself in the foot by alerting her to our interest in Phillips.

But, in a sense, so had Phillips himself. If he was the man with the email address. And I was sure he was. One thing was certain: he would be furious if he ever found out that Donna Lodge had been stupid enough to abandon the computer with all that valuable information on it. And given what we'd learned about his mercurial temperament, that might well have put her life in danger. It behoved us to find him as soon as possible. But he was proving to be a devious bastard and it wasn't going to be easy.

We took the computer with us. We'd got what we wanted, and the recently departed occupants knew we were interested in them, so it didn't matter if they found out that we'd searched the house. If they ever came back.

I scrounged a piece of Sellotape from Linda and used it to stick a copy of the search warrant to the mirror in the hall. 'That prominent enough for you, Dave?'

'Yes, sir.'

'What sort of place does this Nick Lloyd live in, Frank?' I asked DI Mead when we'd returned to Curtis Green and I'd explained the story so far.

'It's a block of service flats,' said Frank, and after a moment, seeking recall from the ceiling, added, 'Number six, Mayberry Court, Tanley Road, Richmond.'

'Tell me about him.'

'Single guy about thirty-five, give or take. Works in the City, something to do with high finance. Spends all day shuffling huge amounts of money around the world apparently. Drives a Ferrari. Said he'd never heard of Patricia Hunter and was at a party the night of her murder. Not that I mentioned the murder, just talked about a missing person. I checked out his story and there were about fifty witnesses to say he was there. In Chichester.'

'What, a party on a Tuesday?' I said.

'So what?' rejoined Frank. 'They don't give a toss, these guys. They've got so much money that by the time they're forty, they're burned out and retire, poor dears. Beats coppering, that's for sure.'

From what Frank had told me, finding Nick Lloyd at home was going to be a hit-and-miss affair. I tossed a coin and determined that Dave and I would pay him a visit tomorrow

232

evening, Saturday. Well, it was as good a day as any other.

In the meantime, I decided it was time to take Gail Sutton out for a meal. A small return for the meal she had prepared for me. And what had followed.

It was a quiet little restaurant that I hadn't explored before. And it was within walking distance of where both Gail and I lived, which was an advantage. It meant I could have a drink. Contrary to popular opinion, there is nothing the Black Rats – as the traffic police are known – like better than to get a positive breathalyser reading from a CID officer.

'Have you caught him yet?' asked Gail before I'd even had time to study the menu. She seemed more obsessed with the progress of my enquiry than did the commander.

'Not yet,' I said, 'but we're getting closer.' Well, I had to say something. That or appear to be totally incompetent. I was now certain that Geoffrey Forman was Bruce Phillips and was running a team of prostitutes, but whether he'd murdered Patricia Hunter was still something to be resolved. And if he had, why? I decided to float the idea.

'D'you think that Patricia may have been a call-girl, Gail?' I asked, knowing full well that she had been a very active call-girl. I broke my bread roll and reached for the butter rather than make eye contact.

I was expecting either confirmation or

outraged denial, but to my surprise Gail's response was measured.

'I suppose it's possible, darling,' she said mildly. 'When showgirls are out of work, they'll turn to anything to make ends meet.' She raised an eyebrow and looked directly at me. 'But if you're thinking what I think you're thinking, forget it. I'm not one of them.' Then she laughed.

'The thought never crossed my mind,' I said.

'What makes you think she might have been?' Gail asked, putting down her menu and shooting a captivating smile at a passing waiter.

The waiter was there in an instant. 'Are you ready to order, madam?' he enquired.

'Well, what makes you think she *might* have been a call-girl?' Gail asked again, once the wearisome business of ordering our meal was out of the way. I hate deciding what to eat, and usually go for the same tried and tested dishes.

'Actually, I know she was,' I said, and told her what we'd learned about Patricia Hunter's activities at the Fenwick Road 'health farm for tired businessmen', as the Sussex Vice Squad had described it. 'That and a bit of shoplifting.'

'Shoplifting?' Curiously, that seemed to have shocked Gail more than learning that her friend had been on the game.

'Yes. We think she was part of a professional shoplifting ring some years ago. Run by an

Australian called Bruce Phillips.'

'You mentioned him before,' Gail said. 'Didn't you ask me if Patricia had ever talked about him?'

'Yes, I did, and we're still looking for him,' I commented, taking the first bite of a rather good terrine that had arrived in record time. It definitely improves the service if you take a good-looking girl out to dinner. 'He's wanted in Australia for a number of offences.'

'And do you think he might have murdered Patricia?'

'It's a possibility I'm considering,' I said, but decided against telling Gail exactly why I thought so.

'What a damned silly thing for her to have got involved in.'

I wasn't sure whether Gail meant prostitution or shoplifting. 'It happens,' I said.

'She was a good dancer, that girl, and she was young enough to have got on well in the profession. What a waste.'

Yesterday afternoon, Tom Challis had obtained details of Jeremy Payne's home address from the credit-card company. It was in a not very salubrious part of Stockwell. That in itself did not sound like the residence of someone who claimed to have a flat in Docklands and a villa in St Raphaël, and who drove a sports car. Nevertheless Dave and I went there. That's what police work's all about.

The woman who answered the door was

235

clearly in the middle of doing housework. She wore an apron and had a duster in one hand.

'Yes, what is it?'

'We're police officers, madam,' I said. 'Does a Jeremy Payne live here?'

'Yes, but he's not here at the moment. Is it something to do with the van?'

'Oh, he has a van, does he?' I clutched at that passing straw with alacrity.

'Well, he doesn't own it. He drives it for the firm he works for.' As an apparent after-thought, the woman opened the door wide. 'You'd better come in, I suppose.'

We were conducted into a shabby front room. An upright vacuum cleaner stood in the centre of the carpet and we'd obviously interrupted the woman's hoovering.

'Are you Mrs Payne?' I asked.

'Yes. What's this all about, Officer?'

'And Jeremy's your son, is he?'

'Yes. Is he in some sort of trouble?' Mrs Payne looked concerned. 'It's not drugs, is it?'

'No. Tell me, Mrs Payne, does your son go to the theatre much?'

'Oh yes. He loves the theatre. He hopes to become an actor one day. He's very keen on amateur dramatics. As a matter of fact he's in a show tonight. It's called *Kiss Me Kate*.'

This was beginning to sound very promising. First we learn that Jeremy Payne drives a van, and then we find that he's into amateur dramatics. And amateur dramatics means access to greasepaint. I took it a stage further.

'Does Jeremy ever go to France, Mrs

Payne?'

'Yes, as a matter of fact he went there last year for a holiday.'

'Whereabouts, d'you know?'

'It was in the south somewhere.' But then the protective mother came to life. 'Look, d'you mind telling me what this is all about?'

'We think he may be able to assist us,' I said smoothly. 'We believe he may have witnessed an incident that we're investigating. At the Granville Theatre.'

A sudden look of fear crossed the woman's face. 'Does that mean he'll have to go to court? I wouldn't like that. You know what happens to people who give evidence against criminals. They usually end up getting petrol poured through their letterbox.'

So much for the commissioner's claim that public confidence in the police had improved.

'Oh, I shouldn't think so, not for one moment,' I said. *Unless I charge him with Patricia Hunter's murder, that is.* 'Have you any idea when he'll be home, Mrs Payne?'

'Not until late tonight. He's working this morning and then he'll go straight to the hall where they're doing the musical. He helps to set things up, you see.'

Armed with the address of the venue for the latest amateur production of *Kiss Me Kate*, Dave and I arrived there at about three o'clock.

'I'm looking for Jeremy Payne,' I said to a passing 'actress'.

'So am I, darling,' said this vision. 'He should've been here an hour ago. It's too bad. People say they're coming here to help and then they don't turn up.'

'Does that often happen?' asked Dave.

'Not with him,' said the girl thoughtfully. 'Come to think of it, he's always here.'

'Does he have a mobile phone?' Dave asked.

The girl looked at Dave as though he'd just emerged from the Ark. 'Doesn't everyone, darling?' she asked, and wandered off shouting for someone called Damien.

'We've done it again, Dave,' I said. 'I'll put money on his mother having alerted him.'

'He'll come, guv,' said Dave, more in hope than in certainty.

All of a sudden, Jeremy Payne had come to the head of the queue of Patricia Hunter's possible murderers.

Despite my initial doubts, Nick Lloyd was at home on the Saturday evening, which was a bonus. But it was some time before he answered the door. When he did so, he was attired in a shirt, unbuttoned at the cuffs, and a pair of jeans. And he was barefooted and his hair was ruffled.

'Yes?' There was something insufferably superior about the way the City trader uttered that single word.

'We're police officers, Mr Lloyd. We'd like a word.'

'Well, I'm afraid it's not convenient right

now. I'm entertaining.' Lloyd cast a scathing glance at Dave and began to close the door.

'We can do it here or at Richmond police station,' I said, gently pushing the door open again. 'Please yourself.' Although it is not an offence to engage the services of a prostitute in the confines of one's own home, it is certainly a crime to murder her. Anywhere. That Patricia Hunter had recorded Lloyd's name and address, coupled with the fact that he had booked Donna Lodge for an 'all-nighter' was good enough for me to regard him as a suspect.

'What the hell are you talking about?' demanded Lloyd, his original hostility beginning to wane quite sharply. He opened the door wide and stepped back. 'If it's about the Ferrari, I've sold it,' he said. 'I'm sick and tired of getting pulled by you people simply because I've got an expensive car. It's just bloody envy, I suppose.'

Lloyd led us into a sitting room that was furnished in somewhat bizarre taste, but nonetheless one in which no expense had been spared. He closed the door and turned to us with an expression of intolerance on his face. 'Well, what's this all about?' he demanded. 'And it'd better be good because my next phone call will be to my solicitor.'

'Why? Have you done something wrong?' asked Dave with a masterful portrayal of innocence on his face.

'No, it'll be to initiate a complaint of police harassment,' snapped Lloyd. 'This is the second time I've had you people here asking intrusive questions about my private life.'

'And it may not be the last,' said Dave mildly, 'unless you give us the answers we are looking for.'

We sat down uninvited.

'Patricia Hunter,' I said.

Lloyd had remained standing, presumably to give himself some ascendancy over us mere policemen. 'I told that other copper that I know nothing about any Patricia Hunter. I've never heard of the damned woman. So perhaps you'd better begin by telling me what the hell it is you want.'

'I don't know if the other officer explained our interest—'

'He said she was missing and mentioned something about my name and address being found in some book of hers,' said Lloyd before I was able to go any further. 'Well, I know damn-all about it. Or her.'

'The reason for our interest,' I continued, 'is that Patricia Hunter was murdered.'

'Christ, he never told me that,' said Lloyd, and at last sat down opposite us. He paused for a moment or two and then added, 'Well, it's nothing to do with me. I don't know the damned woman.'

'Did Fleur turn up last Tuesday?' enquired Dave.

'Fleur? What Fleur?' Lloyd posed the question in an offhand way, but it had obviously struck home.

'The Fleur you ordered off the Internet.

She's a prostitute, and quite an expensive one I should think.' Dave was beginning to enjoy himself.

'Now look here—'

'Before we go any further,' I said, 'have a look at this.' I handed him a photograph of Patricia Hunter. 'And be very careful what you say, Mr Lloyd, because, as I told you, I'm investigating this girl's murder.'

'Oh God!' Lloyd stared at the print of the dead showgirl as if mesmerized. 'It's Dolores.'

'Tell me about her,' I said.

Lloyd returned the photograph. 'I saw her a couple of times.'

'Let's not pussyfoot about, Mr Lloyd,' said Dave. 'She's a prostitute and you engaged her services via the Internet. And at the beginning of the week you also put in a request for Fleur on the same Internet site.'

'There's nothing wrong in that.' Lloyd spoke sharply. 'What I do with my money is my business.'

'But when the woman Dolores is murdered, Mr Lloyd, it becomes my business,' I said.

'Good God Almighty, I didn't kill her,' said Lloyd. There was desperation in his voice now, probably at the thought that we might not believe him.

'Convince me.'

'It's true. I did arrange for her to come here on two occasions and—'

'When?'

'I'll need to look in my diary.' Lloyd reached across to a leather jacket that was draped over the back of his armchair and withdrew a small leather-bound book. He thumbed through it until he found the appropriate page. 'She came here on the first of June and again on the eighth.'

'What time did she get here?' Dave asked.

Lloyd looked a little puzzled by the question. 'It was about midnight, I suppose.'

'Is that the time you asked her to come?'

'No, as a matter of fact, I'd rather have seen her earlier, but I assumed she had another appointment. Why?'

'No reason,' said Dave. But it was likely that her late arrival was because she'd only just left the theatre. Busy girl, combining business with business.

'Was there any reason why you didn't order her again?' persisted Dave.

'I like a change.' There was a return of Lloyd's superior attitude with that statement.

'So you decided to screw Fleur instead. Had her before, had you?'

I could see that Lloyd was not much impressed by Dave's earthiness. I suppose he didn't like to have what he thought of as an adventure, or even a romantic tryst, reduced to the sort of basic language that Dave occasionally revelled in.

'Yes, twice. Now look, I'm getting fed up with this. I told that other copper that I was at a party in Chichester on the date he mentioned, and there were dozens of people who saw me there. But I didn't know this girl had been murdered.'

'You didn't see her picture in the paper?' I asked.

'There was nothing about it in the *Financial Times*,' said Lloyd scathingly.

'And did Dolores spend all night with you on those two occasions?' I asked, ignoring his attempt at lofty disdain.

'Yes, she did. So what?'

'Tell me how this Internet thing works,' said Dave. 'What is it, whore-dot-com, or something like that?' He was playing with Lloyd now; we'd got the Internet address from the computer at Barnes.

Lloyd fell back against the cushions of his armchair, visibly deflated. 'There's an email address on the website,' he said quietly. 'You send a message to it asking for the services of one of the girls whose pictures are on the website. You pay by credit card and she turns up. You can either hire her by the hour, or opt for an all-night session.'

'Must cost a packet,' commented Dave.

'So what,' said Lloyd defiantly. 'It's what I flog my guts out for. So I can enjoy myself. And it's not illegal.'

'Not for you, it's not,' said Dave, 'but it is for the guy who runs it. And very shortly we'll be arresting him. You say you paid by credit card...'

'Yes, I did.'

'D'you have your credit-card statement?'

'Yes, why?'

'Would you tell me the name of the account to which your payment went?'

243

Lloyd knew the answer without referring to his statement. 'It was Grind, Isle of Man.'

'Hilarious,' said Dave, and laughed. But the reality behind the irony was that we both knew tracking down a credit-card account based in the Isle of Man was fraught with difficulties. And that meant that any chance of finding the names of other clients was almost certainly stillborn.

Our conversation was interrupted by the door to the sitting room crashing back against the wall. 'If you want to turn this into an all-night screw, ducky, it'll cost you a monkey more than you've paid already,' said a raucous cockney voice. 'Up front.'

All three of us turned.

On the threshold of the room stood a girl wrapped in what I presumed was one of Lloyd's shirts. And nothing else. Her long blonde hair tumbled around her shoulders and she stood, one leg in front of the other, with her hands on her hips, her breasts thrust forward so that her pert nipples showed through the thin material. She didn't seem at all alarmed at seeing Dave and me, and I imagined that, with the innate perspicacity of her trade, she knew that we were Old Bill. And couldn't have cared less. Her coarseness was certainly a marked change from Donna Lodge's sophistication, but perhaps Lloyd liked a bit of rough for a change.

Dave withdrew the printout of Forman's website from his pocket, studied it briefly and then glanced at the girl in the doorway. 'You

244

must be Domino,' he said.

'So what, darling?' Domino pouted at Dave.

'We may have to speak to you again, Mr Lloyd,' I said, as Dave and I stood up to leave.

'I hope the Skoda runs better than your Ferrari,' said Dave.

'*Skoda*?' screeched Domino as we reached the front door. 'You never said you drove a bleedin' Skoda.' Perhaps she thought that his performance would be similarly diminished. Despite what they may say, even prostitutes prefer a good performer.

'What d'you think, guv?' asked Dave as we drove away from Mayberry Court.

'I think we wasted our time, Dave.'

'Yeah, but it was good fun, wasn't it?'

'But it's about to get better,' I said. 'I get the distinct impression that Domino's not going to be there that long. I think we'll hang about and have a chat with her when she emerges.'

Dave reversed back to the space where we'd parked originally and switched off the engine.

Fifteen

It was about half an hour later that Domino emerged from Nick Lloyd's flat. She was dressed in tight-fitting black leather trousers, and a black, sleeveless, high-necked, crop-top. A leather bag was slung across one shoulder.

And she didn't look happy.

Whether it was Dave's throwaway suggestion that Lloyd now drove a Skoda, or whether Lloyd had been so disconcerted by our visit that he had gone off the idea of forking out an extra five hundred pounds for an 'all-nighter' didn't really matter.

Dave crossed the pavement and confronted her.

'My guv'nor would like a word with you, Domino. Why don't you step into our office?' he said, opening the rear door of the car.

'What the hell's this all about?' Domino's response was truculent, but she got in.

'Bruce Phillips,' I said, once the girl had settled herself in the centre of the back seat.

'I don't know no Bruce Phillips,' said Domino.

'Really? He's the guy who fixes up your appointments and then pays you. Having

246

taken a hefty whack for himself, of course. In other words he's your pimp.'

'No he ain't.'

'Well, who is, then?'

Domino looked from me to Dave and back again. 'Dunno what you're talking about,' she said.

'When did you last see Patricia Hunter?' asked Dave.

'Never heard of her.'

Dave showed her the photograph.

'That's Dolores,' said Domino without hesitation.

'And did she work for Phillips too?' I asked.

'I told you, I never heard of him.'

'I don't think you realize just how serious this is, Domino,' I said. 'Patricia Hunter – Dolores – has been murdered. The police fished her body out of the river over three weeks ago.'

'Christ!' said Domino. 'I never knew that.'

'It was in all the papers.'

'Don't never read 'em, do I?'

'Not even the *Financial Times*?' asked Dave impishly.

'Do what?'

'Did you ever meet Dolores?' I asked.

'Nah, course not. We all work alone, see. Because—' Domino stopped suddenly, presumably realizing that she was about to compromise the pimp she worked for.

'Because your pimp keeps you all separate in the vain hope that he won't get done for living on immoral earnings. Is that it?'

247

'Yeah, summat like that,' mumbled Domino.

'Have you got another job, Domino?' asked Dave.

The girl gave Dave an arch look. 'Do a bit of temping,' she said.

Dave laughed. 'Yeah, I can see that,' he said, 'but have you got another job?'

'In an office, dimbo,' said Domino cheekily.

It was a good question. Dave was obviously thinking that if all Phillips's girls had another job, he could claim that he wasn't living on their immoral earnings. That could explain why Patricia Hunter was working as a chorus girl. But such elaborate precautions wouldn't wash with a judge.

'Who is your pimp, then?' I repeated.

'You must be bloody joking, mister.' In common with most prostitutes, Domino was reluctant to reveal the name of her 'minder', especially to the police. Such treachery could have unpleasant results. Even fatal ones.

'You might be next,' said Dave mildly, as if reading the young tom's thoughts.

'You don't mean...?' For a few seconds, Domino reflected on the implication of Dave's comment. ''Ere, this ain't going no further, is it?' she asked, leaning forward, a hopeful expression on her face.

'Your secret's safe with me,' I lied.

'Forman. Geoffrey Forman,' said the girl.

'And how does the system work, Domino? Incidentally, I'm not going to keep calling you Domino. What's your real name?'

248

There was a further hesitation before Domino replied. 'Marlene West,' she said eventually.

'So, how does it work, Marlene?'

'Geoff's got a website and we advertise on it. Any john what wants a good screw orders one of us by sending Geoff an email. We've all got laptops or mobiles and Geoff sends us an email or a text message telling us where to go and when.'

'And how does he pay you?' asked Dave, although we both knew the answer to that. Or thought we did.

'We meet him in the Kookaburra Club and he gives us our money. I have to go there at five o'clock Tuesday evenings. If I miss the five o'clock slot on a Tuesday, I have to wait another week. He's very particular about that.'

'I'll bet he is,' I said. 'And where does this Geoffrey Forman live?'

'Haven't a clue, darling,' said Domino, giving me a cheeky smile.

'And where do you live, Marlene?' Dave asked.

'What d'you want to know that for?'

'In case you get a visit,' Dave said ominously.

Marlene misunderstood Dave, as he had meant her to. She thought he was concerned with her safety, whereas he was hoping Phillips might turn up there one day. It was a forlorn hope, but we had to try everything in the book if we were going to amass enough evidence to convict this elusive Australian of murder. Assuming he had committed the murder, that is. However, I was not losing sight of the fact that our recent enquiries had also put Jeremy Payne firmly in the frame.

And so Payne's name had been added to the police national computer along with the others in whom we were interested.

Marlene gave us her address but, I suspect, not without some misgivings, misgivings confirmed by her final utterance.

'You ain't never seen me. Right, copper?'

'Doesn't look like we're any further forward, guv,' said Dave as Marlene West alias Domino sashayed off into the night.

Linda Mitchell's report on the fingerprints found at Barnes was on my desk on Monday morning. Fortunately, the Australian police had included a set of Phillips's dabs in their request for his extradition. And they tallied with one of the sets found at 13 Ridgely Road. The other prints, unsurprisingly, were those of Donna Lodge. But that's all there was: just two sets of prints.

'Either Phillips *is* Forman, or Donna Lodge has some explaining to do as to why we found Phillips's prints at Barnes,' I said to Dave.

'It's got to be him,' said Dave. 'We know they were shacked up together at Petersfield Street. At least, Don Lacey was sure they had been when he went chasing Phillips with an extradition warrant.'

But further debate was cut short by the

arrival of Kate Ebdon.

'G'day, guv,' she said brightly. 'He was there.'

'Who was where?'

'Phillips. I spent the evening in the K Club and he turned up at about half nine.'

'Did you get to talk to him, Kate?'

'Sure. He bought me a drink and we got chatting.'

'Did he say anything interesting though?' I asked.

'Not really, no. We talked about Down Under and the places we both knew in Sydney. But I'd only been chatting to him for about half an hour when he offered me a job.'

'What sort of job?' I asked, a smile on my face.

'He said it was a position – he emphasized the word "position" – where a good-looking sheila like me could make a lot of money.' Kate smirked at the recollection.

'What did you say to that?' I asked.

'I told him to go screw himself. But he just laughed. Anyway, when I got around to asking him what he did for a living, he clammed up. There was one interesting thing though: about ten o'clock some girl turned up and sat at the bar. Phillips walked across and gave her an envelope. She finished her drink and pissed off. Neither of them said a word.'

'Did you ask him about it?'

'Too right. He said it was his ex and he was paying her alimony. Well, that was obviously a

251

'load of bullshit, but I didn't press it.'

'What did she look like, this girl?' I asked.

'Why don't we get Kate to have a look at the website, guv?' said Dave.

'Good idea,' I said, and the three of us adjourned to the incident room, where Colin Wilberforce had set up the computer we'd seized from Barnes.

'That's her,' said Kate, pointing to a dark-haired girl whose 'stage name' was listed as Petal. 'Ah! She was there too,' she added, pointing to the photograph of Fleur. 'Funny that, though. She came in, saw Phillips talking to me and buggered off a bit smartish.'

'That,' I said, 'is Donna Lodge.' I explained about the raid on the Barnes house. 'And that's where we got this computer.'

'Looks as though Donna had to go without her fee on Saturday, guv,' said Dave. 'But in view of what Domino said about sticking to a day and time, I reckon Donna must be more important than just one of his girls. I reckon she's his second-in-command, and meets him whenever she feels like it.'

'I think I've made a decision, Dave,' I said.

'Blimey, sir, be careful.'

'I think it's time we nicked Donna Lodge and found out what she's got to say for herself.'

'When do we do that?'

'*We* don't, Dave. I'm not going to dignify a tom with being arrested by a detective chief inspector. I'll let Appleby do it. Get him in if he's there.'

252

'What d'you want me to do, guv?' asked Kate.

'Carry on as usual. I'll be interested in Phillips's reaction to one of his star players getting knocked off. If he mentions it.'

'Sir?' Appleby appeared in the office doorway.

'Come in, John. I've got a job for you and Sheila Armitage.'

'Yes, sir?'

'I want Donna Lodge arrested. But don't do it in the K Club. Wait until she leaves and nick her in the street.'

'Yes, sir.' Appleby grinned, presumably at the thought he was about to do something positive.

It was at eight o'clock that evening when the call came in.

'I've got John Appleby on the line, sir,' said Gavin Creasey, the night-duty incident-room sergeant. 'He's arrested Donna Lodge.'

'Where's he taken her?'

'West End Central nick, sir.'

'Put him through.' I grabbed the phone. 'Well done, John. DS Poole and I will be there shortly. What was her reaction?'

There was a pause while, I imagined, Appleby selected the right words to describe Donna's response. 'Well, sir, after a few profanities on her part, she seemed to be somewhat put out.'

I laughed. 'That sounds about right,' I said. 'Did she, by any chance, meet Phillips in the

253

club?'

'Yes, sir. It was the usual routine except that Donna Lodge was there first this evening. She was sitting at the bar, as usual, when Phillips came in, and handed her an envelope. She left straight away, and we arrested her outside.'

'What did Phillips do ... after he'd paid her?'

'Went and sat down at DS Ebdon's table, sir.'

It was an entirely different Donna Lodge from the one we'd interviewed at Barnes. Immaculately dressed in a black, two-piece suit with a white jabot, black tights and spike heels, she was reclining in a chair in the interview room, smoking a cigarette, despite the no smoking sign. But we had more important things to discuss than that.

'What the hell is this all about?' she demanded when Dave and I entered the room. 'I want a lawyer.'

'Where's Bruce Phillips living, Ms Lodge?' I asked, by way of an opener.

'I don't know how many times I have to say this, but I don't know anyone called Bruce Phillips.'

'Really?' I made a pretence of riffling through the file I'd brought with me. 'Apart from paying your shoplifting fine, you've met him several times in the Kookaburra Club. This evening included. And when you were brought to this station and searched, you

254

were found to have an envelope containing a thousand pounds. An envelope that Phillips had handed you only minutes before you were arrested.'

'What have you got in *your* wallet?' Donna asked sarcastically. 'Have I been arrested for possessing a thousand pounds?'

'Why did Phillips give you that money?'

'I keep telling you that I don't know a Phillips. The man who gave me that money was Geoffrey Forman. As I told you when you came to Barnes, he's my partner and, strange though it may seem, he gives me housekeeping from time to time.'

I couldn't help laughing. 'Good try,' I said. 'So you meet up in the Kookaburra Club so that he can hand you your housekeeping money? Funny that. Most people give their partners the housekeeping money at home.' What she didn't realize, or perhaps didn't care about, was that she had just confirmed that Forman *was* Phillips. 'When did he get back from Düsseldorf then?' I asked.

But Donna greeted that question with stony silence.

'We searched your house at Barnes, Ms Lodge,' said Dave, 'after you'd done a runner, and we found a computer on which was a website advertising the services of prostitutes. On that website was a rather revealing photograph of you, beside which was the name Fleur and some numbers: thirty-eight, twenty-six, thirty-six, if I remember correctly. The website also gave an email address through which clients could obtain your undivided attention for as long as they were prepared to pay for it.'

Donna said nothing, but was obviously shaken by what we knew and, probably, the sudden realization that she'd been foolish enough to leave the computer behind when she fled. And, no doubt, she was wondering what Phillips would say when he found out.

'By the way,' Dave continued, 'Nick Lloyd is not best pleased with you. He sent an email asking for you to turn a trick for him last Tuesday night.'

'I don't know what you're talking about,' said Donna, 'and I want to phone a friend.'

'Why?' I asked.

'To tell him I've been arrested, of course.'

'Have you got a mobile?'

'Of course I have, but that sergeant at the desk took it off me when I was brought in here.'

'Get the lady a phone, Dave,' I said.

A couple of minutes later, Dave returned with a phone and plugged it into a socket. 'There you are,' he said. 'Dial nine for an outside line.'

'I'm entitled to make the call in private,' snapped Donna.

'No you're not,' said Dave. 'That only applies to a discussion with your legal representative.'

Donna shot Dave a scathing glance and tapped out a number. 'Hello, it's me. I've been arrested ... West End Central ... I don't know why ... Yes, all right.' She replaced the receiver and sat back in her chair, a smug expression on her face, before lighting another cigarette. 'And don't bother trying to trace it,' she said. 'It was to a pay-as-you-go mobile. And now perhaps you'll tell me what you're going to charge me with. It certainly won't be prostitution, because I don't solicit in a public place.'

'You should have become a lawyer,' Dave observed mildly.

'Which reminds me,' said Donna. 'I asked for a solicitor.'

'You won't be needing one,' I said. 'You're not being charged with anything. You're free to go.'

Donna sat bolt upright. 'Then what the bloody hell did you bring me in here for?' she demanded with a flash of temper that had not been apparent before.

'On suspicion of harbouring a fleeing felon,' said Dave, conjuring up an impressive bit of legalistic jargon that was more eloquent than accurate.

'Oh? And who might that be?' asked Donna and laughed.

It was time to bring this mouthy tom down to earth. And time to play the next hand.

'We are looking for Bruce Phillips in connection with the murder of Patricia Hunter, whose body was found in the Thames on Wednesday the twelfth of June,' I said.

I could see that Donna Lodge had paled, even beneath her make-up. There was a moment's hesitation before she recovered herself. 'I've not heard of either of them,' she said, but there was little conviction in her protestation of ignorance.

'That's all right then,' I said. 'Because anyone withholding information about Bruce Phillips is likely to find themselves standing beside him in the dock at the Old Bailey.' Not that I thought there was much chance of that.

The moment Donna Lodge had left the police station, I rang Kate Ebdon's mobile, but the result was disappointing.

'He left about twenty minutes ago, guv,' she said.

'So he didn't get a call on his mobile *before* he left.'

'No, guv.'

And so we were no further forward. My elaborate plan to arrest Donna, despite there being nothing with which to charge her, had come to nought.

But I still had Plan B up my sleeve. I'd arranged for her to be followed, the moment she left the nick, by some of the officers whom Alan Cleaver, the commander's deputy, had lent me. I reckoned that my last statement would have thrown Donna into a panic, and that she wouldn't be able to resist telling Phillips, as soon as possible, what we had wanted from her.

But as it turned out, I was wrong about that too.

* * *

Dennis, the CSE who was a dab hand at computers, was unable to offer any further assistance either. His report confirmed what he had said last Friday at Barnes: the email address on the website could be picked up anywhere in the world. I rang him and asked him to explain what Donna had said about a pay-as-you-go mobile phone being untraceable.

'She was quite right, Mr Brock. Any one of the shops that specializes in mobile phones will sell you a pay-as-you-go phone. They'll allocate you a number and away you go. You top it up, so to speak, by purchasing talk time from just about anywhere. Even supermarkets, these days.'

'I get the impression, Dennis, that you're telling me that I'll have a hard job tracing this guy.'

'I reckon so, Mr Brock. For a start you don't know where he might have bought it, so you can't find out the number, and even if you were lucky to get the number, the guy might have bought it second-hand anyway. It's virtually impossible to trace it. Even if you'd done a one-four-seven-one after Donna Lodge had finished her call from the nick, you'd only have got a number, but trying to track down who owns it...' Dennis gave an expressive shrug. 'Well, forget it.'

'Thanks, Dennis,' I said, trying to keep the disappointment out of my voice.

'No joy, guv?' asked Dave.

'No. This bugger's too clever by half, Dave.'

'I think we'd more or less come to that conclusion,' said Dave.

The mistake I'd made – one of many I'd made in this damned enquiry – was to assume that Donna Lodge would leave the police station and get a taxi to wherever it was that she was living now. But she didn't. She walked back to the Kookaburra Club, went past it and got into her own car. And the cab that the surveillance officers had managed to hire was no match for the Alfa Romeo. That one of the following officers had evidence of at least three counts of reckless driving and one of ignoring a red traffic light, before they lost her completely, did little to help. Oh well!

'I think we'll do the Barnes address again, Dave,' I said, more out of desperation than anything constructive.

'I doubt that Phillips will have gone back there, guv,' said Dave.

'So do I, Dave, but when we found the computer, we thought we'd got all the answers. I'm not sure that we searched thoroughly enough.'

'We could bugger him up completely, guv,' said Dave, peeling yet another banana.

'In what way?'

'How about ordering up Phillips's entire collection of birds for the same night in different parts of London and then knock 'em off.'

'What for? They're not committing any offence. Do it if you like, but you can use your credit card. Sure as hell I'm not using mine.'

'Ah,' said Dave, 'I never thought of that.' He seemed as gloomy as me about the whole business.

'It's not a bad idea, even so, Dave. We might try calling up say, Petal, and seeing if she can shed any light on Phillips's whereabouts.' However, it didn't take long for me to abandon that brainwave. 'On second thoughts it'd probably make the commander's eyes water if I claimed that on expenses. And I doubt that Petal would say any more than Kimberley, Domino or Fleur. I think we'll scrub it.'

On Tuesday morning, we returned to 13 Ridgely Road with another warrant, and Linda and a couple of her CSEs. Our last warrant was still stuck to the hall mirror, from which, detective that I am, I deduced that no one had returned since last we were there.

'What are we looking for, guv?' asked Dave.

'Everything and anything,' I said. 'But in unlikely places. The sort of places we didn't look in before.'

It took an hour. And then Linda appeared flourishing a piece of paper.

'Donald thinks he's found something that might be useful, Mr Brock,' she said, handing me the slip. 'It was tucked in behind a tea caddy in one of the kitchen cabinets.'

'What is it?'

'It's a request for information from the local council.'

I studied the drab official form. It noted that Geoffrey Forman had rented a lock-up garage at the rear of a block of flats in Breda Gardens, Barnes. It went on to ask whether Forman was responsible for paying council tax on the premises, or if this liability would fall upon the owner of the said garage.

'Where the hell's Breda Gardens?' I asked of no one in particular.

'No idea,' said Dave. And neither had anyone else.

'Well someone find out for God's sake,' I said, somewhat brusquely.

Dave rang the local nick on his mobile. 'Just round the corner from here, guv,' he said, cancelling the call.

The council form had specified that the owner of the lock-up garage was a Mr Thomas of 6 Delilah Court. We promptly visited 6 Delilah Court. But Mr Thomas appeared not to be there. Well, he wouldn't be, would he? But his wife was.

'Oh yes,' she said. 'My husband rented that to Mr Forman about two months ago.'

I was ill-disposed to explain specifically why the garage was of interest to us, but told Mrs Thomas that, in pursuance of a serious criminal matter, we would be obliged to look inside it.

Mrs Thomas demurred at that. 'Well, I don't know,' she said. 'You see, Mr Forman – he's a very nice man incidentally – wanted it to keep furniture in. And as we've got another garage, we were quite happy to let him have it.'

'I can get a search warrant, Mrs Thomas,' I explained, 'but it would make my job much easier if we were able just to have a quick look in there.'

'Oh well, I suppose it'll be all right.' And with that somewhat grudging authority, Mrs Thomas closed the door.

'Don't know why we bothered,' muttered Dave.

Donald, the CSE who'd found the form, removed the padlock in a trice. There was none of Geoffrey Forman's furniture inside the garage, but there was what proved to be an extremely telling piece of evidence: a Ford van.

And that was only the start.

'I think you'd better get the rest of your team up here, Linda,' I said.

But Linda Mitchell was already busy on her mobile.

Sixteen

The garage was fitted with shelving on which were a few half-empty paint pots and an old golf club. Three or four lengths of curtain rail had been abandoned in a corner at the far end, next to a dartboard with a single dart in it, and a piece of carpet. Slung from the rafters was a twelve-foot length of blueish fibreglass that I presumed was a boat mast. All of which, I imagined, was a legacy from Mr Thomas. With the exception, I hoped, of the carpet.

After a cursory inspection of the Ford van, Linda suggested that it should be removed to the forensic science laboratory for a detailed examination.

Dave, in the meantime, had been busy on his mobile. 'The van's registered to a Robert Peel of thirteen Ridgely Road, Barnes, guv.'

'The saucy bastard's taking the piss,' I said. Robert Peel was the founder of the Metropolitan Police. But it did explain why, when checks had been made with the DVLA, they told us that the only vehicle registered to Geoffrey Forman was a BMW.

After several further calls, Dave managed to impose upon the Transport Branch – which is probably called something else now, courtesy of the Funny Names Squad – to send a flatbed truck to collect the Ford. But not before he'd thrown in the commander's name to emphasize the urgency. Transport Branch obviously hadn't met the commander, otherwise it would have had no effect. But it appeared to work in this case.

An hour later, the truck arrived. The crew alighted, sucked through its collective teeth, muttered something about Health and Safety, and was finally imposed upon to winch the Ford van on to its vehicle.

The removal of the van revealed the existence of an inspection pit. But this was no ordinary inspection pit. Once the cover had been removed, we were treated to the sight of a steel safe against the wall at one end of the pit. It was fitted with both key and combination locks, and alongside it was a coil of thin electrical flex.

'Well now, ain't that interesting,' said Dave, and, turning to Linda, he asked, 'Reckon your blokes can banjo that peter?' It was one of his rare excursions into the criminal vernacular. For banjo read 'break into', and for peter read 'safe'.

'I hope so,' said Linda, and jumped into the inspection pit for a closer look at the safe.

'There's only one problem,' I said. 'We don't know that it's Forman's safe. It might belong to Mr Thomas.'

'Ah, good point, guv,' said Dave.

'Which means,' I continued, 'that we'll have

265

to get hold of the said Mr Thomas before we can go any further.'

Leaving the CSEs to guard our find, Dave and I returned to 6 Delilah Court and spoke, once more, to Mrs Thomas.

'We have searched the garage your husband rented to Mr Forman,' I began, 'and we found a safe in the inspection pit.'

'Really?' Mrs Thomas did not seem too excited about this. Certainly not as excited as we were.

'Do you know if it belongs to your husband?'

'No.'

'No, it doesn't, or no, you don't know?'

'I don't know,' said Mrs Thomas, and then, caution dawning at last, she asked, 'Anyway, how do I know you're policemen?'

And to think of all the money the police waste on crime prevention and the equally useless Neighbourhood Watch scheme. I showed her my warrant card but, as she'd probably never seen one before, it didn't count for much. Nevertheless, she seemed satisfied.

'Can you tell me how we can get hold of your husband, Mrs Thomas?' I asked with great patience. 'It is rather urgent.'

'He's upstairs. He works from home.'

Dave glanced skywards, but otherwise re-strained himself from making one of his usual acerbic comments.

'Perhaps we could have a word with him,' I said, still exercising great patience.

Mrs Thomas pondered the request. 'I'll see if he's available,' she said, after due consideration. 'He doesn't care to be interrupted when he's working.'

'Maybe if you were to tell him we're investigating a murder, he could spare us a moment or two,' I said, at last deciding that there was no reason to keep the purpose of our enquiries a secret any longer.

'Oh my goodness!' said Mrs Thomas and disappeared, leaving us standing on the doorstep.

Mr Thomas was a small, bald-headed man with unfashionable glasses and a toothbrush moustache.

'Can I help you?' he asked in the nasal manner one expects of a shop assistant in a gents' outfitters, but rarely finds these days.

'We have reason to believe that Mr Forman may be able to assist us in connection with a murder,' I said. There was little point in disguising our interest in the errant Mr Forman. In the unlikely event that Thomas told Forman, I now believed he wouldn't be telling him something he didn't already know.

'I see,' said Thomas, displaying no change in either his expression or his tone of voice. 'Perhaps you'd better come in.'

At last!

'We have searched the garage you rented to him,' I continued, once we were in the Thomases' sitting room, a sitting room overburdened with bric-à-brac and what I took to be family photographs in silver frames, including, prominently, one of a young man in cap and gown clutching a scroll, 'and we discovered a safe installed in the inspection pit.'

'Really?' Thomas raised his eyebrows.

'Is it your safe, Mr Thomas?'

'No.'

'Were you aware that it was there?' I asked, struggling on.

'No.'

'So I can safely assume it's Mr Forman's, I suppose.'

'Well, I don't know about that,' said Thomas, obviously cautious in assigning ownership of the safe, 'but it's not mine.'

'Thank you, Mr Thomas,' said Dave. 'You've been most helpful.'

We returned to the garage.

'I've had a good look at it, Mr Brock,' said Linda, 'and we're going to have to open it in situ. It seems to be bolted to the floor or the wall, and we'll only be able to get at the bolts once it's open.'

'Can you do it?' I asked.

'Not immediately. I'll have to send for a lance cutter, and that'll take time.'

'How much time?'

'About an hour.'

I glanced at my watch. It was midday. 'We'll send for the cavalry and get some lunch,' I said. 'Ring the local nick, Dave, and get some uniforms round here to mind the place.'

Two PCs eventually arrived and were instructed to stand guard on the garage until we returned.

At one o'clock, following a rushed bite to eat at a local pub, we returned to the garage to find the cutting team waiting for us.

It took them about twenty minutes to remove the door to the safe, but it proved to be well worth the wait.

Inside we found a handbag containing all the usual things that a woman's handbag usually contains: cosmetics, a key, a few tissues and a purse. But it also contained a credit card and a bank card. *And each bore the name of Patricia Hunter.*

'He'll have a job explaining that away,' observed Dave drily. 'I wonder why he hung on to them.'

'There are some murderers who like to keep mementoes, Dave,' I said, 'but God knows why. It usually does for them in the end.'

'So what's next, guv? Round to the Kookaburra Club and knock him off?'

'He won't be there, will he, Dave?' I said.

'There is another thing, guv,' said Dave.

'Which is?'

'Forman might also be Jeremy Payne, and the Robert Peel in whose name the van is registered may be his employer. His mother said he was a van driver.'

'D'you know, Dave,' I said, 'you have a happy knack of fouling up the simplest of enquiries.'

'Just a thought, sir,' said Dave.

'Yeah, but Payne lives in Stockwell. He's unlikely to park his van here in Barnes.'

'Unless the firm he works for is in Barnes, guv,' said Dave, determined, as ever, to have the last word.

But even if Dave's theory turned out to be correct, I realized, too late, that we'd gone about this enquiry all wrong. It had been a mistake to interview Donna Lodge at Barnes before we'd spoken to Dave's mate on the Extradition Unit, and then to have compounded that error by arresting her in the vain hope that she might point the finger at Forman, alias Phillips, for Patricia Hunter's murder. All we'd actually succeeded in doing was to warn Phillips of our interest.

And on top of everything else, Jeremy Payne appeared to have done a runner.

The trouble with criminal investigation is that you never know these things in advance. Making decisions is very easy with hindsight.

But of one thing I was certain: Phillips would never show his face in the K Club again. But we had to try.

Domino was due to show up at five o'clock that evening to collect her pay. Dave lay in wait with Kate Ebdon, but the coarse cockney whore with the prosaic name of Marlene West didn't appear. Nor did Phillips.

For the next five days, teams of officers kept observation outside the Kookaburra Club. On the inside, DS Kate Ebdon and DCs Appleby and Armitage sat around spending some of the commissioner's money, but achieving nothing else. DC Nicola Chance spoke to Lisa, the hostess who had first

270

alerted us to Phillips's presence, but she claimed not to have seen him since the night Appleby and Armitage had arrested Donna Lodge. And Donna Lodge didn't show up either.

Although I was certain that Phillips was not going to return to the K Club, I decided to let the observation run until first thing on Monday morning. There was little doubt in my mind that he'd changed his centre of operations or, at least, changed the venue he'd used for paying his prostitutes.

But in the meantime, I tried one last throw. Dave and I visited the expensive block of service flats in Islington where Marlene West, alias Domino, had told us she rented an apartment. Perhaps she could be persuaded to tell us what the new payment arrangements were.

But according to a neighbour, Miss West had left at nine o'clock on Sunday morning. *Twelve hours after we'd talked to her outside Nick Lloyd's apartment.* The helpful neighbour further volunteered the information that a man had arrived to help Miss West shift her belongings.

'You didn't happen to notice the number of the car, I suppose?' I asked hopefully. 'Or the make?'

'It was a blue one.'

We didn't bother to ask for a description: we knew bloody well who it would have been. Bruce Phillips was turning out to be a master

271

of damage limitation. And it seemed that he frightened Domino more than we did.

No sooner had we returned to Curtis Green from Islington than we were off again.

'I've just had a call from Brixton nick, sir,' said Colin Wilberforce. 'About ten minutes ago a Mrs Payne walked in with her son Jeremy. According to the station officer, she practically had him in a hammerlock-and-bar.'

Mrs Payne and her son, guarded by a uniformed constable, a rare sight indeed, were in an interview room at Brixton police station.

'I've brought him here because you want to talk to him,' said Mrs Payne. 'He only came home this morning. I don't know where he'd been, and I suppose it was my fault telephoning him to tell him that you'd called at the house. But I told him it's no good running away from the police because they'll always find you.'

Oh, such faith.

'Thank you, Mrs Payne,' I said. 'I'll interview him on his own, if you don't mind.'

'But—'

'How old is your son, Mrs Payne?'

'He'll be twenty-six next birthday.'

'In that case the law does not require the attendance of an adult.' I turned to the PC. 'Perhaps you'd take Mrs Payne for a cup of tea,' I said.

Jeremy Payne was a good-looking lad in a

weak sort of way, and I could quite understand why he had aspirations for the acting profession. Doubtless his friends had told him that, with his looks, he ought to 'go on the stage'. *Oh well!*

'I know what this is about,' said Payne before I had a chance to say anything. 'It's about Patricia Hunter, isn't it? I saw in the paper that she'd been murdered.'

'Yes, it is. So why did you run away?'

'I thought you must have known what I'd done.'

Heavens above, it can't be this easy.

I toyed with the idea of cautioning this young man, but decided that if he had murdered Patricia Hunter, he would undoubtedly repeat his confession if, later, I *did* caution him. In the coppering game, one develops an instinct for assessing character.

'So what *did* you do?'

'I told her I wanted to marry her.'

'And did you want to marry her?'

'I wouldn't have minded, but I knew she wouldn't want to marry a van driver from Stockwell, so I pretended I was something else.'

'Such as?'

'I told her I had a swish flat in Docklands and a place in the South of France.'

'Where in the South of France?' asked Dave.

There was a moment's hesitation. 'St Raphaël. I knew the place, see, because I went there for a holiday last year. It was only a

273

package holiday, but it meant I could sound quite knowledgeable.' Payne's accent had become more sophisticated during the telling of this tale, and I could understand that he was probably quite good as an amateur thespian. It certainly appeared that he'd fooled Patricia Hunter with his acting.

'And you told her you had a Ferrari, too,' commented Dave.

'No, a Porsche,' said Payne, as though the technical details of his lie were important. 'But I haven't.'

'Where were you between the tenth and twelfth of June, Mr Payne?'

Jeremy consulted a small diary. 'On stage,' he said, somewhat loftily.

'What, all day?'

'No, of course not. I was working during the day and went straight from there to the hall where we were doing *Cabaret*.'

'Bit ambitious for an amateur company, wasn't it?' suggested Dave.

'We're really very good,' said Jeremy, preening himself slightly, 'even if I do say so myself.'

'Is there anyone who can verify that?'

'Well, I was delivering all day. I work for an electrical wholesaler. You can ask my boss. And as far as the evenings are concerned, you could check with Lorraine.'

'Lorraine who?' Dave took out his pen and opened his pocket book.

'Can't remember. Martin, I think, but she played Sally Bowles. She's very good. I played

Emcee.'

'And after the show, you took her to bed, did you?' asked Dave, making a shrewd guess.

Payne blushed. 'How did you know that?' he demanded.

'I guessed,' said Dave. 'What tales did you tell *her*?'

'Well, I er—'

'Don't bother,' said Dave with a grin. 'And what's more, the only reason you spun this fanny to Patricia Hunter was so that you could get her into bed, wasn't it? You knew bloody well that you couldn't keep up the pretence, because once she found out the truth she'd've been off like a long dog.'

'You can go, Mr Payne, once we've taken your fingerprints,' I said, 'and I advise you not to tell stories of that sort to any more prostitutes, because their minders have a reputation for turning nasty with people who bullshit in order to get a freebie.'

'She wasn't a prostitute,' exclaimed Payne angrily, 'she was an actress.'

'Oh dear!' said Dave, 'you do have a lot to learn, Mr Payne. But take it from me, Patricia Hunter was a professional whore.'

However, the possibility of Payne's involvement in the death of Patricia Hunter was ruled out by the report from the forensic science lab that was waiting for me when Dave and I returned to the office.

The traces of oil and particles found on the garage floor matched those that had been found in the grazing on Patricia Hunter's back. And the fibres found in the dead show-girl's hair tallied with those taken from the piece of carpet that had been in a corner of the garage. The coil of electrical flex had been examined and the scientist who had taken Sarah Dawson's place at the laboratory was convinced that the ligature used to strangle Patricia Hunter matched it. Significantly, it also revealed traces of greasepaint.

But the best bit of all was that Phillips's fingerprints had been found *inside* the safe. *And on Patricia Hunter's credit card.* And they didn't tally with the set we'd taken from Jeremy Payne.

'Got him, the careless bastard,' I said.

'All we've got to do now is find him,' said Dave, selecting a large orange from his canvas briefcase. 'What about the van, guv?'

The Ford van had revealed traces – albeit minute, but that was good enough – of the same carpet fibres that had been found in Patricia Hunter's hair, and satisfied me that Phillips had used it to convey her dead body wrapped in the carpet we'd found, to wher-ever he had pitched her into the river. And given that the crucial evidence had been found at Barnes, it's likely that he had driven less than half a mile to do it.

I hate a waiting game and to fill in the time I decided to deal with some of the loose ends that inevitably crop up in a murder enquiry. And given that we now knew that Phillips

276

masqueraded as Forman, it was also possible that he had assumed other identities. There again, either Tim Oliver or Edward Archer could have been the murderer. The weary business of elimination went on.

Both the St Malo harbourmaster and the French customs had confirmed the presence of the judge's yacht during the crucial period. And although the harbourmaster had seen a man and a woman on deck from time to time, he was unable to confirm that it was the judge.

Tim Oliver, however, was a different ball game. To start with, his secretary told us, somewhat sniffily, that Mr Oliver had certainly been at a business conference in Birmingham, which, happily for him, had lasted from Monday the tenth of June to Wednesday the twelfth. But, when we told her that we would check – because this was a murder enquiry – she eventually admitted that he hadn't been in Birmingham at all. He had spent the relevant period in a hotel in Winchester, and most of it in bed. *With her.* Oh well!

Frank Mead had made several attempts to see Edward Archer, another of the names in Patricia Hunter's address book, but Archer had not been at home on the occasions Frank had called at Wilmslow Gardens, Stockwell. However, he had verified, from what we call local enquiries, that that was where he lived. I decided to pay him a visit.

And he wasn't at home this time, either.

The man who answered the door was about forty, tall and well built, with a completely shaven head and an earring in his left ear. 'Ted Archer? No, mate. He's away at the moment. Who wants to know?'

Could it be a coincidence that this man spoke with an Australian accent?

'We're police officers,' I said, producing my warrant card.

'What again? You're the third or fourth lot of coppers we've had round here. Christ, what's he done? Ted's as straight as a die.'

'Is Mr Archer, by any chance, an Australian?' I asked.

'Yeah, we both are. Why d'you ask?'

I was suddenly possessed of a gut feeling that we should have tracked down Edward Archer much earlier in this investigation. Was he Phillips alias Forman in yet another guise? 'I think it would be better if we came in and had a chat, Mr, er...?'

'Palmer. Ned Palmer. Yeah, sure, come in.' He nodded in Dave's direction. 'He a copper an' all?'

'Yes,' said Dave. 'Life's full of little surprises, isn't it?'

'Have you any idea where Mr Archer is?' I asked, once we were settled in the living room.

'Not a clue, mate. Last time I rang him on his mobile, he was in India. Least, that's where he said he was, but he could've been anywhere, I suppose.'

'Yes,' I said, not without a measure of misgiving. 'What exactly does Mr Archer do for a living, Mr Palmer?'

'Christ, mate, call me Ned. That's us: Ted and Ned.' Palmer gave a throaty laugh. 'We've never been ones to stand on ceremony. Now then, let me think: what *does* Ted do?' Palmer gazed up at the ceiling. 'He's something in the City. God knows what and God knows where, but he's always off round the world somewhere.'

'When did you last see him?'

'Must have been a week ago, but he was in and out like a bloody rocket. Trouble is, I work all hours, and sometimes we don't see each other for weeks on end.'

'What do *you* do, then?' asked Dave.

'I hope you blokes don't mind me asking, but what the hell's this all about? Has Ted got himself into some sort of bother? It's not an immigration thing, surely? I mean, we've both got work permits and God knows how many other bits of paper.'

'We think Mr Archer may be able to assist us with enquiries we're making regarding a murder, Ned,' said Dave.

Even though Palmer had asked us to call him Ned, he seemed somehow disconcerted that Dave had done so. Or perhaps it was mention of a murder. His next utterance proved it. '*A murder!* Bloody hell. Ted's had nothing to do with any murder, for Christ's sake.' For a moment or two, he stared at the floor, shaking his head.

'My sergeant asked what *you* do for a

living,' I said.

Palmer was obviously taken aback by the realization that Archer might be able to help us solve a murder or, worse, might have committed one. 'Me?' He looked up. 'I'm a deep-sea diver. I've been working off the Isles of Scilly lately. Sometimes I don't get home for a week at a time. Sometimes it's months. Matter of fact, you were lucky to catch me now.'

'D'you know the Kookaburra Club?' Dave asked.

'Yeah, sure I know it,' said Palmer. 'Go for a drink there sometimes. Not that often though. It's usually full of bloody Aussies.' And he laughed.

'And Mr Archer? Does he go there too?'

'Yeah, I think so. Now you mention it, we've been there together a couple of times.' Palmer paused. 'Is that where this murder happened?'

'No.' Now it was my turn to pause. 'D'you know if Mr Archer ever used a website to engage the services of a prostitute?'

Palmer laughed outright. 'Yeah, sure he did. It's not illegal, is it? Is this what this is all about?'

'Did *you* ever use such a website?'

'Yeah. Why?'

Dave produced the computer printout on which Fleur, Domino and Kimberley, among others, appeared. 'D'you recognize any of these women, Mr Palmer?' he asked.

After a few moments' scrutiny, the Australian pointed to a black girl who traded under the name of Ebony. 'Had her a couple of times. She's great. I'd recommend her to anyone.' Rather pointedly, Palmer glanced at Dave.

'D'you happen to know if Mr Archer ever engaged a girl known as Dolores?'

'Damned if I know, mate. I know he had Ebony once or twice, but you'll have to ask him about the others.'

'How about this girl, then?' Dave asked, showing Palmer the photograph of Patricia Hunter.

'Don't know her. Who's she?'

'She's the one who was murdered. That's Dolores.'

'Christ, what sick bastard would want to croak a pretty kid like that?'

'That's what I'm trying to find out, Ned,' I said. 'Have you any idea when Mr Archer will be back home?'

'No, mate, sorry. The first I usually know of it is when he comes crashing through the door. He's a noisy bastard is Ted.'

'How long have you been in England?' I asked.

'About a year.'

'And Mr Archer?'

'A lot longer than that. About six or seven years, I suppose.'

'And where in Australia does Mr Archer come from?'

'Sydney,' said Palmer without hesitation.

'When were you last in Brighton, Ned?'

asked Dave with a suddenness designed to catch Palmer on the hop.

'Brighton? Now let me see. Must have been about seven or eight years ago.'

'But you said just now that you'd only been in England a year.'

'That's right, mate. I'm talking about the Brighton in South Australia. I was born in Gleneig, not far from Adelaide. Brighton's the next town of any size south of there.'

Dave and I returned to Curtis Green with a feeling of foreboding. Was Archer really Phillips? He came from Sydney, had been in the country about the same length of time as Phillips, and had had dealings with the prostitutes in Phillips's stable. But we only had Palmer's word for it that Archer had engaged their services. For all we knew, he could be running them. After all, Palmer had admitted that he hardly ever saw the bloke. And they'd both frequented the Kookaburra Club.

We had to find Archer as soon as we could. And that wasn't going to be easy, because I had a nasty feeling that Palmer was not telling us the truth. If he'd been living in the same house as Archer for a year, how come he didn't know exactly where Archer worked? Unless Archer didn't want him to know. On the other hand, I'd come to the conclusion that Palmer wasn't the brightest of individuals. But, as every policeman finds out sooner or later, appearances and first impressions can be deceptive.

282

Seventeen

By now, I had done a number of things that policemen always do.

Some time ago, Phillips's name had been entered on the Police National Computer as being wanted for extradition, and I'd now added the information that I wished to question him in connection with the murder of Patricia Hunter, and for good measure included the name of Edward Archer as a possible alias. In addition to listing the BMW registered in Forman's name, I also included details of Donna Lodge's Alfa Romeo, with instructions that she was to be detained in connection with the same matter.

I was not surprised that it was Donna Lodge who was found first.

It was four o'clock on that Monday afternoon that Dave and I once again came face to face with the prostitute known to her clients as Fleur.

A traffic car patrolling the Notting Hill area had spotted her driving sedately along Holland Park Avenue, and had given her a pull, as the Black Rats are wont to say, and promptly arrested her. She was now in

Notting Hill nick.

'I want to know why I was arrested by two common policemen,' she began. 'And if you're going to talk about Bruce Phillips again, I'll tell you what—'

'Save your breath,' I said. 'Bruce Phillips and Geoffrey Forman are one and the same, as we now know and you've known all along. Last Tuesday we found a lock-up garage at the rear of a block of flats in Breda Gardens, Barnes. That garage had been rented by Phillips in the name of Forman. When the garage was searched, we found a safe containing various items of property belonging to Patricia Hunter, also known as Dolores.'

'I don't believe it,' protested Donna. 'You're making it up.' But judging by the speed with which the blood had drained from her face, she had been shocked at how much we had discovered.

'The interesting piece of paper that led us first to find and then to search that garage,' I continued, 'was found in the kitchen cabinet at thirteen Ridgely Road, Barnes. Your kitchen cabinet, Ms Lodge.'

'I didn't know anything about that. Nothing at all.'

'In that case, you will appreciate how important it is for us to find Bruce Phillips as quickly as possible. By the way, we also found a Ford van in that garage.'

'Really?' Donna lit another cigarette.

'Registered in the name of Robert Peel.'

'I know nothing about it. And I don't know

anything about any Robert Peel.'

Which confirmed all that I'd read about the school history syllabus having gone to pot in recent years.

'I suppose that was Geoffrey's doing,' continued Donna. 'He must have put that name on the form, or whatever it is one does.' All the fight had gone out of Donna now. 'I knew that he was wanted in Australia for something,' she said quietly, thus confirming to my satisfaction, yet again, that Forman was Phillips, 'but he told me it was all a mistake. Something to do with outstanding debts. I'm sure he wouldn't have killed anyone.'

'Where is he, Ms Lodge?' I persisted, certain that she knew the answer.

'I don't know,' protested Donna. 'I honestly don't know.'

'After you were arrested by my officers last Monday and I interviewed you at West End Central police station, you telephoned Phillips and told him what had happened to you. And that led him to panic because he knew that if the police had found *you* it wouldn't be long before we found *him.*'

'I admit that I phoned *Geoffrey.*' Donna put emphasis on the name, apparently still intent on denying that Forman was Phillips.

'Furthermore, we've learned' – actually it was an assumption – 'that he has ceased to use the Kookaburra Club as a venue for paying you girls what you earn from prostitution. So where do you have to go now to collect your pay?'

'We don't. He rang me, and I suppose he rang the other girls, to say that in future he would send the money by post.'

'What, cash?'

'Of course not. By cheque.'

'Do you have one of those cheques?'

By way of a reply, Donna withdrew a cheque from her handbag. It was for a thousand pounds drawn on a well-known high street bank. *And signed by Robert Peel.* I handed it to Dave, who took a note of the details before returning it to Donna. But we both knew that we wouldn't find the mythical Robert Peel at the address the bank had for him. Even if we managed to persuade the bank to reveal it. But I did wonder why Donna had parted with the cheque so easily. It was only later on that I discovered why.

'Where are you living now?'

'In a hotel in the West End, just for the time being, but I'm going back to Barnes.'

'Not today you're not,' I said.

'Why?' asked Donna. 'What's going to happen now?'

'You will be detained here pending further enquiries, Ms Lodge. I'm by no means satisfied that you were not involved in the murder of Patricia Hunter and the disposal of her body.'

At that point Donna Lodge broke down completely. Great sobs wracked her body and she ferreted about in her handbag for a tissue. By the time she recovered and looked up, she was an absolute mess: eyes red-rimmed, mascara running down her cheeks and her hair – previously well coifed – disarranged. But despite the compelling histrionics, I was convinced that she was play-acting.

'If I tell you all I know, will that help me?'

I glanced at Dave. He knew what I wanted him to do, and he knew I could never remember the words of the caution. And I'd lost my little card with it all on.

He switched on the tape recorder, told it what it needed to know and began. 'Donna Lodge, you do not have to say anything, but it may harm your defence if you do not mention when questioned something which you later rely on in court. Anything you do say may be given in evidence.' And after a pause, he added, 'You are entitled to the services of a solicitor if you wish to have one present.'

'No, I don't.' Donna shook her head and, after a lengthy pause, added, 'I suppose that in a sense it was Patricia's own fault really.'

Well that was hardly original. Strange how the victim always seems to be responsible for his or her own demise. At least in the eyes of the killer.

'Go on,' I said.

'It was after she was arrested for shoplifting. Patricia wanted no more to do with it because the magistrate remanded her on bail for reports and said he was considering a custodial sentence. He said he knew it was a hoisting ring. Well, Patricia went into a blind panic, but Bruce told her not to worry, that worse things happen at sea, or something trite like that. Then he was stupid enough to tell her that he was wanted in Australia and that he'd take care of her. He knew how to avoid going to prison, he said, and he'd make sure she didn't go either.'

'But she was fined,' I said.

Donna smiled. 'I know, but Bruce told her that if she got done for prostitution, she'd go to prison just the same, which was nonsense, of course. That's why he told her to keep moving from one address to another. Patricia was a devious little bitch though,' she continued, 'and she threatened to tell the police where he was if he didn't pay her double for getting laid. It was blackmail really.'

'Which is why Phillips kept moving as well, I suppose,' I commented, but Donna didn't respond to that.

'And that wasn't all,' Donna continued. 'To begin with, he did pay her extra, but that wasn't good enough for her. She wanted to marry him, the silly little cow. Well, Bruce wasn't up for that.'

'So he killed her?'

'I didn't know that. In fact, I still can't believe it. All I do know is that she disappeared. I thought that he'd paid for her to go to the South of France. Just to get her out of the way. That's what Patricia said he'd told her anyway.'

Funny how the South of France kept cropping up in this enquiry.

'Three years ago, you and she shared a flat

at Petersfield Street, Fulham, where you ran a call-girl service. Where was Phillips then?'

'He'd gone back to Australia. He'd heard somehow that he was wanted there, so he decided to lie low for a while. But a year later he was back.'

'Are you saying that he went back to Australia, knowing that he was wanted there?' I was beginning to think that Phillips wasn't so clever after all, or that Donna was still not telling the whole truth. Or didn't know what the truth was.

Donna shrugged. 'I don't know why he went. Perhaps he didn't go at all. All I do know is that he disappeared for a while. He said he'd been to Australia, but I don't really know where he went.'

That sounded more like it. It would have been crass stupidity for him to return to the very country that wanted him for several counts of long-firm fraud. And Phillips wasn't stupid. The likelihood was that he had taken refuge elsewhere in the United Kingdom. Created a new identity for himself perhaps, but he wouldn't have dared risk attempting to leave the country, even less entering Australia.

'But then he came back?'

'Yes, but he decided that the shoplifting game was too dangerous. That's when he set up the website for us. There were about ten of us girls altogether and he took our photographs in the nude' – Donna gave a coy little smile – 'and gave us names like

Fleur and Domino and Dolores, and set up what he said was a foolproof way of getting business for us without getting into trouble himself.'

'And you've no idea where he is now?'

'No, honestly.'

'But you do now admit that Geoffrey Forman and Bruce Phillips are one and the same.'

'Yes,' said Donna softly.

'To your knowledge, did Phillips ever use the name Archer, Edward Archer?'

'No, I've never heard that name.'

Which might have been the truth. There was no telling with this woman.

'When did you last see Patricia Hunter, Ms Lodge?'

Donna gave a convulsive sob, maybe at the thought that the man she'd been living with could be a ruthless killer. There again, it may have been the thought that she too could finish up in prison. 'About six or seven weeks ago, I suppose.'

'And where was that?'

'Bruce and I were having a drink in the Kookaburra Club when she came in to collect her money. Bruce usually handed the girls an envelope and they left, but she started a row at the bar, shouting and screaming at him. By the time she eventually left, Bruce was in a furious temper.'

'Did he say why?'

'Yes, he told me that she was trying to put the arm on him again and he wasn't having any of it. He was really steamed up about her. I told him to forget it, but he said that if she did what she'd threatened to do, which was to tell the police, he'd finish up behind bars in Australia.'

'Did he say anything else?'

'He said that she'd have to be stopped, but I didn't think he meant he was going to kill her. I still can't believe that he would have done.'

'Why was she working as a chorus girl in *Scatterbrain*?' asked Dave.

'She'd always said that she wanted to go on the stage. She reckoned she was fed up with being screwed every night for peanuts. I don't know where she got that idea. We only turned a trick three times a week at the most, and got five hundred a time for it. And that was after Bruce took his cut.'

'What was so special about you that Phillips allowed you to live with him?' I asked.

There was a long pause and then Donna flashed me a superior smile. 'We're married,' she said, and lit another cigarette. 'So you can forget any ideas about me giving evidence against him.'

Terrific! The icing on the cake. If she really *was* married to Phillips, she would be neither competent nor compellable to give evidence against him. Damn and blast the bloody woman!

And she'd known it all along, the smug bitch. That's why she'd told us all she knew. But even then, I thought that she'd only been

291

telling us half-truths. And when we analysed it, she'd really told us little that we didn't know already.

But why had we not found a trace of that marriage when the usual checks were made at the General Register Office at Southport?

'Where were you married?' I asked in a voice that even I thought was remarkably restrained.

'Scotland,' said Donna.

Which, of course, explained it.

'But even though you're married, he still sends you out to get screwed three times a week.'

'I enjoy my work,' said Donna.

It was nigh on eight o'clock by the time a frustrated Dave and I returned to Curtis Green. I was on the point of abandoning the day and going down to the Red Lion for a drink when Gavin Creasey, the night-duty incident-room sergeant, rang through to my office.

'I just got a phone call from the station officer at Brixton, sir.'

'Not Mrs Payne again, surely?'

'No, sir.' Creasey sounded somewhat puzzled, but he wasn't as conversant with the twists and turns of the enquiry as the rest of us, and Payne's name probably didn't ring any bells with him. 'The sergeant there said that an Edward Archer walked into the nick about ten minutes ago. Apparently he thinks you want to talk to him. The station officer said he checked the PNC and you've got Archer flagged up.'

'Too bloody right, I have, Gavin. Get back on to Brixton nick and tell them under no circumstances to let this guy go until I get there. I don't care if they put him in a straight-jacket and bung him in a cell, but they're to hang on to him. Got it?'

'Yes, sir,' said Gavin.

'My mate Ned Palmer reckons you've been looking for me,' said Archer. 'What's the problem? Ned said something about a murder.' He shook his head in apparent bewilderment. 'I don't know anything about any murder.'

Was this guy a great actor, or what?

Dave produced the photograph of Patricia Hunter. 'Did you know this woman?' he asked.

'That's Dolores,' said Archer without any hesitation. 'Ned told me she's the one who was killed.'

Archer was about the same age as Phillips, and could have been him. At least from the rather vague descriptions that we'd been given by the various people who'd claimed to have seen him. Or thought they had.

'How did you meet her?' I asked, not prepared to believe what Ned Palmer had told me.

Archer ran his hand round his chin and grinned inanely. 'Found her on a website. She's a prossy.'

293

'Yes, I know that. How many times did you meet up with her?'

'About three, I reckon. She was pretty bloody good for a pommy sheila.'

'Where did this take place?'

Archer thought about that for a moment. 'A couple of times down my place in Stockwell, when Ned was at work, like, and once at some flat in Fulham. Petersfield Street, it was. I remembered that because I've got a mate called Peter Field back in Oz.'

'When was this?'

'What, at Petersfield Street? About a year back.'

'Anyone else there at the time?'

Archer laughed. 'You joking? No, mate, it was a one-to-one. Mind you, I wouldn't have minded a threesome. Never thought of it really.'

'And the last time you saw Dolores?'

'Must have been six months ago, I reckon. To tell you the truth, I couldn't afford her any more.'

'Bruce Phillips,' said Dave suddenly.

'Who?' The name seemed to have no effect on Archer.

'Bruce Phillips is an Australian from Sydney.'

'Really? I'm from Sydney too.'

'Have you ever heard of him?' Dave asked.

'No. Should I have done? Damn near every other Australian's called Bruce.'

'He frequents the Kookaburra Club. I understand you occasionally go there,' I said.

'Been there a few times, yes. Never heard of him though. What does he do?'

'He runs the team of prostitutes on the website that you use.'

'Is that a fact?' Archer shook his head. 'No, never heard of him.'

'What do you do, Mr Archer. For a living, I mean.'

'I'm a courier. Carry diamonds and important documents all over the place. It doesn't pay much, but I get to see some good places.' Archer laughed. 'Get to meet some pretty exotic sheilas, too.'

'And where were you the week beginning Monday the tenth of June?'

Archer reached down and picked up his briefcase. Extracting an A4 diary, he riffled through its pages until he found the entry he wanted. 'Week beginning the tenth of June,' he murmured. 'Yeah, got it. On that Monday, I took off for Lagos, Nigeria...' He looked up. 'That's a godforsaken place, I can tell you. Not a decent hotel anywhere. And the bloody beer's warm,' he added in final condemnation. Glancing down at his diary again, he said, 'And I got back here on Thursday the thirteenth, having gone via Kenya with a pile of securities that weighed a ton. Finished up back here in London on the Friday of that week. Here, see for yourself.' And he handed over his diary.

I looked at the entries and, as far as I could tell, they appeared to be genuine. Nevertheless, I asked the name of the firm he worked for. He gave me a business card and invited me to check with his boss.

I did, and Archer was telling the truth.

Another one off the list.

Eighteen

In my book, we now had enough evidence to charge Bruce Phillips with the murder of Patricia Hunter, and possibly even enough to convince the sceptical Crown Prosecution Service to take him to trial. But all of that remained academic until we actually laid hands on the man.

But Phillips was a crafty bastard, and I suspected it would be some time before I had the pleasure of taking him into custody.

Although we still had Donna Lodge banged up in Notting Hill nick, I knew that the law wouldn't allow me to keep her there indefinitely, and there just wasn't the evidence to charge her with anything relating to the Hunter murder. But I was hoping to hang on to her long enough for me to arrest Phillips before she was able to tell him how much we knew and, for that matter, how much she had told us. If he learned of that, he might just kill her. These days you don't get any more porridge for two murders than you do for one. In any case, he would certainly become even more elusive than he was now. If that were possible.

But we'd have to move fast. Even with a

297

superintendent giving the OK for an extension, she'd have to be released by four o'clock on Wednesday morning. Realistically that gave us only tomorrow to catch up with Phillips.

Late on Monday evening, I rang Inspector Steve Granger at home and told him the story so far. He laughed. 'Bad luck, mate,' he said.

Undaunted, I continued. 'Steve, any chance you could get back to Canberra and ask them to send everything they've got on Phillips, whether it seems relevant or not? It's pretty urgent.'

'No probs, mate,' was Granger's confident reply.

Halfway through the following morning, Colin Wilberforce stuck his head round my door. 'Mr Granger at Australia House has got the information you wanted, sir,' he said. 'He suggested you meet him for lunch at the usual restaurant at one o'clock.'

'Splendid,' I said, as ready as ever to take a lunch off our generous colonial friends.

What I didn't know was that the kaleidoscope was about to be shaken again.

The Australian Government, in common with the United States and one or two others, believed in encouraging the police officers attached to their respective missions to entertain their British counterparts in the hope that they might obtain some useful intelligence, *without giving too much in exchange.*

298

The plan was cocked up a bit because the British took a similar view: that the intelligence flow should be incoming rather than outgoing.

The result was something of a cagey stalemate until sufficient mutual confidence had been engendered between the individuals concerned. And then they swapped information quite freely and enjoyed eating at the expense of their respective governments. And laughing up their sleeves while doing it. Metaphorically, of course.

As a result, the restaurant where Steve Granger and I usually met was one of the better-class eating establishments in the West End.

Steve was already there, and there was a large malt whisky waiting for me, but it was not until the meal was over that he produced a slim file from the briefcase at his feet.

'This is just about everything that we've got on this guy, Harry. He's got a few previous convictions. Minor stuff really: a bit of thieving, selling cannabis at rock festivals when he was a youngster, that sort of thing. But then, as I said the last time we talked about him, he got into long-firm fraud. In every bloody state in Australia. Cunning bastard.'

'How come he never got captured then, Steve?' I asked.

'I suppose he'd worked out that if he moved from state to state it would take our fragmented policing system ages to catch up with him. And he was right. It wasn't until the

Commonwealth Police started putting things together that they were able to build a case. But by then the galah had taken off.' Steve broke off to order brandy. 'Each time he reneged on the payments for his last order, he'd shoot through to a different part of the country. He pulled his first scam in Sydney and promptly moved to the Northern Territory. After he'd pulled a couple of strokes there – in Darwin of all places – he opened up in Perth. From there he went to Rockhampton, out east in Queensland, and then to Adelaide.' He passed the file across the table. 'It's all there, Harry. Take it and digest it at your leisure.'

I took the file and flicked it open to the first page. 'Now that's interesting,' I said.

'What is?' Steve took a sip of his cognac and leaned forward, his arms on the table.

I pointed to the scrap of information in the Australian file that had attracted my interest and explained why I thought it could be relevant.

But Steve Granger was an experienced detective, and the coppering game varies very little from one country to another. 'I reckon that's a bit tenuous, mate,' he said. 'A hell of a lot of women who were born there were given that name. Although I say it myself, Aussies can be an unimaginative crowd when it comes to things like that.'

It was but a scintilla of suspicion, but it had to be followed up.

'Any progress, Mr Brock?' The commander drifted into the incident room, polishing his glasses with his colourful pocket handkerchief.

'I'm thinking of going to Edinburgh, sir.'

'Really? Why?' The commander replaced his glasses and peered at me closely. 'Holiday? I've heard that the area around the Kyle of Lochalsh is very pleasant at this time of year.'

'No, sir, business.' I explained the reasons, not that they sounded too convincing, and certainly not to our tame, paper detective.

'But is that really necessary? Just because Phillips was married to the Lodge woman up there makes your assumption seem rather tenuous in my eyes.' As always the commander was thinking of the expense, cost-conscious *apparatchik* that he was.

'It will have been worthwhile if it means the arrest of Phillips, sir.'

'Mmm, I suppose so. But make sure you use one of those budget airlines.' And with that throwaway line, the commander retreated to preside over his paper empire. One of the DCs had once suggested that he had a black belt in origami. I gave the DC a bollocking; you can't have junior officers going about slagging off commanders.

Donna Lodge had been released from custody at four o'clock on Tuesday afternoon, there being nothing with which I could charge her. I'd floated the idea of assisting an offender, but the Crown Prosecution Service would have none of it.

On Wednesday morning, we arrived at Edinburgh Airport and were met by a detective inspector of the Lothian and Borders Police who introduced himself as Charlie Nicholas. And he was an Englishman.

'What the hell's an Englishman doing up here?' I asked.

'I was in the navy at Faslane,' said Nicholas. 'Married a local girl and when I'd finished my time I joined the job.' He grinned. 'Beats coppering in the Smoke,' he added. 'Anyway, what are you after?'

'An Australian called Bruce Phillips,' I said, and went on to explain our interest, and the reason Dave and I had come to Scotland.

'I know a bit about that,' said Nicholas. 'It was one of my blokes who did the original enquiry for you.'

We drove into the heart of Edinburgh and straight to the private nursing home that was now at the centre of my investigation.

A pretty young matron – she didn't look old enough to be a nurse, let alone a matron – introduced herself as Connie McLachlan and told us that she was in charge.

'I don't know how much you know about Alzheimer's disease,' she began, 'but I doubt that you'll get much out of this lady. Some days, she's quite lucid, but on others, she makes no sense at all. I don't know exactly what you want to ask her, but her short-term memory isn't very good. With this complaint, it's the one that goes first, and half the time she can't remember what you said to her five minutes ago. Her long-term memory's usually all right though. At the moment.'

'How often does her husband come to see her?' I asked.

Connie McLachlan gave me a questioning look. 'She doesn't have a husband,' she said. 'At least, not as far as I know. But her son comes to see her occasionally. Peter Crawford, that is.'

I was suddenly possessed of that feeling that detectives get when they're sure a solution is imminent. And that what I had thought when Steve Granger had showed me Phillips's file was about to be confirmed. 'How old is Mrs Crawford, Matron?'

'We have her down as sixty-five – anyway, that's what her son told us when he brought her in – but she could be older.'

'And how long ago was she admitted?'

The matron paused, calculating. 'It must be three or four years ago, I suppose. I can look it up for you if you want.'

'No, that's good enough. May we see her?'

The matron smiled. 'Aye, you can if you wish, but as I said, I doubt that she'll know what you're talking about.'

I decided that it would be detrimental to my professional standing to admit that, right now, I didn't know what I was talking about either. Crawford had been adamant that it was his wife who was here, not his mother. Admittedly he'd told us that at forty-five she was a little older than he was, but the fact that the hospital authorities believed her to be at least twenty years older than that merely served to heighten my suspicion of Peter Crawford.

Even so, we may have been wasting our time. Perhaps Alzheimer's disease accelerated the ageing process. I didn't know enough about it to offer an opinion. A sketchy first-aid course when I'd joined the job, coupled with what I'd picked up attending post-mortems, did little to expand my knowledge of medicine.

When we entered the airy, sunny room, Mrs Crawford was sitting in an armchair watching television and sipping a drink from a plastic beaker. Even though she was seated, I could see that she was probably a tall big-boned woman.

'Alicia, these gentlemen have come all the way from London to talk to you,' said Connie McLachlan.

The confused old lady gazed at us and smiled a vague smile. 'Oh, how nice,' she said. 'I don't get many visitors.'

'Mrs Crawford—' I began, but got no further. The woman's mood changed instantly, and she hurled the beaker at the television, leaving a trail of liquid across the carpet.

'Now, now, Alicia,' said the matron gently, 'there's no need for that. These gentlemen are friends.'

'I've told you before, my name's not Crawford. It's Phillips. Why does everyone call me Crawford? It's not my name.' Alicia began

304

rocking backwards and forwards in her chair, hammering the armrests with clenched fists. 'It's not my name. Not my name!' she shouted.

Connie McLachlan turned to us with a sympathetic expression on her face. 'I don't know what it is,' she said, 'but she's always going off like that the minute anyone calls her Mrs Crawford. I'm sorry, I should have warned you. I doubt whether she'll answer any questions now. It'll take some time to calm her down.'

'It's all right, Matron,' I said. 'Believe it or not, she's told me all I wanted to know.' I glanced at Alicia Phillips. 'Were you born in Alice Springs?' I asked.

'How did you know that?' growled Alicia, and glanced around as though seeking a missile to throw at me.

The mistake I'd made was to ask the Edinburgh police to check whether Peter Crawford had visited Alicia Crawford without telling them he'd told us she was his wife. If the Scottish officers had known that and had informed me that she was Crawford's mother, we might have resolved this enquiry a damned sight sooner. How easy it is to be wise after the event. But at least the commander would be satisfied that the expense of our trip to Scotland had been justified.

'What are you going to do now, Harry?' asked DI Nicholas.

'D'you know this house that Crawford claims to own and where he said he'd stayed,

Charlie? It's in a place called Colinton.' And I gave him the full address.

'Soon find it,' said Nicholas. 'It's about six miles out of the city. Want to stop off for lunch on the way?'

Crawford's house, the sort of stone dwelling typical of Scottish architecture, was set back from the road sufficient to allow two cars to be parked on the drive. And two cars were there. Nearest the house was a BMW – we knew from Dave's check with the DVLA that it was Forman's – and behind it was Donna Lodge's Alfa Romeo.

'Blimey!' murmured Dave. 'That's a bit of luck.'

If the owners of those two cars were in the house, it was good luck indeed. And about time, too.

The three of us, DI Nicholas, Dave and me, walked up the drive, but Dave and I stood to one side of the door, out of sight.

'This is what I want you to say...' I whispered to Charlie Nicholas, and gave him brief instructions.

'Good afternoon, madam,' said Nicholas when the door was opened. 'I'm a police officer. Is Mr Crawford at home? It's about his mother.'

All right, so it was a dirty trick, but not as dirty as murdering a prostitute. Prostitutes have rights, too.

'I'll get him for you,' said the familiar cultured voice of Donna Lodge, or more

306

correctly Donna Phillips. We had established from the Scottish General Register Office that she and Phillips had indeed been married in Edinburgh a year ago.

Dave and I moved into view as Crawford appeared in the doorway. We were probably the last people he expected to see on his doorstep, and there was a stunned look on his face as he recognized us and realized that we knew who he was and why we wanted him.

Then he turned and ran back up the hall. But he didn't run fast enough. Shoving past me and the Edinburgh DI, Dave sped after Crawford and laid him low with a flying tackle that would have brought the crowd to their feet at Twickenham.

'Peter Crawford, also known as Bruce Phillips, you are wanted on a warrant of extradition issued by the Bow Street magistrate in respect of offences alleged to have been committed by you in Australia,' I said when Dave had dragged our quarry upright again and handcuffed him.

It didn't sound much of a finale to all the convolutions of the murder enquiry that had brought us, eventually, to the door of a very ordinary house on the outskirts of Edinburgh, but it was enough.

'You can't arrest me in Scotland,' said Phillips smugly. 'You don't have the authority.' The very English tones in which he'd spoken when we'd interviewed him in Chelsea had now given way to an Australian accent, but it hadn't affected his knowledge of British law.

'I'm not arresting you,' I said. 'Allow me to introduce Detective Inspector Nicholas of the Lothian and Borders Police. He will arrest you.'

By the time we were ready to leave, Charlie Nicholas had summoned a police van crewed by two burly constables to take us to the airport.

'If you want to borrow these lads to accompany you to London, Harry, you're more than welcome,' said Charlie.

'Thanks,' I said, 'but I reckon Dave and I can take care of him. You could telephone my office though, and ask them to send an escort to meet us at Heathrow.'

It was seven o'clock that evening before we'd lodged Phillips in the cells at Charing Cross police station but, tired though we both were, the Police and Criminal Evidence Act clock had started ticking and there was no time to waste. Not that I intended to waste any on Phillips. From what we'd learned of him, he was a devious bastard. And his opening statement in the interview room proved it.

'I won't fight extradition, mate,' he said. 'You can put me on a plane for Sydney first thing tomorrow morning.'

'It'll be a bloody long time before you see Sydney again... *mate*,' said Dave.

Phillips gave Dave the sort of scathing glance that he probably afforded Aborigines who had the audacity to live in their own country. 'I'm talking to the organ grinder, not the monkey,' he said.

But black policemen live with that sort of racist insult all their professional lives. And probably their social lives too. Dave just laughed, switched on the tape recorder and cautioned Phillips once again. You can't be too careful when there are lawyers lurking in the wings waiting to catch us out in even the most trifling of mistakes.

'Bruce Phillips, I shall shortly charge you with the murder of Patricia Hunter on or about the twelfth of June this year,' I began.

'Is that right? And what makes you think I'm Bruce Phillips?'

'Donna told me,' I said, and had the satisfaction of seeing a dark look of hatred spread across Phillips's face. 'And your mother.'

'You leave my mother out of this!' snapped Phillips.

'The one thing that puzzles me,' I said, 'is why you contacted the Granville Theatre after you'd murdered Patricia Hunter.'

'I didn't murder her,' Phillips sneered. 'She was my girlfriend and I was worried about her.'

Like hell he was. Phillips, in the guise of Crawford, had made that call in an attempt to mislead us into believing that he was a concerned and innocent party. I had to admit that it had been a pretty cunning ploy, but he would have many years in prison, I hoped, to reflect that that call had been the beginning of a train of events that had eventually caused his downfall. A downfall that was aided by the overconfidence that led him to believe he could outwit the police, by his carelessness in leaving a credit-card receipt on the floor of Patricia Hunter's room at Coping Road, and the irresistible urge of many murderers like him to keep a memento of their victim.

But best of all was the fatal error of leaving his fingerprints on the *inside* of the safe we'd found in the garage, and on the dead girl's credit card. And that's how we knew for certain that Crawford was Phillips, because the first thing we'd done on arrival at Charing Cross police station was to have him finger-printed. And those prints also tallied with the ones the Australian Commonwealth Police had sent us with their request for Phillips's extradition. Clever that, ain't it?

And the Crown Prosecution Service went for it too, without demur. I suppose there's a first for everything.

On the Thursday I charged Bruce Phillips with the wilful murder of Patricia Hunter, took him to court and got an eight-day lay down. The next time he surfaced it would be in front of a circuit judge. But the real fun would begin quite a while after that.

And along with the rest of Fleet Street, Fat Danny had plastered it all over the front page of the disreputable tabloid that he dignified with the term newspaper.

The following evening, I took Gail Sutton out to dinner at Rules, my favourite restaurant. And it was she who brought up the arrest of Phillips.

'You got your man, then, Harry.'

'You make me sound like a Canadian Mountie,' I said.

'I read all about it in this morning's paper. And I saw a shot of you on television.'

Gail was certainly much more cheerful this evening than she had been in the month or so since I'd first met her, and I can only imagine that it was because Patricia Hunter's murderer – although that had yet to be proved to the satisfaction of the court – was now in custody.

We finished our meal and stepped out into Maiden Lane. I looked up and down for a taxi to take us to Waterloo, but in vain. We walked along to the corner of Southampton Street, but fared no better there.

'You know, Harry, there's something I've always wanted to do,' said Gail.

'And what's that?'

She took hold of my arm and steered me towards the Strand. 'Stay the night at the Savoy Hotel.'

There was still some unfinished business that had yet to be resolved. The following week we flew to Edinburgh once again and met up with Charlie Nicholas.

The advertising manager of the company Crawford claimed to have visited on the Monday that Patricia Hunter was murdered, was an attractive, willowy redhead with a

311

typically Scottish complexion. She introduced herself as Morag Wilson, and was all bright-eyed and bushy-tailed. Until we told her who we were and why we were there.

'Mrs Wilson, I understand that a Peter Crawford visited you on the tenth of June last in connection with a television advertising project.'

'That's right.' Mrs Wilson beamed at us.

'Really?'

'Yes, really.'

'That's interesting. Because we have charged Peter Crawford, who is actually an Australian called Bruce Phillips, with the murder in London on that date, of a young woman named Patricia Hunter. And he will shortly appear at the Old Bailey.'

Morag Wilson blanched and began to shake, and gripped the arms of her chair so hard that her knuckles showed white.

'I don't believe it,' she said in a whisper.

'Why did you provide him with a false alibi? And before you answer, you'd better listen to what Detective Inspector Nicholas here has to say to you.'

Charlie Nicholas reeled off the caution and began to make notes in his pocket book.

'He told me that some men were after him and if I could say he was up here, it'd be all right. He said it was something to do with a gambling debt.'

That was obviously rubbish, unless you counted us as the men who were after him.

'What is your relationship with Crawford?'

Nicholas asked. Thanks to the vagaries of British law, the prosecution of the case against Morag Wilson would be in his hands.

There was a lengthy pause before Morag Wilson replied. 'We're lovers,' she said.

'And presumably, therefore, you'll have done anything he asked you?' Nicholas said.

'Yes,' she whispered. 'But if I'd known that he was a murderer—'

Nicholas held up his hand. 'Don't bother to say any more, Mrs Wilson. The matter will be reported to the Procurator-Fiscal and I have to tell you that legal proceedings for assisting an offender may well follow.'

And with that we left Morag Wilson in tears, doubtless wondering, like many others, why the hell she had ever become involved with the smooth-talking man known variously as Peter Crawford, Geoffrey Forman and Bruce Phillips.

Phillips's trial took place at the Old Bailey some months later. With all the money he had acquired from his nefarious activities, Phillips, as was to be expected, had briefed one of the bar's leading Queen's Counsel.

But even so eminent a silk was unable to do much to counter the mass of evidence we had built against his client. Not that he didn't try, but then that was what he was being paid for.

When my turn came to be cross-examined, Phillips's QC rose languidly from his seat on the front bench, hitched his gown back on to his left shoulder and regarded me – for a few silent moments – with all the hubris that his class, education and social standing could muster.

'Chief Inspector, I understand that you arrested my client in Scotland—'

'No, sir.'

Momentarily disconcerted, the QC glanced down at his brief, an elegant, well-manicured finger flicking through the pages until he found what he wanted. 'But Mr Phillips was arrested in Colinton, near Edinburgh, was he not?' He affected an air of amusement designed to indicate that he'd caught me out.

'Yes, sir, he was arrested in Scotland, but not by me.'

'But you were there, were you not?'

'Yes, sir.' I do enjoy a bit of legal fencing.

'So, what you are saying is that you did *not* arrest him. Is that correct?' The silk glanced across at the jury box, his expression implying that he'd got this dim policeman on the spit and was about to roast him.

'That is correct, sir, yes.'

With a theatrical gesture that may have fooled the jury, but didn't fool me – and certainly didn't impress the judge – the QC moved his spectacles down an inch and stared at me over the top of them. 'Then who did arrest my client?' he asked, with just the hint of exasperation.

'Detective Inspector Nicholas of the Lothian and Borders Police, sir.'

'But why should a Scottish officer have arrested him, pray? After all, you were the officer investigating the alleged murder with which my client stands indicted, are you not?'

'Detective Inspector Nicholas had the authority, sir, and as I was not in physical possession of the warrant, I did not. But he was not arresting your client on a charge of murder, he was executing a warrant of arrest on behalf of the Australian Government. Your client is wanted for extradition to that country.'

Gotcha! And it hurt. Visibly.

With a convincing display of outrage, Phillips's counsel turned to the judge. 'My Lady, that is irrelevant to the case before the court, and I must ask that the chief inspector be directed—'

'If you don't want answers, don't ask questions,' said the judge dismissively.

And so it went on, the QC nitpicking at trivia in an attempt to discredit police evidence, but it failed. Even without a confession from Phillips, the circumstantial evidence was so overwhelming that the jury took slightly less than an hour to convict him.

The judge sentenced him to life imprisonment and announced that the count of living on immoral earnings would remain on file, a pronouncement that didn't seem to worry Phillips too much.

Some weeks later, the Lord Chief Justice placed a tariff of twenty years minimum on the life sentence. I wasn't there to see Phillips's reaction, but I imagine he wasn't too chuffed about it.

* * *

After the trial, I rang Steve Granger at Australia House.

'I guess you'll have to wait about twenty years to get Phillips back,' I said. 'He's just gone down for life.'

'No worries, mate,' said Granger. 'We don't mind you paying for his board and lodging.'

'Your lot learned to play rugby yet?' I countered.

Because the prosecution of Morag Wilson depended upon the outcome of Phillips's trial, it was not until a week after his appeal had been disallowed that she appeared before the Edinburgh sheriff's court.

However, we were not obliged to travel north again to give evidence, as the case against her was now in the hands of DI Nicholas. Morag Wilson pleaded not guilty, but it did her little good. Once Charlie Nicholas produced the certificate of Phillips's conviction and gave details of Morag Wilson's admission, the fifteen members of the jury found her guilty within thirty minutes.

The Scottish courts, like their English counterparts, take a dim view of people who assist offenders, particularly when those offenders are murderers. She was sentenced to a year's imprisonment, but she didn't complete it.

Six weeks later she was found hanged in her cell at Inverness prison.

* * *

But the whole Phillips thing still irritated me.

'We never did find out who she'd had it off with just before her death, Dave, because Phillips's DNA didn't match the seminal fluid that was found in Patricia Hunter's body,' I said when we were having a pint in the Red Lion not long after the trials of both Phillips and Morag Wilson.

'So what?' said Dave. 'It's all water under the bridge. Waterloo Bridge.'

'Or why there was greasepaint on the wire with which Phillips strangled Patricia Hunter. Neither he nor Donna Lodge had ever had any direct contact with the theatre.'

But that's police work for you. Real police work, I mean. It's not like it is in the police 'soaps' that abound on television, where the scriptwriter insists on tying up *all* the loose ends.

'Never mind, guv,' said Dave, as he got another round in.

'What's more,' I said, determined to beat myself up, 'you've had a lesson in how to make a cock-up of investigating a murder. To think I alerted Phillips by mentioning him to Donna Lodge before we knew that he was also Forman. If I hadn't done that, we might have captured him much sooner. And if only we'd known that Alicia Crawford was Peter Crawford's mother, not his wife, we might have homed in on him before we did, and saved ourselves a lot of time.'

'Yeah, but we got lucky, guv, and that's all

that matters. We got a result,' said Dave. 'What's more, you met Gail Sutton.'

'Yes, Dave,' I said thoughtfully, 'there is that.'